THE END
OF
EVERYTHING

ALSO BY MEGAN ABBOTT

The Street Was Mine
Die a Little
The Song Is You
Queenpin
Bury Me Deep

THE END OF EVERYTHING

a novel

MEGAN ABBOTT

A REAGAN ARTHUR BOOK

LITTLE, BROWN AND COMPANY

NEW YORK   BOSTON   LONDON

Reagan Arthur Books / Little, Brown and Company
Hachette Book Group
237 Park Avenue, New York, NY 10017
www.hachettebookgroup.com

First Edition: July 2011

Reagan Arthur Books is an imprint of Little, Brown and Company, a division of Hachette Book Group, Inc. The Reagan Arthur Books name and logo are trademarks of Hachette Book Group, Inc.

The publisher is not responsible for websites (or their content) that are not owned by the publisher.

The characters and events in this book are fictitious. Any similarity to real persons, living or dead, is coincidental and not intended by the author.

Library of Congress Cataloging-in-Publication Data
Abbott, Megan E.
    The end of everything : a novel / Megan Abbott. — 1st ed.
        p. cm.
    HC ISBN 978-0-316-09779-6
    Int'l ed. ISBN 978-0-316-18564-6
    1. Teenage girls—Fiction.   2. Best friends—Fiction.   3. Missing persons—Fiction.   4. Secrecy—Fiction.   5. Psychological fiction.   I. Title.
    PS3601.B37E63 2011
    813'.6—dc22   2010031574

10 9 8 7 6 5 4 3 2 1

RRD-IN

Printed in the United States of America

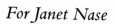

For Janet Nase

THE END
OF
EVERYTHING

One

She, light-streaky out of the corner of my eye. It's that game, the one called Bloody Murder, the name itself sending tingly nerves shooting buckshot in my belly, my gut, or wherever nerves may be. It's so late and we shouldn't be out at all, but we don't care.

Voices pitchy, giddy, raving, we are all chanting that deathly chant that twists, knifelike, in the ear of the appointed victim. *One o'clock, two o'clock, three o'clock, four o'clock, five o'clock...* And it's Evie, she's it, lost at choosies, and now it will be her doom. But she's a good hider, the best I've ever seen, and I predict wild surprises, expect to find her rolled under a saggy front porch or buried under three inches of dirt in Mom's own frilly flower bed.

Six o'clock, seven o'clock, eight o'clock, nine o'clock, the cruel death trill we intone, such monsters we, *ten o'clock, eleven o'clock, twelve o'clock, MIDNIGHT! Bloody murder!* We all scream, our voices cruel and insane, and we scatter fast, like fireflies all a-spread.

I love the sound of our Keds slamming on the asphalt, the poured concrete. There are five, maybe ten of us, and we're all playing, and the streetlamps promise safety, but for how long?

Oh, Evie, I see you there, twenty yards ahead, your peach terry cloth shorts twitching as you run so fast, as you whip your head around, that dark curtain of hair tugging in your mouth, open, shouting, screaming even. It's a game of horrors and it's the thing pounding in my chest, I can't stop it. I see you, Evie, you're just a few feet from the Faheys' chimney, from home base. Oh, it's the greatest game of all and Evie is sure to win. You might make it, Evie, you might. My heart is bursting, it's bursting.

It was long ago, centuries. A quivery mirage of a thirteen-year-old's summer, like a million other girl summers, were it not for Evie, were it not for Evie's thumping heart and all those twisting things untwisting.

There I am at the Verver house, all elbows and freckled jaw and heels of hands rubbed raw on gritty late summer grass. A boy-girl, like Evie, and nothing like her sister, Dusty, a deeply glamorous seventeen. A movie star, in halter tops and eyelet and clacking Dr. Scholl's. Eyelashes like gold foil and eyes the color of watermelon rind and a soft, curvy body. Always shiny-lipped and bright white-teethed, lip smack, flash of tongue, lashes bristling, color high and surging up her cheeks.

A moment alone, I would steal a peek in Dusty's room, clogged with the cotton smell of baby powder and lip gloss and hands wet with hair spray. Her bed was a big pink cake with faintly soiled flounces and her floor dappled with the tops of nail polish bottles, with plastic-backed brushes heavy with hair, with daisy-dappled underwear curled up like pipe cleaner, jeans inside out, the powdery socks still in them, folded-up notes from all her rabid boyfriends, shiny tampon wrappers caught in the edge of the bedspread, where it hit the mint green carpet. It seemed like Dusty was forever cleaning the room, but even she herself could not stop the constant, effervescing explosions of girl.

Alongside such ecstatic pink loveliness, Evie and I, we were all snips and snails, and when permitted into her candied interior, we were like furtive intruders.

You see, knowing Evie so well, knowing her bone-deep, it meant knowing her whole family, knowing the books they kept on their living room shelf (*The Little Drummer Girl, Better Homes and Gardens New Cookbook, Lonesome Dove*), the banana bark chair in the living room and the way it felt under your fingers, the rose milk lotion on Mrs. Verver's dressing table—I wanted to sink my face into it.

I couldn't remember a time when I wasn't skittering down their carpeted steps, darting around the dining room table, jumping on Mr. and Mrs. Ververs' queen-size bed.

There were other things to know too. Secrets so exciting that they were shared only in hushed giggles under the rippling flannel of sleeping bags. Did you know? Evie whispers, and tells me Dusty is named after the singer whose album her parents played sixteen times the night she was conceived. It is thrilling and impossible. I cannot, even in my most devilish thoughts about the hidden wickedness and folly of grown-ups, imagine Mrs. Verver turning her child's name into a lurid, private wink.

Not Mrs. Verver. Living next door all of my life, I never knew her to laugh loudly or run for the phone or dance at the drunken block parties every July. Tidy, bland voice as flat as a drum, she was the fleeting thing, the shadow moving from room to room in the house. She worked as an occupational therapist at the VA hospital, and I was never sure what that meant, and no one ever talked about it anyway. Mostly, you'd just see her from the corner of your eye, carrying a laundry basket, slipping from hallway to bedroom, a fat paperback folded over her wispy hand. Those hands, they always seemed dry, almost dusty, and her body seemed too bony for her daughters, or her husband, to hug.

Oh, and Mr. Verver, Mr. Verver, Mr. Verver, he's the one always vibrating in my chest, under my fingernails, in all kinds of places. There's much to say of him and my mouth can't manage it, even now. He hums there still.

Mr. Verver, who could throw a football fifty yards and build princess vanity tables for his daughters and take us roller-skating or bowling, who smelled of fresh air and limes and Christmas nutmeg all at once — a smell that meant "man" to his girls ever after. Mr. Verver, he was there. I couldn't remember a time when I wasn't craning my neck to look up at him, forever waiting to hear more, hungry for the moments he would shine his attentions on me.

These are all the good things, and there were such good things. But then there were the other things, and they seemed to come later, but what if they didn't? What if everything was there all along, creeping soundlessly from corner to corner, shuddering fast from Evie's nighttime whispers, from the dark hollows of that sunny-shingled house, and I didn't hear it? Didn't see it?

Here I was knowing everything and nothing at all.

There are times now when I look at those weeks before it happened and they have the quality of revelation. It was all there, all the clues, all the bright corners illuminated. But of course it wasn't that way at all. And I could not have seen it. I could not, could not.

Sometimes I dream I'm playing soccer with Evie again, all this time later. First I'm alone on the field. It's all green-black and I'm knocking the ball around between my feet. My round little legs beneath me. My funny little thirteen-year-old body, compact and strange. Bruise on my thigh. Scab on my knee. Ink on my hand from doodling in class. Wisped hair pressed by cool girly sweat onto my forehead. Arms like short spindles and stubby fingers protruding. Barely buds under my shiny green V-neck jersey. If I run my hands over them, they will hardly notice. Hips still angular like a boy's, rotating with each kick, passing the ball between my feet, waiting for Evie, who's there in a flash of dark heat before me. Breath splashing my face, her leg wedging between my legs and knocking the ball free, off into the dark green distance, farther than she ever meant it to go.

When I remember Evie now she is always slipping through shadows. Big, dark, haunted eyes rimmed with red. Running across the soccer field, face flushed, straight black sheet of hair rippling across her back. Running so hard, her breath stippled with pain to go faster, hit the grass harder, move forward faster, like she could break through something in front of her, something no one else saw.

Tw o

It is May, the last month of middle school, and Evie, who is my best friend, is propped up on Nurse Stang's examining table, so steely cold it stings my teeth to look at it.

"Does it hurt?" I ask, and Nurse Stang throws me an irritated look. She is holding a large pack of ice over Evie's left eye.

"You only get one set of these," she says, and makes to poke Evie right between the eyes. "What kind of girl hooks her stick into another girl like that."

"It was her sister," I say, and I'm smiling a little at Evie, from underneath Nurse Stang's raised arm."

"I was near the goal," Evie says, mush-mouthed, her eye tearing. "It's what she had to do."

Dusty had been showing us her moves. High school star, the golden goddess of the Green Hollow Celts, she was getting us ready for August, for our first high school tryouts. She plucked our twig arms and said, *You two paper dolls have wasted years knocking soccer balls.* Chin high, hand on hip, she told us the time was ripe, we must make our move and ascend to the one true sport, to the deeper glories of field hockey.

I'd do anything Dusty said. I'd let her drill us forever. Even when it made you so tired, almost sick from the exhaustion and heat, it didn't matter, because you were with her, and she was everything you wanted. You'd be about to collapse, then you'd look up and there she'd be, face gleaming, telling you, without saying it: *You can do better, can't you?* And you could.

Nurse Stang calls Evie's mom, watching us the whole time.

"You should have been wearing something," she says, hanging up the phone. "They're supposed to put goggles on you girls..."

"We were just messing around," I say.

Just then Evie spits out her mouth guard, red speckled. All three of us look at it.

"What in the world," Nurse Stang says, her voice pitched suddenly high. She tosses the ice pack at me and peers deep into Evie's mouth, thrusting with her fingers, looking for something.

"I bit my tongue," Evie says, her voice thickening. "I bit into it." A strand of blood slips down her chin, and I start to feel dizzy. I look at the mouth guard, which is split clean through.

"You," Nurse Stang says to me, holding Evie's tongue between newly scarlet fingers, "get the needle and thread."

We're walking home and Evie is leaning close, wagging her tongue out at me, the cloudy gauze nearly tickling my face. She's flaunting it mercilessly. We're always eager for war wounds. Oh, her fury when I sprained my arm falling from the top of the rusty old slide in Rabbit Park.

"Your dad is going to be mad at Dusty," I say, scraping my stick on the sidewalk, which I'm not supposed to do, but the sound is so satisfying.

"I don't think so," Evie lisps. "That's the game."

I think of ringletted Dusty, goalkeeper mask propped up daintily over her forehead. "Show me what you got, runt."

"You don't know the game," Evie adds.

"I know as much as you, *mamacita*," I say, leaning in and flicking the bandage on her stuck-out tongue with my finger.

We stop at her house. There's no car in the driveway and all the lights are off. These are moments to be seized on, never wasted.

"Do you want to go to Perry's?" she says, tugging the bandage off for good. I can see the threaded x-marks-the-spot on the tip of her tongue. One, two, three, four. One for each pointy tooth.

Peppermint-stripe awning, wall-to-wall white like the soft vanilla filling of a Creamsicle, Perry's is the place all the kids in our class go. Next fall, when we're in high school, we'll have to go to the Ram's Horn restaurant instead, where my brother, Ted, goes, and there is nothing under five dollars there, and there are no counter stools to spin on and the lighting is grown-up low.

I am eating an Oreo sundae, picking wedges of cookie carefully from my molars. With great concentration, Evie is eating her favorite: a Reese's Peanut Butter Cup sundae—the kind where they give you the long spoon to get all the peanut butter silted up in the narrow bottom. She shoves the spoon far into the back of her mouth, to miss the stitches.

Some boys from school are at the counter, knocking over canisters of straws and punching one another, practically jumping from their skin. Their donkey-bray laughter fills the place.

One of them, Jed, spots us and starts throwing wadded-up straw wrappers in our direction. I am itching to go. Evie, though, keeps looking at me and shaking her head, her bangs veiling her eyes. I reach out and push them back and I can see the bruise beginning to bloom on her face. I wriggle in my seat, my thighs itching against the vinyl. Jed has curly yellow hair and a nose that hooks at the end. I remember once he tugged the back of Evie's shorts in gym class. She said he pressed his fingers against her skin and everyone was watching.

We wait too long and Jed gets his blood up, pigeon-strutting over to us. I look at Evie, trying to catch her eye. The bangs have shaken loose once more and she is staring down at her sundae, sloshing her spoon around the frothy Reddi-wip. But I see her pinkening a little, so I know she sees Jed.

She curls her tongue into the corner of her mouth.

"Hey," he says, hands shoved in pockets, head cocked to one side.

"Hey," I say, kicking Evie lightly in the shin.

Jed stands in silence for a few moments, then reaches over to Evie's sundae and dips his knobby pinkie in and lifts a sticky strand, lacing it across his hand. With a nasty grin, he shoves a pair of caramel-webbed fingers in his mouth and smacks his lips.

She watches him, we both do, and I can feel things jumping in me, and I have to stop myself because this is about Evie, this is hers, and I'm not sure what's skittering behind those dark eyes.

But she does nothing, she looks at me and asks me if I'm ready to leave, and I say I am. She is so cool, so regular-day, as she gathers her things and we very nearly glide to the front door.

Jed follows, and of course he would, and he's saying boy taunts like, "What's a matter, girls, don't you like to share? Don't you want to lick my fingers?"

The rest of the boys are out front, watching the show. Evie adjusts her backpack and begins walking, but I can't stand it anymore. Eyeing the swampy old fountain where the little kids grab slimy pennies, I drop my bag and dunk my hands under it and, with one heaving hurl, splash Jed. Oh, do the boys laugh, and Jed, sludge-drenched, is elated.

Why, that's what he wants me to do, I figure out, that's all they ever want.

Then, Jed grabs me around the waist, tight on my ribs so it hurts, and shakes his wet hair against my neck from behind. I can't fight the deliciousness of it, all the kids screaming, but I pull free, nearly tripping, tugging up my fallen bra strap.

I barely have a chance to turn to Evie when Jed grabs her next, and drags her, sneakers skidding, to the fountain. They wrestle around the browning spout briefly, Evie's legs kicking, and, next thing, she has elbowed him hard in his scrawny ribs and pushed herself from those freckled arms.

She stumbles back and somehow is in the center of all of us.

We all see Evie's pale yellow T-shirt is skin-soaked with the mucky stuff.

The sight, it has a stone-turning power. Jed can't take his eyes off her.

Evie doesn't cover the hard outline of her small breasts, though I want her to. I want to cover them for her, those pebbly nipples. I feel my face go hot and I drop my head, I want to fold my own arms across my chest. I feel a weird laugh coming from me.

But Evie, she puts her hands on her hips and stares Jed down with her slate eyes. The clinging shirt is pulled even tauter by her pose.

I'm laughing with my hand over my whole face.

"The boys come for her," Evie told me once. Late into the night, both of us snug in her twin bed, we'd been talking about Dusty. We love to talk about her, to spin speculations into looping tangles at our feet. *What if Becky Hode tries to take team captain from her? What if it's true about Mr. Douglas, the lantern-jawed science teacher? Did he really say there was no better example of the sublime poetry of hydraulics than Dusty walking down the third-floor corridor?*

"Bobby Thornhill sits across the street in his car," Evie told me. "He doesn't think anyone can see. Do you think that's creepy?"

"Maybe," I said, thinking about Bobby Thornhill, the galloping track star with the black bolt of hair and the marbly eyes that roll around in his head when he's pounding his horse legs on the cinder.

"What does he do?" I asked, careful now. "When he sits out there, does he do things?"

Evie looked at me. "I guess he might."

"Oh," I said, feeling funny, all the air sucked out of me in a big swoop. And I thought of Bobby in the front seat of his parents' car, his forest green varsity jacket with the chenille C. I thought of him hunched there, eyes gazing up at Dusty's bedroom window, its frothy curtains, Dusty's frothy girlness.

It must have been a wondrous thing to him, the curtains and pink light coming from her room. The whisper of Dusty floating by. A whisper he could just catch. And the feeling must have been so great, such a hard pressure in him, and he could, he could—

The thought came to me, *I know this, I know this.* But it was gone before I could wrap my head around it.

I lay there and listened to Evie breathing, fast.

I'm thirteen, did I tell you, and I have soft dimples where my thighs meet my knees, and each night I lie in bed with my hands wedged between my legs and wonder things and the wonder becomes so real, and there's a heat and pressure there, and if I try hard enough I can, like a tightness kept within me, make the whole world break open and break me all to pieces.

There are boys and there are boys, but in my head it's better because there is none of the roughness of these boys, boys like Brad Nemeth, trying to steer me onto his lap at the party at Tara Leary's house, trying to steer me there so my shorts ride up and feel his curling denim underneath the uppermost part of my thigh, and he has such a look, and his face so close to mine.

"He was rubbing on you like it was Boy Scout camp," Evie said later. "Like if he rubbed hard enough he could start that fire, get that merit badge."

Evie would say these things and it made everything easier, all at once. We would laugh and laugh, and boys hate it when you laugh together, at them. "It was like rubbing a pink eraser to the nub," Evie said. "He was gonna rub on you till you were just the metal tip."

That night, that very same night, though, I felt the soft part of my underthigh, the pink stipple of brush burn, tender like new skin. It did things to me.

I wake up with a start, my legs jackrabbiting to the foot of my bed. It must've been a car door slamming, a clap of thunder, a raccoon in someone's trash can, an early-summer bottle rocket, something. I jerk my feet, ankles free from the knot of sheets, and wait for a minute, trying to listen for it, but there's nothing but the heavy buffering of the sleeping house. That lonely, lost feeling where it's like everyone else has sunk into some velvety splendor-world except you.

My retainer sliding against my teeth with a tickle, I lie back and fix my eyes on the bleary whites of the soccer ball corkboard hanging on the back of my door.

It takes only a few seconds before I remember it was the dream. The dream woke me up and the dream was this:

Evie is on my bedroom floor, tucked in her sleeping bag, deep pink like two plush lips, on the floor by my bed. I glance down at her and see her mouth is stuffed with plumes of cotton, like from the top of an aspirin bottle. Eyes dark, loose in her head, she's looking up at me and one hand darts out in tan, bony twitches, the cotton sputtering from her mouth in wisps. And I can't decide if she's laughing. It seems like she must be laughing, like we're in the middle of a joke together and I should be laughing too, but I keep hearing things, strange, bleating sounds, and I am unfocused.

I feel a hard tug on my ankle, her fingers gnarled, her eyes large and stricken, and she whispers, and it's like a slumber party movie with glinting hacksaws and bright cleavers, and my heart runs cold. "Is it now? Is it now?"

The dream fresh on me, I sit up again, try to shake off the murk of it, but it's hard. That face, the feel of Evie's hot hand wrapped around my leg, I am still there. I count to ten three times, like when I was a kid and the thunder rolled over the house. It always works and it does now too.

Just as I feel myself settling into sleep, though, I think I hear my mother's voice, chattering and then lifting into a long sigh.

That strange, untethered feeling comes back, like things have slipped from their right place while I'd slept. I can't think of any time since the screaming maw of the divorce that she would be on the phone at such an hour. And then it was always a grasping, urgent voice, filled with sobs and gnashing teeth.

This one lilts, filled with coaxing laughs.

It sounds like she's outside, and I remember how it was that time right after my dad left, finding her in the driveway, cord stretched outside, crying behind the screen door, her face behind her hand.

But then I hear a deeper voice and I know. I know she's not on the phone at all. I know it means that man is with her. My brother, Ted, saw him first, from his bedroom window. He told me about it the next day and then I watched for it. Dr. Aiken, that's his name, Ted says so.

And check out the wedding band, Ted said, but I've never been close enough to see it.

He always arrives very late and he never comes inside. That's how I know they're out on the screen porch together again and they're drinking tumblers of whiskey sour and he's rubbing his face in his hand and saying, again and again, "I know I should go home, Diane, I know I should."

But he doesn't, or only at five, when I see him, shoes in hand, tie hanging around his neck, tripping across the front lawn to his car.

The next day, Evie and I are standing in front of the school, tapping our sticks against each other in time. The dream from last night is hovering in my head, and I think I might tell Evie about it, but I keep stopping myself. No one ever really wants to hear your dreams.

Anyway, we are having a day of no talking, just being, walking together, tapping our new hockey sticks and yanking our sweaty shirts from our chests.

Still, I can't keep my eyes off the violet stain flaring over Evie's temple. It looks like it could move without you, get up and go. It's like a purple butterfly, I tell her, flitting from her face.

She puts her fingers on it and I can almost feel it pulsing on my own face, a gentle throb.

"What did your dad say?" I ask, and I imagine Mr. Verver's wrinkled brow, like when I slipped on their stairs, running way too fast in my stocking feet, skidding down three steps, and making brush burns all up my calves.

"He bought me a raw steak at Ketchums to put on it," she says. "Mom said it cost more than their anniversary dinner."

It sounds like Mrs. Verver, who says everything with a yawn.

"All night," Evie says, a grin creeping, "he kept calling me Rocky."

We both roll our eyes, but we love it. When the boys tease, you don't want it to be you, but with Mr. Verver, his teases are like warm hands lifting you.

Evie thrusts her hockey stick out in front of her like Zorro. "Dusty said I looked more like a battered wife on a TV show," she says.

Then she tells me how, after dinner, her dad took her for pecan pie at Reynold's, the good kind, gritty-sweet on your teeth. The waitresses felt sorry for her and gave her an extra scoop of ice cream.

I think of sitting with Mr. Verver, gooey pie plates between us, and how the waitresses probably always give him extra scoops. Waitresses were always doing that with Mr. Verver, just like the mothers who buzzed around him at the PTA meetings, filling his plate with sugared cookies and inviting him to their book clubs.

I wish Evie would have invited me to Reynold's. Like other times, with Mr. Verver dabbing Cool Whip on my nose.

Out of the blue, my ankles feel itchy and I wish I could take off my gym socks.

I look down the street, which has that four thirty hush. The summer heat seems early, hovering above the asphalt.

"Where's your mom taking you?" Evie asks, watching a car flutter upward at the speed bump in front of the school.

"The mall," I say. "Are you going to wear your sister's old dress?" I remember the lavender Laura Ashley with the gored skirt that Dusty wore to her own middle school graduation. All those ringlets dangling down her back and her face bright with achievement—it wasn't something you forgot.

A maroon car shimmers out of nowhere and glides past us quickly.

"I don't know," Evie says, kicking her shoe toe into the pavement.

Squinting, she looks down the street. "I think I see her."

We both watch as my mom's tan Tempo floats before us on the horizon.

"We'll give you a ride," I say.

"That's okay," she says, twirling her hockey stick over her shoulder. I hear the stutter in my mom's car as she pulls up.

The moment stretches out, I'm not sure why.

Evie is looking past my mother's car, down the street.

"Someone's lost," she says.

"What—" I start, but then we both watch as the same maroon car drifts past us again soundlessly. Something in my head flickers, but I can't place it.

I turn back around and there's that Evie face, cool and orderly, the line for a mouth and her smooth, artless expression, like a soft sheet pulled fast, hiding every corner.

I twirl my stick around and clatter it against hers.

"Call me," I say, turning toward the idling car. My mother is looking at us from behind big sunglasses, smiling absently.

I open the door and lean in. "Mom, can Evie come with us?"

But when I turn around, Evie's gone, slipped behind the tall hedgerow, behind the stone columns of the old school.

Do I see it in her expression, as she looks at me, as she pulls her face into blankness? Do I hear her say, in some low register, a creeping knowingness always between us? Do I hear her say, *This is the last time, this is the last time*?

This face, my face, gone forever.

Three

The phone rings. It's ten thirty at night. I'm brushing my teeth when it happens, and I hope it's not my dad calling from California, calling from his apartment balcony, a sway in his voice, talking about the time we rented canoes at Old Pine Lake, or the time he built the swing set in the backyard, or other things I don't really remember but that he does, always, when he's had a second glass of wine.

But it's not him, and my mother sounds rattled and confused.

"I'll be sure to speak to her right away," she says, and I try to think of things I might have done. Late for Algebra twice last week. Would they call your parents at ten thirty at night for that?

After she hangs up, she drops her arms to her sides, and I can see her take a long breath.

Pushing wisps of hair behind her ears, which is what she does when her nerves run high, she sits me down at the kitchen table.

"I'm going to ask you something," she says, "and I need you to tell me the truth."

I say of course I will.

"Okay," she says, and her hands tremble, and I feel bad about whatever I did even though I can't imagine what it might be. "Do you know anything about Evie not coming home from school today?"

I shake my head and say I don't know anything. I don't know anything at all. Even though I'm telling the truth, it somehow feels like I'm lying.

My mother, her face gone soft and pink, takes my hand in hers and asks me again. And then once more.

But I don't know. I don't know, I don't.

Somewhere, though, somewhere in my head, in the back pitch of it, there's something. There's something. I just can't reach it.

Four

It's happening, that's what I think, but even as the words come to me, I don't know what they mean. In some tucked-off way, it seems like whatever is happening had already been happening, for so long, a falling feeling inside, something nameless, a perilous feeling, and I don't know what to do with it.

I saw her, that hank of dark hair, sports socks tugged high over knees. I saw her.

Evie was there, and then Evie was gone.

Fingers pushed between the blinds in our den, I peek through to the Verver house, lights blaring in every room.

Just five nights before, I slept over, trading pj's and listening to music and even reading aloud a chapter from the thick paperback Mrs. Verver kept by her lounge chair, the one with the woman's mouth on the cover, open, and a man's finger touching it. Evie said the finger looked hairy, and she didn't like how they were always having sex standing up. But we read some of the scenes two, three times, taking turns. I kept thinking what it might be like, all those bodies and rushing blood and thrusting tongues. Everything seemed rough, bruising, wet. It made my stomach go tight and we put it away and I was glad.

I kept thinking about the book after we went to bed, Evie's room dark, my eyes on the soccer ball mobile making lively shadows on the wall. Dusty and Mr. Verver were in lawn chairs on the back patio, their voices floating up. I could hear them laughing and his laugh always so serene, so serene, like he is.

You always feel Mr. Verver through the whole house, that laugh of his, deep and caramely. He makes the house feel so full, crowded with bright things and mischief and fun. When we were younger, he'd play board games with us and he always cheated, but you couldn't care. He'd announce it, like it was his own special strategy, and then he'd wink at you, and it was like you were in it with him. You found yourself wanting to help him. Dusty always scolded him and sometimes took his turn away. The games would go on for hours, and you never wanted it to stop.

"Dusty's back from her date," Evie whispered, and it was only then that I realized she was listening to them too. I sat up in my sleeping bag and nudged toward her bed.

"With Tom Mullan?" I asked, and Evie said shush.

"Listen," she mouthed. "Just listen."

Dusty and Mr. Verver's voices hovered, so delicately, through the window. We could hear Dusty, wry and giggly at the same time, which is how she always is with her dad and no one else.

"So then he stops the car and—"

"Just tell me he didn't say he was out of gas."

A peal of Dusty laughter. I remembered the week last summer when my brother took Dusty out a few times and wondered if she sat back here with Mr. Verver and they laughed together about him.

"No, he just stops the car and turns to me and says, 'Babe—'"

"Babe? He called you 'babe,' did he? Poor kid. He's in way over his head."

"He says, 'In that white dress, you look like an angel.' And then—"

"But you *are*, babe, but you *are*...," Mr. Verver said, and I could practically see his grin.

"Dad, stop!" Dusty was wheezing with laughter, trying to get words out. "So he leans over, and next thing I know he's practically swallowing my ear."

"Well, did you return the favor? I raised you with manners, didn't I? I mean, he promised you dinner, didn't he?"

Dusty's laughter was just breathless squeaks.

"C'mon. What did you do?" Mr. Verver chuckled. "The poor little squirt."

"What could I do? He swallowed my pearl drop earring and nearly choked. I couldn't stop laughing. I hit him on the back, and it popped out."

"I bet it popped out," Mr. Verver said, and there was the briefest of gasping pauses before both of them let loose a new stream of uproarious howling.

Evie kept staring at me, waiting for me to smile or say something, but I didn't because I didn't know what she wanted.

All I could think was how wondrous it was—oh, the two of them. Everyone wanted to fall under their enchantment, her gaze hard and appraising, his so soft, so welcoming.

That was how it was in that house, and there was so much fun to be had. Wouldn't it be wonderful, I remember thinking—was it just five days ago?—to talk about boys with Mr. Verver? To play Uno with Evie for hours and watch Dusty try on her pastel dresses and listen to music with Mr. Verver until dawn?

It is a long night and my mother walks the halls, checks the window latches three times, the front door. She seems to walk all night, bumping into chairs, turning the television off and on.

And I try to sleep, I try to sleep away the thoughts spreading dark stains through my head.

But I have thoughts, and the thoughts feel like they will be very bad dreams.

My mother walks me over to the Ververs the next morning. On TV you have to wait twenty-four hours. Twenty-four hours before it means something. It's been only a half day. This is what I tell my mother as she holds my hand so tightly for the seven steps between our houses.

She stops and looks at me, her face pinched. "Not with children," she says. "They don't make you wait with children."

"Oh," I say, and she looks like she wants to say more but is stopping herself, making herself stop. But then she can't.

"With children," she says, "every minute matters. Everything can be ruined in a half hour. You have no idea."

I feel a hard rake across my chest. It's the most awful thing I've ever heard. What could she mean? What does that mean?

Wired so tight, she doesn't notice my flinch, and before I know it, she's yanked me through the Ververs' side door.

There are two detectives in the living room, and they ask my mother to wait while they lead me upstairs. I'm still thinking about Mr. Verver's face when he'd answered the door for us, brimmed high with feeling, his whole body jumping, his hands scratching at his upper arms, bouncing on his feet.

He's trying so hard, that's how I see it. He's trying so hard, and Dusty was making coffee, her whole body cocooned in a big sweatshirt that made me perspire to look at, and she was trying to concentrate, and the grounds kept scattering, and when she knelt down, I saw the long swoop of a tear hang off her eye, but she covered it quick with her ballooning sleeve, and by the time she rose and turned to me, she was dry-eyed, focused.

Upstairs in Evie's room, with the two men in blazers and ties, my head feels hot, and everything's twitching in me, like nerve endings snipping and snapping. It's all too much and here I am, and I have to know things, tell things.

I take breaths, many of them, deep ones. First, they ask me if anything in the room looks different, but it doesn't. They make me look around, but there's nothing to see. Nothing I can see. All I can think of is how strange it is to see the room that's all Evie — a soccer ball lamp, tidily arranged schoolbooks, neat rows of pencils with bright eraser toppers, and that Magic-8 Ball she keeps on her desk (*Ask again later,* it always said) — filled up with two men in striped ties who have to bend their heads to avoid the eaves.

Then, for half an hour or more, they ask me many questions, over and over again. They sit me down on the twin bed, that nubby yellow bedspread of hers. I don't know where to look, so I focus on the luscious strawberry crusted over my knee from practice, running my fingernails under its hard edges, tugging ever so gently.

"Lizzie," one of them says, "did Eveline — Evie — did she say she was waiting for someone?"

"No. She was just going to walk home."

"Do you usually walk home together?"

"Yeah, but I was going to the mall."

They repeat the earlier questions. I repeat my answers, running my fingers over my knee, the crinkles of the scab. The questions shift.

"Did Evie have a boyfriend?"

I feel my face rash up with red, and then I feel silly for it.

"No," I say.

"Did she ever talk about boys to you? Boys she liked, or who maybe liked her?" One of the detectives sits down beside me, crunching the tiny bed lopsided.

"No," I repeat. "Never."

MISSING: *Eveline Marie Verver, age thirteen years old. Five feet, one inch tall. Eighty-nine pounds. Hair: Dark brown. Eyes: Gray.*

Last seen en route from JFK Middle School, 5/28. Wearing yellow T-shirt with butterfly on front, blue shorts, tennis shoes.

Identifying marks: Bruise above left eye. Small white scar on inside of upper left thigh.

It's posted on all the electrical poles, in store windows. Everything about it seems wrong, beginning with the name.

When you're girls growing up like we did, you're so body-close. Sometimes, I'd look at my own left thigh and wonder where the white curl went, the scar like a half-moon, a nail dug deep, from falling off Dusty's Schwinn in second grade, Dusty pushing so hard, hands on Evie's back. Then I'd remember it wasn't my scar, my leg, but Evie's, even as I could sometimes feel it under my fingertips, like the soldiers with the phantom limbs we read about in History class.

The body-closeness, it comes from all those nights knotted together in the tent in the backyard, or showering the chlorine off in the bathhouse at the pool, lying in the plush grass by the soccer field, comparing injuries, pushing our fingers in each other's violet bruises. Tugging at our bathing suits, seeing who'd get that bra first, even as Evie knew it would be me, but she was the one with the hot cramps that made her bend over, that made her turn white. Sometimes I felt them too, with her. Sometimes I felt my insides turning as hers did. I wanted to.

We shared everything, our tennis socks and stub erasers, our hair elastics and winter tights. We were that close. Sometimes we blinked in time.

Back in second, third grade, all the parents always saying, *Do the dance, do the dance.* The first time was at the tap recital. "Me and My Shadow," in our matching silver leotards and shiny top hats, our hair the same muddy color, the baby curls sprayed to shellac by Madame Connie, our teacher. Then everyone made us do it again and again, at birthday parties, on Easter. A hundred times in the Verver basement, my living room, at school, *step-shuffle-back-step, step-shuffle-back-step.* Over and over, cheeks painted red. Until I grew two inches and Evie's hair went dark and finally we never did that dance again.

But I bet I still could do it. I bet I could do it right now.

These things, though, they end.

And with Evie gone, I can see things had been changing for who knew how long. It was like the scar on her thigh, the one I could feel beneath my own fingers, had slithered from my own leg back to hers. "Maybe I won't try out for field hockey," Evie'd said one day, even as we'd talked of little else all year long, aiming for a shot at JV. And there Evie is on Friday nights, and she doesn't want to do the backyard table tennis tournaments with Dusty and Mr. Verver, the ones that last till long past dark, fireflies flicking in the deep night majesty. She just doesn't anymore, and these are things I can't account for.

We're no longer two summer-brown kids with tangles of hair and jutting kid teeth. I don't know when it happened, but it did. Lately, things had been hovering in her face, and I couldn't fathom it. I had things too, new things twisting under my skin, but I didn't know what they were. It felt like she knew her own zig-zagging heart, and I was just killing time.

★　　★　　★

"He's b-a-a-c-k..." That's what Kelli Hough says at school, a group of us ribboned around her locker. I'd missed the first three periods, talking to the police, and I feel unsteady, somehow lost. And there is Kelli, shrill-mouthed, French braids tight enough to pop veins.

"Corrine Willows," someone whispers. It's the name sizzling through the halls, behind locker doors, in the steaming cafeteria line. We were all in second grade and Corrine was two years ahead of us. Someone had climbed into her bedroom window during a slumber party, grabbed her, and disappeared into the night. The details, you remembered them. The Strawberry Short-cake sleeping bag, the shiny purple nightgown, the finger splint on her left hand, from when she jammed her finger in gym class. There were search parties. They dragged the lake and the Milky River.

"Willows was a nine-year-old kid," Tara Leary says, ruddy-faced and imperious. "It's not the same." Tara's father works for the district attorney. "Besides, all the cops know it was her dad, a custody thing. They just couldn't prove it."

It all made sense, but you didn't feel that kind of truth in your gut, so stories flew, knocked around, shimmied back, that it wasn't the father at all but someone in our very town, a child killer in our midst, who had hid Corrine's lifeless body in some place it would never be found, like under the floorboards of the high school gymnasium or the ice rink at the community center.

That whole day, and on buzzing phones that night, all the girls hiving around me, saying the child killer has struck again. There is a breathlessness about it.

"White slavery. That's what my mom says. She saw it on TV.

Evie's probably been sold to some sheiks, is on her way to the Arabs now."

"It's a perv. And they always kill them in the first twenty-four hours."

It's what the kids are saying, in tight little knots in hallways all through the school, they are giddy with it, with the fever of Evie being gone. But I don't believe them. I would know if Evie were dead. Something would hollow out in my chest and I would know. She's not gone, not gone like Corrine Willows, a name more than a girl, a bloody stitch we like to wedge our nail under and poke. Corrine Willows is only a hiss-whisper, an eerie blankness. That could never be Evie. We might not be body-close like we were, but we are close enough for me to know this: Evie never stops moving, her legs pumping, her smile fanning—*that* girl, I know. That girl I know better than me.

In bed that night I let my mind go anyplace but to Evie, to what might have happened.

I put my face to the window screen and look down at the furred night lawn.

Thinking of things, pondering in the dark. There's something nagging at me and I grapple for it. I'm not even sure what I'm tugging at, what that speck is in the corner of my head.

It's one thirty and everyone is asleep, or trying to be. I tiptoe down the stairs, my nightshirt twining between my legs, key chain flashlight curled in my hand.

The front door is right there, but I know its epic creak, like the sliding patio door, the way it squeaks open, then rattles after. Instead, I lift the half-open window in the family room, and crawl up on the sill, my knees wedging hard into the grooves.

I wish the pain weren't so pleasing, searing into my knees like that. I hate it when it feels like that, so solid I want to put my mouth to it. These are things too embarrassing to say. Only Evie would . . .

Tucking the flashlight in my mouth, I slip out the other side, my feet landing lightly on the grass, itching between my toes. Darting across the Verver driveway, I feel like a ghost.

There's a deliciousness to it, like so many times with Evie, our Brownies tent in the backyard, mouths and fingers sticky with marshmallows, rolling in nighttime grass, jittery with every sound, every echo, every katydid rubbing toothy wings, just for us.

There's something. What it is, I can't place it.

I press my palm to the brick wall because I feel like I might fall.

There was something here, something that might mean something. Something found, something that put an aha catch in my throat, but I can't reckon it now. I can't hold the ends together and lift it to my eyes.

I stumble around to the back of the house, stubbing my toe three times, the last time feeling a hot push of blood under my toenail.

Something's there, wedged beneath my foot.

I bend down and look upon it.

The fluorescent bend of the garden hose, the spike from its hard nozzle.

But it reminds me. It puts form to that hovering thought.

Three weeks, a month ago, Evie and I running our bikes to the back, out of the way for the gutter man to come with this big telescoping pole, raining down a spray of pinecones, twigs, and silt. Shake, shake like maracas, and there's more, more. Once a nest of baby sparrows came down, all dead, and since then Mrs.

Verver stays in her room with a cold washcloth on her forehead until it's over. "Who wants to see it all?" she said. "Who wants to see what's up there?"

We leaned our bikes against the pear tree in the center of the lawn, and that is where Evie shows me.

I remember thinking it was funny how little time we spend in the far reaches of the lawn now. When we were little we spent all our time there, bitty hands gnarled around the bark of the pear tree, clattering our way up to the top.

Evie crouched, her hands resting on the garden hose, which we are supposed to twine up on the big wheel for Carl, the gutter man.

"Do you want to see something?" she asked, and I settled down eagerly, always expecting such wonders, like a five-leaf clover, a two-headed worm, a piece of pottery from ancient times.

We hunkered down together, but all I saw were three cigarette stubs, spent matches curled upward. The word "Parliament" wraps around one of the white tips.

"Your sister?" I asked, although I can't picture Dusty—all those doll curls, her scrubbed face and smooth barrettes—sneaking smokes.

"No," she said, although I didn't know how she could be sure. I went to poke one with my finger, but she stopped me.

"My dad quit," she said, and I remembered Mr. Verver telling us how he did it, chewing on coffee stirrers, pipe cleaners, and bendy straws until he almost choked in the car one day, ran up over a curb.

"Maybe," I said, and I grinned at her. "Maybe not."

It would be fun, and then I could tease him about it, like Dusty, like she teased him when his friends came by to play cards and they left a pile of beer cans and she called him a degenerate. I could never say such things, but Dusty used marvelous words, and laid them forward, like a ladies' fan, spread. And Mr. Verver loved it, and wouldn't it be wonderful to make him smile, just for you?

Evie peered down at the grass, the papery stubs.

There was something in her face, a graveness. She was thinking, and I couldn't see my way into it. Charging through the back of my head came that thought: *It's happening again. More and more, Evie isn't exactly Evie any longer.* Something hung heavily, moody, behind her eyes, and I wanted to see. Like she had a weight hanging behind there and I could tap on it, swing it back and forth, but it wasn't mine.

How dare she keep it from me?

I gave her shoulder a shove. She, kneeling, toppled over backward, catching herself with her spindled arms.

I laughed, but it sounded wrong, a retchy laugh like Tara Leary's when she saw my sad little training bra.

Evie looked hard at me, weighing things, and said, "Sometimes, at night, he's out here."

The words plucked a quiver in me. I couldn't think what she must mean.

"You mean your dad," I said.

"No, another man."

"What man?" I said, my voice slow, confused. "A boy, you mean, one of Dusty's boys?"

She shook her head and looked up at her bedroom window, and I turned and looked up at it too. Dusty's window faces the front of the house, while Evie's faces the back. From where we were kneeling, you could see into Evie's room, the slant in the ceiling, the soccer ball mobile.

"What man, Evie?" I repeated.

And she pressed her palm flat on the cigarette butts. "I guess it was a dream. I guess it's all confused, like a dream."

She rubbed the side of her head and smiled, a goofy smile with all her teeth, and her arm darted out and shoved me too and I keeled back fast, my head sinking into the grass, and Evie was on top of me and laughing, and we were both laughing until Mrs. Verver shouted out for us to unlatch the gate for Carl.

And now here I am. And there are four cigarette butts, two pressed flat and two like curved seashells. You could put your ear to them and hear the sea.

They are there.

"Hi, Lizzie," Mr. Verver says. It's the third day. His eyes are threaded red and his stubble is thick like it was the time Dusty had to go to the emergency room, her appendix popped like a balloon.

"Hi," I say. "My mom said you wanted me to come over."

It all feels so funny because, having grown up with eyes always lifted to Mr. Verver, I can barely remember ever getting to talk to him without Evie there, except that time when we were seven and he took us to the Halloween Harvest at the county fairgrounds. Everyone wanted to go into the Haunted Hollow, where ghouls with pitchforks were supposed to chase you through a maze of corn. Clangs and screams thudded from the speaker behind the spook house door and I didn't want to go inside. Bantam Dusty spurred Evie on, and the two of them went, terror roistering up their faces, while Mr. Verver stood outside with me and assured me that haunted houses were for kids anyway. He bought me a sack of candy corn and showed me how to toss them high and catch them in my upturned mouth.

Later, he told Dusty I was shaking the whole time, tugging on his belt, eyes wide and mouth rigid. But I wasn't. I wasn't scared at all. That wasn't what it was.

"Lizzie," he says now, his voice cracked and stretched, "Evie needs your help. I need your help. We all do. You can tell me anything."

He reaches out and taps two fingers on my hand and makes me look straight in his eyes.

"No one's in trouble," he says. "You're not in trouble. But you may know something, even if it doesn't seem important. You were the one—" And he leans toward me and I can see the crinkles in his shirt and feel all the tiredness on him.

"You were the last one to see her. You're the closest link we have to what happened."

I can't pretend it doesn't startle me, the jangling look on Mr. Verver's face. I've never seen it on him before. It's not a look you see on adults, least of all Mr. Verver, who always carries himself so lightly, who runs on glimmers and grins and ease, laying his hands on things—broken bicycle handles, split hockey sticks, your arm so he could see the bug bite—as though, if he turned them just so, he could heal them, without even so much as a squint. Just by his hands.

But here he is, with the jangling look—and it disarms me.

My head feels clogged and I try and try.

There is something else, too, another faint, smoky smudge in the corner of my head, but I can't make it real.

Upstairs, I hear a lot of clomping and I know it's Dusty because Mrs. Verver never makes any noise. My mother told me, in her confidential tone, that Mrs. Verver had been throwing up for hours. I keep picturing it now. Once, after my dad left, my mom drank pink wine all night at the dinner table and got sick in the kitchen sink. It is a favorite tale of my brother's, who regales others with heaving imitations.

"Why was Mrs. Verver throwing up?" I'd asked my mother, who'd sighed and said, gravely, "I don't think you understand what's happening."

And that's when I stopped listening, shut my ears from the gloom and murk of her. It's almost like she savors the terribleness— everyone does. Like it does things for them, makes everything seem more exciting, more momentous, more real.

Evie's not gone, I wanted to say to her, and now as I sit on the Verver sofa, the sofa Evie and I used to wedge our hands into, sneaking crusty quarters after dinner parties, I know Evie's right here, watching, giggle-faced, that snaggletooth in the left corner of her mouth, where her chin hit the Benedicts' deck as she ran fast to get into their new fiberglass pool and under the water and down, down, down to its burning-chlorine center.

"Lizzie," Mr. Verver is saying, and his voice brings me back. "Is there anything else you can remember about that day? Anything she said, anything maybe out of the ordinary the last time you saw her?"

"I don't know," I say. "I can't think. She said she was going to walk home. She was behind the hedges and then she was gone."

He nods, like what I'm saying makes sense, which it does not. I'm trying hard to picture it all, to fall back into it like a dream you can make yourself dream twice.

"She said she didn't want a ride. I asked her if we could give her a ride. But she didn't want a ride. Is that weird? It doesn't seem so weird. It's weird because of this, but if it hadn't been for all this, I don't think it'd seem weird."

Mr. Verver nods, looking across the room at nothing in particular. "Everything seems weird now," he says. "It's all upside down."

I look out the window and see the detectives talking on the front porch, one of them smoking, like a cop on a TV show. I'm thinking about the cigarette butts again.

I feel dizzy and ask if I can use the bathroom. Standing in the Ververs' pink powder room, I look in the mirror and count to ten three times.

When I come out, I see Mr. Verver again, making coffee in that old dented pot he takes on fishing trips.

"Dusty broke the other one this morning," he says, trying for a smile. "Nerves."

"It might not be anything," I blurt.

He stops, the water running over his hand.

"What?"

"It's just—it's probably nothing," I stutter. I can see his face lifting and something swells in me.

"I know," he says. "But nothing is okay. It really is. Right now, nothing is more than we have."

We walk to the backyard, and I hope they're still there. My heart pit-pats and I worry that I dreamed those cigarettes into sputtering life.

Mr. Verver's hand is on my shoulder and I feel a weight on my chest.

Twenty paces walking to the knobby pear tree, but it seems, now, so far. I feel, with each step, every twig, kicked-up dirt, curling leaf, the sharp cut of a rake thatch. Soon enough, I am nearly running.

My eye catches the white first, and I see them, still there from last night, matted fast into a root corner of the tree.

Mr. Verver is already crouched down, and it's no dream. They are there. Hands on his thighs, he doesn't touch them.

"You found these?"

"Evie did. She showed them to me. Or ones like them. About a month ago."

His eyebrows rise. His face is doing all kinds of things, calculations and divinations.

"What did she say about them?"

Sometimes, at night, he's out here. That's what Evie'd said.

"Nothing," I lie. I don't know why, but the lie comes so easy that I feel its rightness.

He rises and looks at me and I think he can see the lie on me. I know he can.

I stare at the cigarette butts, flat and soggy, like a peel slipping from a hard center.

"Nothing," I say again, and look up at him, at those tangled eyes of his.

He *says thank you, then, he does, he puts his hands on my shoulders as if to hug me and he nearly hugs me but instead slips his fingers around one braid and tugs it soft and smiles. His face is popping with light and I feel my neck flushing, my face too, because I thought he might hug me, I did. Or throw me over his shoulder like a sack of potatoes when we were little and underfoot and he would swing Evie and me to and fro with our pigtails swaying and our squeals so loud and Dusty sitting at the kitchen table doing long division and yelling at us to stop and she always hated it when Mr. Verver played with us. But soon enough he hoisted her too, hoisted us all, one by one, from kitchen to living room, and flung us onto the sofa, the laugher was loud, Mrs. Verver running down the stairs to see who was on fire...*

Mr. Verver is talking with the detectives in the backyard. They're all circling the cigarette pile like it's a bonfire.

I'm watching through the kitchen window, the coffeepot chugging.

Sometimes, at night, he's out here.

That's what Evie had said.

When she said it, it was just a cold-spiny feeling, a bit of nighttime spookiness. But later, it snuck back into my thoughts, and I wondered about all the boys who trailed Dusty, who swarmed her in the school corridors, who wedged notes in her locker and buzzed around her. So many of them might flit around at night, like Bobby Thornhill, might conspire to watch for her, might end up, even, in the backyard, mistaking Evie's window for hers.

I thought, nastily, of their disappointment, catching a glimpse of Evie's post-rail frame, her barely bud breasts, lying on her bed, her stick legs crossed, rocking gently, her white socks with pom-poms jittering.

Mr. Verver walks into the kitchen, his whole body jumping with energy. "They think it could be something," he says. "They don't know, but they think it could be."

I feel a tingle on my tongue. I feel it because I think, Doesn't he see what this means? Isn't this scarier, a hundred times, the idea that wherever Evie is she might be with someone who watched her, for nights on end, from the dark sweep of a back-yard tree, who watched, unhurried, unbothered, puffing and breathing and watching and—

Something clicks and shutters in my head, and there it is, there it is, tumbling from my half-open mouth:

"The car. Twice. I saw a car go by twice."

"What?" Mr. Verver says, cautiously, gently, his fingers touching the edge of the counter. "A car?"

"The maroon car. When we were waiting for my mom, it went by twice. At least twice." I feel very excited, bobbing slightly as I stand, sneakers tapping the linoleum.

"Do you know what kind of car, Lizzie?" he asks, and his eyes are suddenly so bright, so clear.

"I don't know." I can barely say it. "But . . . but I know that car. I've seen that car."

I'm not even sure what I mean when I say it, but it's true.

The detectives, perched all around, show me pictures of cars from a big, fat binder. Pages and pages of cars. But it doesn't work because it's not how the remembering of it happened. I can't picture the car itself, it's the feeling when I saw it, the flicker of curiosity, the question dangling there, *Why is it driving so slowly, isn't that the same car—*

A flicker, and then it was gone.

Someone's lost, Evie said. Didn't she say that?

And I can picture almost recognizing the car in that second, that fleeting second when she spoke, the recognition hovering just out of my reach, I had only to tug it down.

An hour or more passes, Mr. Verver pacing, and Mrs. Verver sedated, and me not knowing what to do, going to the kitchen to fill my water glass two, then three times. Once, I walk past the staircase and hear Dusty sobbing in her room.

Finally, the phone rings and it's for Detective Thernstrom and he talks for a while and then comes back and asks me if I know the car because in fact I see it every day, every day on Cloverly

Way, which is on the way to school, the same six blocks I walk every day, twice a day. Isn't that where I've seen it?

And I begin to feel thoughts plunking at me again, at some back corners in my head.

"It's a Skylark, isn't it? A Buick Skylark?" he says and points to a picture of a shiny black car that looks like any other car to me.

I start to say, "But it was maroon," but I stop myself because I know it sounds stupid.

I squint at the picture and press my finger on it. It's the car. It is.

That's when everything scatters into a thousand pieces and reassembles with pinpoint clarity. A picture in my head of the car, the man, the man in the car.

"Mr. Shaw," I say. "It's Mr. Shaw's car."

Five

I have said the words, I have said his name and slapped my hand on the photo of the random Buick. I have said the words and everything springs to hectic life.

I'm not sure what's happening, but everyone seems to be moving, and one detective is on the phone again and Detective Thernstrom is talking to Mr. Verver in the corner and Mr. Verver is listening intently, his hands clenching and unclenching as he stares at the carpet. From the look on his face, I don't know whether, like in the fairy tale, I've found magic balm from the hollow center of a tree, or whether I've opened the ground beneath us all, and we're now plummeting fast into the dark earth.

"Shaw's wife called the station this morning," Detective Thernstrom is saying to Mr. Verver.

I'm at the dining room table, looking at pictures of cars. One of the deputies is talking to me, but I'm not listening. I'm listening to Detective Thernstrom's slow, calm voice, and to Mr. Verver's raspy uh-huhs.

"She said her husband was supposed to be at an insurance convention upstate. When she didn't hear from him, she started calling the hotel and the convention staff. They all say he never checked in. She hasn't seen him in two days."

"And we know that's his car?" asks Mr. Verver, a voice darty and hectic. "Harold Shaw. I've known him—not well, but known him—ten years. We know that's his Skylark?"

"That's his make and model. If that's the car she saw, well, this is a big break. We have two officers heading up to the convention hotel now. We put out the APB. We're interviewing everyone who knows the Shaws. All our resources are on this... it's our number one priority."

Detective Thernstrom's voice lowers, and I strain to hear. I feel like Detective Thernstrom's talking about me now. Like he's saying, *She might know more. She might know everything.*

But that's when the deputy starts poking me with questions again. "How fast was the car going? You're sure you saw it twice? The same car?" And I can't think of anything at all, and sometimes their voices spike again, and I hear Mr. Verver say, "But what can I do here? What can I do?"

That sound, the creak at the center of his throat, it's something I've never heard from him, and it hums in me, powerfully.

Now, in my head, when I picture that Skylark going by, I can see Mr. Shaw behind the wheel. Though in my head, it's not even maroon anymore but black, like the one in the book they showed me, the picture lodging in my brain.

I can see Mr. Shaw behind the wheel.

Mr. Shaw carries a briefcase and wears brown loafers and tie-pins. He's my mother's insurance agent, or was, and the Ververs' too. He's old in the sport-jackety way of math teachers and principals and doctors, older by decades, it seems, than Mr. Verver.

Mr. Shaw has the glass-front office on Cloverly Way, right where the street slopes down fast. When I picture him, he's there. I'm on my bike, riding past, coasting, sneakers kicking up, and I turn my head, glancing in, seeing him there, blue blazer, wispy brown hair, a pen in his hand, holding it like he's not sure what it is or how it got there. And then he's gone.

Or no, no, another time, walking by and seeing him standing, hands on hips, looking out the window as he talks soundlessly to someone, his mouth moving but the rest of his face still.

Or there, there, over on, what street is it? Huntington? Washing that maroon car in his driveway, golf shirt spattered, his son, Pete, the one in Dusty's class, twisting a big golden sponge, Walkman cord dangling, and Mr. Shaw, face so plain, arms pale, chin faintly shadowed.

"I've never talked to him," I tell the detectives. "I never saw Evie talk to him."

Why would Evie ever talk to him? It all seems so impossible. Like it's a big mistake, and somewhere up north Mr. Shaw is stiff-backed in some convention room chair, doing whatever people at conventions do, unaware of all the wretched scenarios spinning around him.

But elsewhere in my head, I seem to know something, or guess at it. The look I've been seeing on Evie's face, behind her eyes. But I don't talk about that. I don't tell them about Evie's face and what it carries because it's just a guess, a feeling, because I know Evie so blood-thick. I know her so well that I know when I no longer know everything.

And Evie, in showing me those cigarette stubs, was showing me something private, mysterious, a slippery secret, which is what we did. Mouth to ear, we shared everything. Until we didn't.

My mother sits me down at the kitchen table. She quit smoking after the divorce, when she started taking aerobics and got the lemony highlights in her hair. But there is a cigarette flaring in her hand now, slipped from that Benson & Hedges pack she keeps wedged under the leg of one of the lawn chairs on the back patio.

"Lizzie, how well do you know Mr. Shaw?"

It seems a funny way to ask it. I tell her I don't know him at all, which is true. I know him like I know anyone's dad. They're all dads.

She takes a deep breath and shakes her head. "It's so terrible. I don't know how Annie is managing. Either of them. I don't know at all."

"It's okay, Mom." I can't think of what else to say. This is not the way she usually talks to me and it seems like if I say the wrong thing, it will make her more nervous.

She looks at the cigarette in her hand, turning it like she doesn't recognize it.

"Do you think he's hurt her?" I finally ask. I don't think I've let the idea really cross my mind until that moment.

"No," my mother says, jerking up suddenly, face set, eyes on me. "No, honey. It's a mistake. It's all a crazy mistake."

Her lie is somehow meaningful and I can feel the weight of it.

No one is saying it, but everyone seems to be so sure. Why would Mr. Shaw take Evie if he didn't mean to touch her, to do things to her?

But no one's actually saying it, no adults can say the words aloud. And I fight the ideas in my head, shake them off. They're ugly things, and I don't even know where they've come from. They're like choppy collages, pieces pulled from cable movies caught late at night, hand-wringing school assemblies, leering reenactments on news shows, and snapshotted Evie in her soccer jersey, clipped in, her face pasted on bodies nude and scandalized.

I go to my room, pull out a stack of old, gold-spined horse books, and read them for hours.

S i x

Mr. Shaw. He's the one. The way they talked at school, the
way everyone had been talking, you'd think it had to be
some lurching drifter, claw for a hand, living out of his truck.

But it's Mr. Shaw.

A hundred times, you would see him paying the newspaper
boy, or filling his gas tank, and he was just a man, and now he's
the one who took Evie in that Buick. He has taken her away and
has maybe done things to her and done, done, done.

A hundred men like him in the five blocks on either side, and
I never noticed one.

It's that night, the third night. It's after the emergency PTA meeting, my mother's on the phone all night with parents, the phone
ringing all the time, and my brother is walled up in his room, TV
on, stereo on, everything on, and the vibrations, when I press my
hand to the door, thunder through me. It's like some booming,
screeching spell struck across the threshold to keep me out.

So I walk from room to room. It's like I think I'll find Evie
there, crouched under the window seat, twined in the shower
curtain, and she'll be laughing, laughing that we all cared so
much.

"Harold Shaw," my mother says, standing in the doorway of my room. "It doesn't seem possible. It really does not." She shakes her head.

I don't say anything, but I turn off the light on my bedside table and she drifts away down the hall.

There's a picture in my head of my mother at one of those Memorial Day picnics, stringing up fairy lights with Mr. Shaw, asking him to help her off a ladder. Did it really happen, and did she giggle girlishly when he lifted her and set her daintily on the ground? And that makes me think of all the parents at block parties when we were kids, the way they would huddle with one another's spouses, sneaking off for smokes like teenagers, dancing too close, dropping beer bottles and tripping across lawns. Like married people love to do. And they love to make their husbands, their wives, act the knuckle-rapping parents all day so they can play the wayward kid. Is being young so magical that they must conjure it up again, can't help themselves? I don't see any magic in it at all.

That night, in bed, I picture the way it was. Twice a day, five days a week, all school year long, Evie and I walking, running, biking past the big windows of the All-Risk office, with Mr. Shaw there. Mr. Shaw always there. Looking out with those gloomy eyes of his.

He looks so sad, Evie said once. Oh, the sudden remembering of it now brings on a shiver.

He's so sad, she said. We were looking at the sign in the window: LIFE INSURANCE, FIRE INSURANCE, FLOODS. *He must hear sad stories all day long.*

He always looks like his dog died, she said, and I laughed, but Evie didn't.

$\star$ $\star$ $\star$

Last night's emergency PTA meeting, and everything's changed. There are many announcements, from teachers, from the gravely voiced principal across the PA. The new rules.

"It's lockdown," Joannie groans.

Trapped in the gym, with the windows covered with GO, CELTS! in streaks of swampy green paint, we all wait.

My legs are still shaking from practice, that aching, stretchy feel that's so delectable, like my body being pulled in five ways and sprung back strong and magnificent.

It never lasts.

Some days, Evie and I lie on the soccer field and take turns pulling each other's legs as hard as we can, pulling until we feel torn in two. I have two inches on Evie and she says it's because she's stronger and could pull harder and I owe those two inches to her.

To escape the noise from the boys doing basketball drills, the bunch of us girls nest up in a corner of the bleachers and do not acknowledge their hoarse-voiced, bare-limbed, flaunting presence.

Intermittently, we play Flame, a folded-paper game of mammoth complexity, where you add up the vowels in your name and some boy's and get a number and then count the letters in F-L-A-M-E, crossing out "hits" until you have one letter left. It tells you your future with the boy: F equals "Friends," L equals "Lovers," A equals "Affair," M equals "Marriage," and E equals "Enemies."

We talk about the difference between an affair and being lovers. Tara says that affair means one-time sex. Joannie says affair means sex any number of times, only with not caring. I can't decide, but I shake my legs out and wonder where the stretching feeling went. My whole body's gone tight, pleated inside.

Most of the time, though, we talk about Evie.

"She's probably in some basement somewhere," someone chirps, "tied to a pipe."

"Pete Shaw wasn't in school today."

"He'd better not be. They'd swing him from the goalposts."

Everyone seems to know that Mr. Shaw is, as Joannie keeps putting it, the "prime suspect," and there's much talk of my seeing the car, which can only have come from Tara, with her assistant prosecutor dad. It has made me tremendously popular.

"It might've been you, Lizzie," Joannie says, pointing at me with her curving dolphin pen with the finned tip. "It just might have been you."

The thought had not come to me. Now it rockets around in my head. Could it be true? If I'd been the one left alone, the one on the empty street in front of the emptied-out school? What if it had been me yanked from everything to some dark place? Could Mr. Shaw have—

"No way," Tara says, shaking her head definitively. "He had his target in his sights."

I remember the cigarette stubs, and I know she's right. It was never me.

With that, the furtive shimmers that shimmered briefly in my head snuff out.

I see him, when my eyes are shut, standing under the dark boughs of the pear tree, standing in the middle of the yard, waiting. What did he see in spindly Evie, her big rain-puddle eyes, her jumpy little body, the way she sucked her teeth when thinking, hard, over algebra, the way she picked the frilled edges off her spiral notebook, one by one?

This girl, this girl, and he a man with a business and a secretary and a house with a furnace and bills and a son and a roof with three torn shingles and a pretty birdbath made of stone that I sometimes see Mrs. Shaw, her hair tied back with a scarf, cleaning with a dainty skimmer.

How does this man, a man like this, like any of them, come to walk at night and stand in a girl's backyard, and then, smoking and looking up, suddenly feel himself helpless to her bright magic?

Seven

My brother, Ted, picks me up after school. His eyes lost behind sunglasses, he is confident and impressive as he flicks the steering wheel to and fro, his long limbs poking from every corner of the front seat, his hair long over his ears.

As he rounds corners, I pinball back and forth in my seat. The streets look so empty, like it's Christmas. All those packs of raucous kids, all that rabid energy, gone. I picture all of them in their family rooms, their dens, staring at TV screens, their parents lurking in the doorframe, standing guard.

We drive by the All-Risk office, heavy-metal guitars crunching on the car radio, Ted with his enormous basketball-player hand fisted over the gearshift.

The office is dark, the red watch face on the CLOSED sign grinning from behind the smoked glass.

"Sick motherfucker," Ted shouts as we pass. The car windows are closed, but he shouts anyway.

Something about it makes me want to laugh. Ted heaves the steering wheel, and we charge down our street, the bass tickling in my thighs, my hands fast on the door handle, holding on tight. I hear my backpack fling across the backseat.

The screech when we roil up the driveway jolts me and I see

the blinds sway in Mrs. Darlton's next-door window, her tsk-tsking face thrusting through.

"Listen," Ted says, turning down the music as I gather my books, fanned across the floor of the backseat, "you lock everything up. I have to be someplace. You can't leave, though, or Mom'll kill us both."

"Okay," I say.

It's the longest exchange I have had with him since he taught me how to fill my bike tire in the fourth grade.

I open the car door and climb out. We both stare at the house, which looks so very still. From the corner of my eye, I see the Ververs' screen door, the way it puckers out and you can peek in, but now the heavy front door is closed and the curtains drawn across all the front windows, like wintertime when we'd frost the glass with spray snow from a can.

It's all closed up, and our house too. It's like coming back from a week at the shore and pulling up the drive and thinking, Is this our house? Could this really be our house? It's like the doors and windows shut and shuttered themselves, tucking themselves within.

Ted clears his throat, and I see that I'm still holding onto the open car door, my fingers tight on it.

"We're okay, right?" he asks. I can see myself in his sunglasses and I think I look thick and monstrous, with a grave line furrowed across my forehead.

"Yeah," I say, and I watch myself say it, and we both turn and look at the house again.

Inside, it's so quiet and lonely and I wish I could knock the soccer ball around in the yard, but I don't want the Ververs to see me.

Walking from room to room, feeling like a burglar, I poke in errant places, touch my fingers to the peach-skinned covers of *Hustler* on the floor of Ted's closet, the womens' mouths so open and red, and the way their legs open so redly. It makes me touch my hand to my neck and the dizziness comes fast.

Ted, who's likely buried at this moment in a swirl of his girl-friend Nina's white blond hair, her fingernails always painted lilac, her fingers always clawed over Ted's denimed knee.

In my mother's room, I finger her bottle of Je Reviens, screwing off the gold-tone top and running the dauber along my wrists like when I was seven years old and would stare at the box: "Recommended for romantic wear" in foil script.

The room is orderly, hushed, and my socks spark on the carpet. It's a room I've hardly been in since the first few weeks after Dad left and she'd ask me to crawl into bed with her and, phone cord wrapped around us both, call him and ask him how he could do this to us and did he mean to destroy the family.

Later, she made me promise to forgive her for all that because she should never have been so weak and she meant to set a good example of self-proud womanhood. But she could say it and say it and say it, yet I wondered if I'd ever see that tender-soft way about her again, the way she'd put on her special silky wine-colored dress for Dad and the Je Reviens daubed on the bow in the middle of her bra—a secret mother passed to daughter, even as she blushed to tell it. I was nine and it was the most enticing slip of adulthood that had ever passed through my fingers.

It's with a stub of my toe now that I nearly trip and my eye catches something peeking out from under the creamy doily-edged duvet on my mother's bed. Leaning down, I see it, a man's dark sock curled on the floor like a bat wing. Plucking it between thumb and forefinger, I lift it, turning it around.

I think imaginative thoughts of him, her nighttime guest, her

Dr. Aiken, tripping down the hallway, like a man on fire, hurtling out the front door, bare foot to gas pedal in his silver Lincoln before he realized what he'd left behind.

My tour landing me in my own room, I pull my new graduation dress from the closet, still in its plastic bag, slickery silver. The cabbage roses blare grotesquely. It didn't seem that way in the store at all. Turning fast in the dressing room mirror, shaking off my mother's barks ("Pull your hair off your face, Lizzie"), I'd surveyed myself and felt glamorous, the roses spread across my chest, sprouting there, the illusion of full-flower breasts, and across my hips the illusion of curves and womanliness, or teen-girlness at least. On my bare tiptoes, battered shins hidden by starchy folds, I was nearly Dusty, if you squinted, from far away.

I think about how, while I was spinning, ballerina style, before the trifold department store mirrors, it was all happening. Evie, gone in the blink of an eye. Did he blindfold her and shove her in his backseat? Or worse, like in that TV movie, was she locked in the trunk where she might, if canny, disconnect the brake-light wire? We'd watched that movie, together, hadn't we, lying on the family room floor? Maybe Evie remembered the way the girl had been so smart and kicked out the taillight and pushed her arm through the broken plastic and waved and waved until the handsome police officer spotted the arm, the white, waving arm. Dusty, wry on the couch above us, saying it must be an old movie because all trunks have emergency releases now, but Evie wasn't so sure and I wasn't either.

Thinking of Evie trapped in some dark space like that, it makes me want to tear and tug, and I pull at the silvery plastic dress bag until the plastic pops over my knuckles and the dress slides from its padded hanger to the floor and I kick it into the back of the closet.

I slam the door and the mirror on it rattles, and I feel very dramatic: this is what you do when your best friend has been taken, it's what you do. You fear for her and feel for her and slam doors and sob.

But there is something creeping in the back of me, and it makes me know things. Like that Evie was never in Mr. Shaw's trunk. This, I know. I don't know how, but I do. Like I know too that she is not dead, not buried in three feet of dirt, not coated in pearly lime. No, she is not dead, she is lost, lost. Missing. Gone. There's lots of things behind those words, and I can't look at them now. But I feel them.

The next day, I wake up, and I don't know what I think, but I guess it was that there'd be news. That all those police skittering across the state would surely have found the breadcrumb trail. But my mother, hand perched on the kitchen radio, keeps shaking her head.

"*. . . Verver girl . . . Police have received more than two hundred calls on the tip line, but have nothing to report . . .*"

What I thought was this: I'd given them what they needed, hadn't I? The cigarette stubs, the car? What was stopping them now? Couldn't they just hurl out their long hook and pull him—both of them—in?

Ted picks me up again, but he forgets his Spanish book and we have to go back to the high school.

While he's inside, I wait in the parking lot, kicking at one of the curbs and looking out to the hockey field, thinking of things, dreaming things into their right places, versus how they are, so broken and askew.

I see someone running, a green flicker. I find myself reaching for the car door, but when I spin around again, the flicker's not there and instead it's Dusty, in uniform and a thick runner's turtleneck, stopping now, wrapping her stick with tape, her knee raised high on a wood bench, her shin streaked with dirt.

I start to say something and stop myself, but she hears me, lifting her head and looking at me through the blond disarray, her fulsome bangs loose from her tight, toothed headband.

"You want me to drill you?" she says.

I think of walking by the Verver stairwell, hearing her crying upstairs.

"I didn't know you were in school," I say as she stands upright.

"Here I am," she says, composed, but, for a second, something hitches in her face. How could it not, even as serene as she is, so serene and poised.

"Get midfield," she says, picking up one of the composite sticks left behind after practice and handing it to me. "I'll shadow. See what you learned last week."

I don't know what to say, but I don't see how it can be no, so I take the stick and breathe in hard, hard as I can, because I feel like she's going to pitch everything at me, just to get it off herself, lift it from her shoulders, and I need to be ready. Before I can think, the ball whistles toward me like a battle shell and I drop to the ground to stop my face from splitting in two.

I keep trying spin dodges, but she's everywhere all at once, her arm like a scythe, and I wonder if my brother will arrive to save me from certain death.

It's five terrorizing minutes before I breathe again, the force of her coming at me, the speed with which she is on me, stick, arm, jab, the gust of her hair, the sucking sound of her stick sweeping, slicing, my legs spiraling beneath and dragging me down with a thud three, four, five times.

Five times, ten times, she takes it from me. Three, four times, I feel the hard kick of the ground knock my chin backward, my teeth rattling like loose pennies.

Then, I think I finally have it, I have a shot, one shot, but just looking at her in front of me, legs apart, puts a fear in me I can't shake.

She could always do that to me, since we were little kids, me standing, wide-eyed, stunned by that gold-sparked perfection. She could tear you down with a glance, a flicked wrist, a slow-blinking eyelash.

Then the ball is there, and the toe of her stick down like a guillotine and the block comes so fast, my head jerks like it might pop off.

I am sitting on the ground, my breath like scraping metal, and Dusty is far afield, her face flush, her breath coming fast too, but in excited fits and starts. She smiles at me, wry, and is saying something about how I've done good, or something like it, amid all the ringing in my head.

She's above me and her hand is outstretched and I wobble to my feet and that's when, with her swinging me up, so strong, I see the change in her face. The gleaming triumph breaks into something soft and desolate, and the breath in sounds almost, almost like a sob, our hands interlocked.

"Dusty, I—" I start, but she whips around, stick to her side, nearly slicing me, and she's running off the field, curls swinging.

Later, I wonder if she went back into the locker room and let herself cry, head between her knees. But I think that's my dream of Dusty. The way she is, which is lionhearted, magnificent, those few tears she nearly shook fast on the field—that's the most I'd get.

★　　★　　★

That night, the reporter on the Channel 2 news with the blond ledge of hair is holding up a Parliament and saying, "Cigarettes much like these were found in the Ververs' backyard," but adds, gravely, "but whether these cigarettes are linked to the alleged abduction is uncertain."

Watching, my mom is amped up at the kitchen table. She'd brought a casserole over to the Ververs and she says the police were there again.

"They keep getting these endless reports of Harold Shaw sightings," she says. "One of them's got to come through. They sent two detectives up to the border. They think he might be in Canada. The wife—Kitty . . . she said he had an old college friend up in Ontario somewhere."

She goes on like this, and I'm listening, but mostly it's about how Mrs. Verver can't sleep, can't eat, lost seven pounds in five days, and then about how frightening a place the world is for mothers.

I wait until her show comes on, and then I sneak outside and drop into a lawn chair, twist myself into the rubbery slats, wedge feet and toes beneath.

Oh, these long curfewed evenings and no gallivanting, hopping yard to yard with Evie, pedaling bikes up to Rabbit Park to swing on the rusty merry-go-round or pump legs on the squeaky swings. No ice cream, no riffling through magazines at the drugstore and giggling through the feminine products aisle, nose to the tip of the lavender bottles dappled with flowers promising such cleanness, such powdery, perfumed womanly cleanness.

Instead, I sit and contemplate my foot, the cool dent from Dusty's fiberglassed saber, its terrorizing J hook.

There is something holy and badgelike about the injury, about the flaring bruise on my ankle, the hardening scabbed streak up my shin from the cut rendered by my own desperate stickwork.

Savoring my war wounds, I sit, and feel I deserve rich rewards. Spotting my mother's secret Benson & Hedges pack crammed into the wet dirt of a gangly potted geranium, I think about pulling one out and lighting up. Evie and I did it once. It hurt our throats, but the good kind of hurt. That's what we said.

Are there cigarettes in every backyard, every garage, every toolshed or bird feeder?

I spot a lemon wedge sucked dry in the corner of the patio. Sliding my foot out from beneath me, I take my toe to it, kick it loose, watch it wheel across the pebbled expanse, hollow and paper light.

This is where she sits with him, with Dr. Aiken, who wears squared glasses and, in my head, always seems to be carrying a clipboard, wearing a stethoscope, even though I've never seen him with either. He's not my doctor and wasn't my mother's. She met him, Ted confided—but how did he know?—at the snack bar at the pool last summer, but that seems too long ago, so I'm not sure. I think I've felt him in the house only since March, since that night he brought her that book, the one called *The Heart of the Matter*, which he said he'd promised to loan her and which she read even while washing the dishes. I never saw her read like that before, but it was soon after that all the huddled conversations in the backyard started, all the mixing of drinks and long telephone calls and a steamy pink look on my mother's face.

She doesn't talk about him, but he's everywhere, all over the house. Once I saw him through my window at four in the morning, saw him rustling through the patio shrubs, looking for his glasses, which he cleaned with the tail of his untucked shirt.

He leaves himself everywhere, I think. He leaves bits and pieces and scraps and shavings.

It's strange, a little, sitting where he sits, even though it's our patio, my patio.

I can hear the Darltons' television drifting from their living room, the theme music with the big strings and whirling piano. And, from upstairs, Ted's baseball game, *And there's a strike on the outside edge...*

Then, just like that, Mr. Verver emerges from the green of his backyard, a finger shoved into a brown beer bottle.

He swings it back and forth as he walks toward me.

The startled *oh!* that springs from my mouth, I didn't even know it was there, and he looks at me and I feel my face scrub up hot.

"Hi, Mr. Verver," I say. I wonder how long he's been in his driveway. Has he seen me eyeing those cigarettes? Has he seen the awkward way I've been sitting, hands between my thighs?

"Hey, Lizzie." He smiles slightly, forelock dangling like a football player. His shirt looks dirty, like he wore it to sleep.

I feel my hand go to tuck my hair behind my ear.

It's the first time I've talked to him in two days. The first time since I recognized the car, since I told him about the cigarette butts. Since everything seemed like it was hurtling fast toward something, whatever something might be. That's how it seemed two days ago, but here we are, Mr. Shaw everywhere and nowhere at once, and no closer to Evie at all.

I think of how disappointed he must be in me because in some way he thought I had given him a golden key. I wish I had given him a golden key.

He stands over me and pauses, eyes crinkling.

Then, and I can scarcely believe it as I see it, he settles into the chair beside me, legs astride.

"So how are you. How's school," he says, looking off into the hazy stretches of the yard.

"Okay," I say, but it sounds ridiculous. "You know, strange." My hand reaches to scratch a phantom mosquito bite on the back of my knee.

Talking to him, talking like this to *Mr. Verver,* feels so big and important. I don't want it to stop, but I don't know how to make it go forever. I never had this before, never had him like this, just talking to me.

"Everything's been canceled," I say. "Practices and stuff."

I feel my face flushing. I can't really look over at him, but I can feel his eyes on me.

"You miss her very much," he says, with such gentleness, as though I am the one to be comforted, soothed. "Don't you?"

I feel my mouth open slightly, but nothing comes out.

He pats me lightly on the arm with the tips of warm, callused fingers.

Looking at him, I see such heaviness on his face, like I've never seen. I think of dire things. This isn't how it's supposed to be. Not for him.

"Yeah," I finally say, the small hairs on my arms tingling. "But she's coming back."

I say it and I can't believe I'm saying it and I know it's true. I know it.

Mr. Verver encloses my wrist in his hand and smiles sadly, his eyes unfocusing and drifting to someplace over my left shoulder.

"Yeah. Yes, that's right."

He doesn't believe me, and the knowing of it pierces me. I want him to know, really know, in the blood, in the bones, as I do.

Oh, Evie, what you have carved out, unloosed, scooped out clean, such fullness, such wholeness, and what's he to do?

How can I make him believe? I wonder.

I look at him with all the Evieness I can flood my face with. I promise him over and over, without saying one word.

Know it, know it. Know me.

I *don't remember it all, it's in the dungeonmost part of my head, but I was four, five years old, and he saved me. It was at Green Hollow Lake, and so many families, it was Fourth of July or it was Labor Day or it was some big summer picnic and I remember the ashy hot dog buns from the grill and the tang of ketchup warming on paper plates and I was there on my brassy yellow Hawaiian Punch raft, floating next to Evie, so alike then no one could tell us apart, our hair cut in the same bobs, our squirmy little bodies in matching checked swimsuits.*

We were all there and it was before they roped off the beach because of that rough current and there was so much noise and frenzy and I remember the feeling of the raft against my cheek, the way I tried to block everything out, to push myself into the center of the raft and hear nothing but the low pounding of the water, my heart.

Somehow, the shoving and nonsense of older boys, or the slickness of the seaweed snared around my kicking ankles, or something, I tumbled into the lake, and no one saw. There were minutes, centuries, in those murky depths. That is how I think of it now, epochs floating, vanished, forgotten. No one saw. Until Mr. Verver scooped me up, shook me like a wet puppy, lifted me as if by my neck scruff, and saved me then and there.

I remember — do I? — spouting green sludge, lake bottom sorrow, a tadpole wiggling in his arms. The rough towel on me, Mr. Verver there now, his bright white grin. "You slid away like a scaly fish," he said. "You don't get away so easy." Huddled fast against his chest, the warmth then came, like a promise.

I remember that.

Eight

That night, the dream comes, and it's Evie at the foot of my bed, mouth stuffed with cotton, just like before. And I sit up and reach down and pull it in long tufts from her mouth, long tufts that wind through my fingers like swirls of snow.

More comes, more, and I let my hands rise up high, to her chin and to her open mouth, which is now black and bottomless.

Like Nurse Stang, my fingers slip in, touch the wetness there.

Your stitches are gone, I say, as my fingers push against her tongue, rasping cotton free in filmy tendrils.

I don't need them, she says, and sticks her tongue out, propelling my fingers back.

The tongue, it dangles like a red ribbon. But I look closer and see it is split in two, like a snake's. Like the king cobra they showed us at the zoo.

I reach out to it, and her jaw clicks, like it might snap loose, like her mouth might swallow her face. It's then I realize it's not Evie at all but the thing that took Evie deep inside and is hiding her there.

Tara Leary always has things to tell in the locker room after gym. Her pipeline of secret knowledge surges constantly, we are ankle-deep in it. She hears everything, her gaping-mouth mother phoning in dispatches. Before, her dad's job at the prosecutor's office meant only that we all had to go to the morgue for Biology class. Now it means she is the keeper of all life-death knowledge and revelation.

I am her most favored steward. She knows the police have talked to me, and therefore we two are part of a special category, an elite.

We're in the shower stalls, and she's whispering to me through the curtain.

"I heard my dad tell my mom," she says. "They got the search warrant for Mr. Shaw's house."

She tells me the police also got an anonymous tip that he had boxes of pornographic magazines and videos hidden in the garage.

"Whoever called must've seen them," she says. I can see the shadow of her mouth through the curtain as she talks. "He hid them under stacks of old newspapers or something. His wife probably never knew. He probably went out there at night."

I try not to picture it, not to see Mr. Shaw in a garage like our garage, with my dad's old workbench and the transistor radio and the dozens of boxes labeled SHIMS, DOWELS, SCREWS, HINGES/ PULLS. Mr. Shaw in his bathrobe, standing under an overhanging lightbulb, looking, looking, looking—

"It's called kiddie porn," Tara is saying, and I touch my side of the rubber curtain, feeling the vibration of her voice against my fingers, telling myself she is lying.

"I heard there was this one video," she continues, "where they show this little girl and she's a pure virgin because she's, like, nine, and this long line of men, some of them, like, fat or old, they come along and rape her one by one and then they kill her and they really kill her because it's called a snuff film. They snuff her out. My dad said that it's just as well by that point because what's gonna happen to a nine-year-old girl who's been raped by, like, twenty guys in an hour?"

Tara's voice is clear and sharp, sliding through my brain like a hot needle. I want her to stop, but I can't catch my breath or get my voice back.

Here's the thing: Evie is gone, has been gone for six days, and no one can find her and it is not long, another day, before it starts to feel like no one really expects her to be found. It starts to feel like everyone is waiting to hear where the body was dumped and what was done to it.

"If you can think of anything else, anything at all," Mr. Verver says. "Day or night. You can come over, you can call."

This is what he says. We never had anything together like this. Now we do. We have this.

"Sometimes, Lizzie," he says, "we think we don't remember things, and then suddenly we do. Like you with the car. Wasn't that something, the way you were able to summon that up? And then sometimes we don't connect things, but they *may be* connected. Like you did with the stubs. You're smart as a whip, Lizzie, and you've been a lifesaver. Where would we be without your help? So I'm just saying, anything comes to you, anything at all, just come over. Find me. Or call, even if it's the middle of the night. Okay?"

Yes, Mr. Verver, yes, yes.

★　　★　　★

Joannie and Tara and I are perched on our bike seats three doors down from the Shaw house, thick with cops. Tara has been passing tantalizers about the search warrant, so we skip fifth period and now hover madly from afar. It seems certain we'll be caught, grisly truants, rubberneckers, ghouls. But we have to see.

We don't catch even a glimpse of Mrs. Shaw, or Pete, who still has not returned to school.

We're there only ten minutes before a patrolman spots us, follows us back to school, but before he does we got to see the detectives duck under the half-open garage door with flashlights, and Tara nodded so self-satisfiedly. We did not see them come out.

It's on TV that night. My mother, head craned over her tea, listens intently, shushing my brother. The newscaster says police won't confirm it, but that "inside sources" say that a search took place. On all three channels, they keep talking about Mr. Shaw as a missing person who "may or may not be a suspect in the Verver girl disappearance."

On Channel 7, they mention lab testing of the cigarette butts, though "it remains a question if anything can be retrieved, given rain and exposure to the elements." And, the lady newscaster adds, "According to his family and friends, Mr. Shaw was not a smoker."

"He gave it up years ago," says a pinch-nosed woman identified as Mr. Shaw's bookkeeper. "For his health."

"Sources close to the investigation," the lady newscaster says, in closing, "say that no cigarettes were found during the alleged search of the Shaw house."

I feel my mother's eyes on me, watching my reaction. I don't give her anything, even as it hits me, spins me.

I know they were his cigarettes in the Verver yard. I know it.

"Maybe the police just missed them," I say. "You can hide cigarettes anywhere."

"Maybe he stashes them on the patio," Ted says, in that snide, prodding way he has with our mother. "Under a flowerpot."

But we are in such a serious space that my mother doesn't even look up when he says it, doesn't lose her focus for a split second.

"We have to consider the possibility that these may be two unrelated disappearances," the jowly chief of police says. The TV anchor nods with gravity, but in the chief's eyes you can see it: *he knows it's Mr. Shaw, we all know, don't we?*

"Well, I just don't understand this," my mother is saying. "Do they really think, after all this, that..."

But it is Mr. Shaw. I know it, soul deep. Somehow, it's like I even knew before it happened. Must've felt it on some deeper level when I saw Mr. Shaw's car licking past us that day. And didn't Evie share it with me during that momentous second in her backyard, kneeling over cigarette stubs, a secret so perilous she could scarcely utter it?

It is Mr. Shaw, even if Mr. Shaw might not be as they conjure him, this appalling monster in our midst. Even if he might be something else entirely.

It becomes hard to sunder the believing from the knowing.

And then there's this:

It must be Mr. Shaw. It has to be.

Because if he didn't take her, where is she?

★   ★   ★

"They didn't find a-n-y-thing," Tara explains the next day. There was no pornography, no murky snuff films, and nothing to link him to Evie at all.

"He must've really cleaned house before he did the deed," she says.

Part of me was bracing for unimaginable horrors. Something worse than dirty pictures of brace-faced girls lifting their jumper over their head, worse even than muddy videos of dark deeds done to tousled children, eyes wide with terror. What could be worse than that?

But mostly I realize that I never truly thought they'd find anything bad, anything ugly. There's just that squinting part of me that feels sure Mr. Shaw, whatever he's done, was driven not by private sickness but by the purest, most painful love. If I squint my eyes just so, if I push out all the dirty rumors, I can see him differently. I can see him as a yearning nighttime wanderer dreaming his way into Evie's yard, her lighted window. Her face there.

"He probably took all the dirty movies and magazines with him, up to Canada or wherever he's got her," Kelli, sucking on gum, says. "Took them with him so he could make her look at them. So she could see how to get him off."

We all faintly gasp at this. We all shift back, just slightly. There is someplace she has just taken us and all I can think is how dare she?

Because then I do think of such things, of Mr. Shaw sitting next to Evie in his maroon car, the glossy peach of a centerfold laid open, across their laps. I picture it like the one buried under my brother's baseball card collection, where the girls all seemed splayed like bent-back dolls, their mouths bright, enormous, their depthless eyes.

"Maybe it's not him," Joannie says, and we all look at her. "Maybe it really is just a coincidence."

"So where the hell is he, then?" Tara says, clicking her retainer definitively. "My dad says there is no such thing as a coincidence. Coincidences are for bored housewives and defense attorneys."

There are things grinding in my head, chugging mercilessly...

The icky mysteries the Shaw house was expected to hold, the darkening rumors, none of this is in my real imagining. I don't believe any of it.

Didn't I know they wouldn't find a thing? It's not about a rancid need for all girls, any girl. It's about Evie and love. Standing in her yard...

Blood-thick: I know it's nothing's like what they think. They've all got it wrong. I just don't know how, yet.

The sobbing upstairs is loud, helpless, as if to rattle the windows and shake the pillars.

"Dusty wasn't feeling up to school today," Mr. Verver says, and I can tell from his T-shirt and jeans at three thirty in the afternoon that he never made it to work either.

I'm there to deliver the trophy Dusty won at the end-of-year ceremony at the high school. MVP, which is a very big deal, especially for a junior. Ted brought it home, was asked to deliver it to Dusty. ("I can't go over there," he whispered. But I could.)

Mr. Verver smiles at the golden figurine of the ponytailed field hockey player as he turns the walnut base over in his hand. He brings the face close to his eyes, his brows knitted. "She doesn't look nearly fierce enough," he says, staring hard into the gold-plated eyes.

I can't fight the grin and he sees it and grins too.

"Shall we put it in a place of honor?" he asks, and for a second he feels like Mr. Verver from before, the way he made everything an adventure, even having to get our shots before school started, or the time Mrs. Verver was sick and he took Evie and me to the Roberto Salon for haircuts, the way he sat in one of the lilac chairs and tried to read *Woman's Day,* and the way all the stylists preened and cooed over him, and one gave him a free cut and rubbed creamy coconut-smelling lotion into his scalp and we could all smell it for hours, in the car, in the rec room when we played table tennis.

I thought of how the coconut scent must have sunk into his pillow that night.

Once, last summer, Mr. Verver, he pulled up the fallen strap of my bathing suit with one long finger. I still remember the tickly-achy feeling, a feeling I never felt before.

We walk down the basement stairs to the rec room. This is where the Verver kid parties were held, and, for a while, weekly poker night with Mr. Verver and some of the neighborhood dads. And the adults come down here a lot during the block parties and the Verver Fourth of July party to get away from the kids and to smoke. There are family pictures and some German beer posters. An old velvet poster that said, "Mott the Hoople," which I always thought was a Dr. Seuss book.

The floor is hard and when we were little Evie and I practiced tap down here.

"Me and My Shadow," step-shuffle-back-step, step-shuffle-back-step.

Behind the bar, there's a long, thickly varnished shadow box where all the trophies are, except Evie's, which are in her room, because they are always too big for the case—puffy, padded soccer ball sculptures, and Dusty always says they look like cartoons of trophies, not trophies themselves.

Mr. Verver shoves the new trophy into the center, and a fog of dust puffs out at us. When I cough Mr. Verver slaps me hard on the back and makes a funny Three Stooges sound.

The room always smells like laundry, the soft gust of fabric softener. I see a few empty beer bottles on the barrel-slat coffee table and think sadly of Mr. Verver down here, his mournful wife and daughter crying mercilessly in separate bedrooms upstairs, and there's nothing he can do.

It is so terrible.

In the corner of the shadow box, which stretches the full length of the leather-padded bar, there's a small trophy I don't remember noticing before, a green-gold musical note propped on top of a tiny marble stand.

"What's this?" I say, reaching out for it.

Mr. Verver smiles, yanking it from the shelf and handing it to me.

I see the gold lettering half dissolved, as if even setting my fingers on it could erase the rest:

STA E MUS C COMPE T ON — 2 P CE

"It's so old," I say, and Mr. Verver laughs.

"Centuries past. Ice ages have come and gone."

I feel an impish smirk on me. "This is yours," I say.

"Yeah," he says, taking it gently from my hand and turning it around to look at it.

"What did you play?" I ask, even though I know. I remember him telling Evie and me before. I remember how he got so excited when he talked about it.

"Piano," he says. "Keyboards. I played at the state finals. This big theater by the Capitol Building. One of those old-time movie palaces with pipe organs that seem to hit the sky. I remember coming onstage and there was this heavy gold curtain, the tallest I'd ever seen. And the lights. It was like stepping into the sun."

He laughs softly. "It was a lot to take for a scrawny kid like me. But I played my heart out."

I picture Mr. Verver, hunched over a gleaming baby grand, over a silver piano like in an old movie, over a shambling upright piano in a dimly lit bar, his eyes soulful and brooding.

"I bet you were amazing," I say, nearly cringing at myself.

"Not amazing, exactly," he says, "but it got the girl. Annie. Mrs. Verver."

I've never seen Mrs. Verver listening to music. Whenever I hear stories about Mrs. Verver, it's always like this. They're always old stories, like she's someone everyone used to know. Stories about how when we were little Mrs. Verver and Mrs. McCann smoked pot behind the garage at the Fourth of July party, or how, back in high school, she played Ado Annie in *Oklahoma!* and flipped her skirt so high everyone saw her underwear, which was midnight blue lace.

These stories seem impossible and I don't believe them. It's like there was this Mrs. Verver once and now there's someone else, tired and bone-skinny, who works evenings at the VA and who reads while watering the garden, one hand on the hose and the other clawed around a yellowing novel from the rummage sale. I wonder if that other Mrs. Verver is somewhere else, like San Francisco or Mexico, doing wild things and never looking back.

"She heard me play at a club," he says. "We were just out of college."

"You were in a band?" I ask, feeling myself lift up onto my toes, leaning over the bar as his head lolls back in reminiscence.

"That'd be a generous way to put it," he says, his eyes glimmering and doing wonderful things. "She was in the back hallway with a guy she thought she was in love with, this cool guy with long sideburns and a ring on every finger. But then she heard me playing and she couldn't stop herself. She left the poor fella and made a beeline straight across the club to the front of the stage."

My head goes crazy with thoughts of Mr. Verver, age twenty-one, a mop of dark hair and a boy's body lurched fast over the keys. Did his collarbones jut, his Adam's apple bob? Did he have that awkward slouch of boys who grew so fast they themselves seemed bewildered by it, faintly dazed in their own skin?

And I could see it so clearly, Mrs. Verver, hair long and sunny, like in that old photo on the fireplace mantel, hips twisting, eyes fixed, walking toward him, hypnotized.

And what if Mr. Verver was, and I bet he was, just as confident, just as cool and easy as he is now? How could she stop herself from walking toward him?

"What were you playing?" I ask.

"I don't remember," he says, but the way he says it, I know it's on the tip of his tongue. And sure enough, as he rotates the trophy in his hand, looking at it like it's a crystal ball, he breaks into another smile.

"'Moonlight Drive,'" he says.

I nod eagerly, even though I've never heard of it, but it speaks of romance, of lost highways, red taillights flashing across dreamy faces, dire love.

"If I can find it," he says, "I'll play it for you sometime."

"On the piano?" I ask. I am bouncing on my feet and I can't stop myself.

"Well, I don't even have a keyboard anymore," he says, his eyes creasing tenderly. Then he nods toward the wire album racks teetering dangerously in the corner. "I'm sure the album's in there somewhere."

I resist the urge to run over and look. Instead, pressed hard against the leather front of the bar, I put my hands on the trophy, hoping he'll keep talking. I've always wanted this, even before I knew it. To hear Mr. Verver talk and talk with no one to interrupt, not Mrs. Verver, not my mother, not Dusty, calling out, always calling out for him.

"I used to play this song for Dusty when she was little," he says, like he read my mind. "She'd dance to it. She'd twirl around, her hair all corkscrewed."

Then everything slows down, as if his words know the dark place they are going, where they will end up. "Little Evie'd try to dance too," he says, his voice softening, weakening. She always wanted to be like Dusty. She'd get caught in her sister's legs and they would both fall on top of each other."

The look on his face, well, it's awful. With each word, the warm flush sinking from him, the fever in his eyes gone. The lovely clatter of our fun struck hard into broody silence.

We look at each other and I want to go home more than anything in the world.

I'm standing at the side door of my house, about to go inside. I can't quite do it because I'm thinking of Mr. Verver, wondering if he went back down in the basement after he walked me out. Is he running his finger along the albums, ridged, with peeling spines, looking for his song? Or is he sitting, broken-shouldered, drinking a beer and thinking about the weight of things?

I'm standing there, and then she flits out at me, and I nearly jump from my skin.

"Lizzie," the hiss comes, and my head thrashes around to see Dusty, barefoot, in a long-sleeved Celts T-shirt and bitty shorts. Her legs are long and creamy-tanned, just one white scar loping around her knee from her famous Stallions injury last year. The other girl had to have her jaw rewired. Her face split like a zipper. Oh, we loved Dusty for it.

"Hi," I say, finding myself leaning back against the side of my house, like a criminal ready for frisking.

"You were talking to Dad," she says.

"Yeah," I say. "I brought over your MVP trophy."

She doesn't respond but glares at me. "Did you see on the news?" she asks. "They can't pin it on him."

And I'm hurled back.

"Not yet," I say. "But they'll find him. They're looking everywhere."

I know it's true. You see the police cars circuiting all over town, across the county. You see them on the news, at the border, standing sentry. How could anyone hide from all that?

"They have no idea where he is," she says, shaking her head, her voice going ragged. "They've narrowed it down to possibly Canada. Those cigarettes don't matter now. He didn't smoke. All they know is she's gone and he's gone."

She looks at me.

"They can't pin it on him," she says again. "And if they can't, how will they ever find out what happened?"

I'm listening, but she makes it all feel so hopeless. The hopelessness in her voice. Which, for Dusty, seems a kind of anger.

I don't know how I can be around any of them anymore. It is too terrible and, by myself, I don't have to think about this part, not at all.

"They'll find him," I say, but I start to wonder what I even mean.

"You said it was him," her voice stutters out, a hard stutter, like gears grinding, "you said you saw him. His car."

She raises her eyes to me, and I feel it. I feel everything rip-
ping through her. I've never seen Dusty like this, words breaking
in her mouth.

"Maybe I was wrong," I blurt, even as the sound of it feels
shakingly rotten. It's not something I've let myself think, not
really. "Maybe it wasn't his car."

Dusty looks at me, her face tightening up again, recovering
from the loose sprawl that had overtaken it.

"It was his car, all right," she says.

"How do you know?" I watch the certainty battening down
in her.

"Don't *you* know?" she says. "You were always smart. I was
sure *you* knew."

"I think so," I say. "I think it was his car." The sureness on
her, it feels so steely. It makes me doubt myself, then doubt the
doubting. I don't know what to think.

Nine

Walking down the school corridor, backpack dragging on the buffed floors, I think about Dusty, and what she might know. Could Evie have shown her those cigarette butts too, or is it something else? Evie never told Dusty anything, did she? When you talked to Dusty, you almost had to rehearse, and every time you felt like you'd better best your game because you were on an egg timer, and it was ticking away.

In my head, I replay it and replay, each time asking Dusty the question I didn't, "How do *you* know, Dusty? How do you know it's Mr. Shaw?" But, with her hawk eyes on me, I'd said nothing.

The door to the teachers' lounge is ajar and I see them all hovering around the TV cart, the one they wheel in the room on the days the teachers don't feel like doing anything and instead show you that old *Romeo and Juliet* movie with all the hippies again.

I pretend my shoelace is untied and bend down, but Mr. Moskaluk sees me and shuts the door.

I don't like it. I don't.

In the school library, I find Kelli and Tara jammed into a study carrel together, nearly sweaty with nervous energy. They wave me over with what seems like a hundred arms.

And it's funny because I never spent so much time with these girls, and whenever I did before it was always with Evie, and we were Lizzie-and-Evie, Lizzie-and-Evie. And now it was like *I* was Lizzie-and-Evie.

They tell me everything and we have to be so quiet, the student librarian with the pink-tinted glasses glaring at us ferociously, that it feels like one long wheezy whisper in my ear. They tell me this:

An old woman who lives on the other side of the hollow called the police to say that at five o'clock in the afternoon on the day Evie disappeared she saw a girl who looked just like her. The girl was walking along Green Hollow Lake, a half mile from school. Stopping by the spillway, the water pushing through its channel, she stood for a minute.

"And then she just jumped in," Kelli says, and her mouth is pressed against me, her hand curled in front of us, her bangled bracelets scratching against my face.

"The lady figured she was going for a swim," Tara jeers. "Don't you always swim with all your clothes on?"

"But then she never saw her come up again," Kelli says, finally leaning back, wiggling her hands and fingers in disbelief. "Figured the girl just swam away."

"That doesn't make sense," I say.

"Guess it makes more sense than a bunch of cigarette butts," Kelli says, smirking.

I feel it burning on me. I feel it under all their breaths, and now, the way they're looking at me, like I made everything up.

"You don't do that in the lake," I say, trying to fight off the clamor in my head. "The current. I fell in there when I was little. And you only go in the swimming areas. You don't just jump in. Not with that current."

In my head is the prickly static of all the drownings, the young men whose dinghy overturned, the girl who hit her head on a rock and drowned in the spillway.

"Well," Kelli says, arching an eyebrow, "you jump in if you don't care about coming up again."

I feel like I want to smack her, but I stop myself and Tara clamps me over the shoulder like she knows.

"But why didn't the old lady call before?" I say. "Why is she all of a sudden calling now, eight days since Evie's been gone?"

"She didn't know about everything. She'd been at her grand-daughter's in Greenvale. She saw the picture of Evie in the paper, and it all came back."

"I don't believe it," I say, because I don't. I don't believe it because of what I know. I don't believe it because of what I'd seen myself. I don't believe it because there's a hollow wrongness to it that echoes forth.

Most of all, I don't believe it because it makes everything so spare and simple. And I now know in a deep, desperate, world-crashing way that there's no simple anymore, and there never was.

Sitting in Algebra I, hearing Mr. Silverston review polynomials for the final exam, my head clogs mightily.

I feel like I should be crying. I feel like I should be begging to go home for the day, how can I go on when Evie might be— might be—and I think of Mr. Verver, and what he must be thinking, feeling. Evie at the sumpy bottom of Green Hollow Lake.

The empty seat looms in front of me, the way Evie used to twist her ankles around the back of her chair, the way I used to kick them loose and make her laugh, rubber-toed tennis shoes skidding against each other.

It's just not so. It's just not so.

I know what I saw. I know what I feel. I know what I know.

I try to will myself back to Mr. Shaw, to Mr. Shaw and Evie. At first, I can't even picture them together. They don't seem to live in the same world. He was a man in suits, in offices, at PTA meetings, in a short-sleeved shirt, iron pressed, a drifting look on his face. But didn't they, all these men, these dads, have that look? Like my own dad.

These are the things I know:

Mr. Shaw was Mr. Verver's insurance agent. Car, home, life.

All the scattered talk and low humming and tilt-head speculation when Mr. Shaw's name first came up. Had he been to the house, seen Evie, and become fixated on her, or had he sold Mr. Verver policies just to get closer to Evie, had been trying to for years?

I sit and balance my chin precariously on the eraser end of my pencil, rocking it this way and that, the lead point skittering across my worksheet.

It is in this state of intense thought that I remember the thing, the thing that puts the two in the same frame, in the same sunlit reverie. Mr. Shaw talking to Mr. Verver in their backyard, a year ago, before everything.

They were sitting on lawn chairs, drinking beer. Mr. Shaw sat more stiffly in his chair, his sport coat on, his briefcase nestled in cool grass. And I saw him from my upstairs window, so I noticed how bald Mr. Shaw was from above, when he was only a little bald face to face, or in pictures like the one in the newspaper.

And another time, later that summer.

Evie and I are twelve.

We are wearing our matching blue bathing suits and shorts.

We are barefoot.

We are doing cartwheels and round-offs, jumping, skinny legs everywhere.

And Mr. Shaw and Mr. Verver come walking down the Verver driveway. Mr. Verver waves at us, then sticks his fingers in his mouth and whistles.

I laugh, a silly chirp, and stop, looking at them.

Evie just keeps going, cartwheel after cartwheel.

Mr. Shaw, eyes set so deep, like holes in his head, has a hand resting on his open car door, and he is watching us, with Mr. Verver.

And I am still laughing and Evie's hair fans out black feathers with each cartwheel.

And Mr. Shaw's keys fall to the pavement of the driveway and Mr. Verver picks them up for him and Mr. Shaw opens the car door wider and smiles funnily at Mr. Verver, his tie loose around his collar from his after-work beer break. The smile is wrong, it lifts in the corners but it's not really a smile, it's a thing he does with his mouth.

And he looks over at us one more time before getting in the car, then he starts his engine and leaves.

And Mr. Verver waves, but I don't think Mr. Shaw sees. He is driving slowly past my house, my lawn.

Evie springing, legs flying, hair whipping around her face, hard body never stopping, and Mr. Shaw still looking, even after he's gone.

Did it happen like this? I don't know. But it's how I remember it and I know Evie's cartwheels, the way she floated through them, like moving through molasses, smooth and dawdling and tongue-sweet, why, that's how it was. I tried, always, to slow them down like she did, to make them linger, lovingly, but mine were always short bursts, tight and fast.

Her dark hair sheeted out, matching her limbs, summer-honeyed.

He saw that and he fell in love. How could anyone see Evie's cartwheels and not fall in love?

Oh, how his heart must have ached with it.

And then the picture comes again.

The picture comes twice. Everything comes at least twice.

Mr. Shaw watching, eyes set so deep, like holes in his head, has a hand resting on his open car door, something square and silver gleaming in his dangling hand.

A cigarette lighter, square and silver, gleaming in his dangling hand.

Mrs. Shaw may not know it, Mr. Verver may not remember. But I do, I do.

He smokes.

And now I can guess how it is. He smokes Parliaments, in his car, around town, on sales calls, on long walks at night, twining through the starry streets. Standing at courtly remove in the Verver backyard, yearning.

Anywhere but home.

Evie is not at the bottom of the lake.

Those are his cigarette stubs, his left-behind longings and woe.

He watched Evie and smoked and made her his dream, over and over, then and later, and then every night, every single night until he couldn't stand it any longer.

Saturday morning, I'm crouching in the alley behind the Tri-County All-Risk office, and that's where I see them, behind the drainpipe.

The two cigarette butts, the gold-edged piece of plastic from a hard pack. I even spot the Green Hollow Pharmacy bag, crumpled in the wire trash can, a receipt still inside. It might be his. It might've been his.

It hits me fast that my hand is shoved in a trash can, and

that I have left home without permission and during a strict curfew.

There's a giddiness in it too.

And I peer in the glass door, into the darkened office, thinking of Mr. Shaw in there, gloomy and yearning.

Everyone else running down blind alleys, everyone doubting me, but I know. I know everything.

At home that night, I imagine placing an anonymous call to the police. "Look in the alleyway!" I'd whisper witchily.

My mother is droning on and on about the old woman and the lake sighting and what it means.

"I haven't seen Annie at all," she says, talking about Mrs. Verver. "I tried calling. What do you say? Do you say you're sure it wasn't Evie. I mean, really. What do you say?

"And him. Oh, it's so sad, the way he stands in the driveway, like he's forgotten something. Or like now. Did you see? He's sitting in the yard with the bottles of beer, and the way he looks into the trees. It's like he thinks just maybe little Evie will suddenly slip from between two trees and walk back into the yard.

"And he doesn't even have Dusty around to lean on. Where is she? The way she usually clings to him — the vine, that's what we used to call her when she was little. Where's she?"

My mom is feeling wistful and semitragic. She has had no late-night visitors in days. She and Dr. Aiken can't lie languorously in our patio loungers late into the night when Mr. Verver's twenty feet away, doing such conspicuous grieving.

"Why don't you go sit with him?" Ted, eating ice cream over the kitchen sink, says. He glances through the screen. "He looks lonely."

I feel a surge of warmth toward Ted, who never seems to notice anything. But part of me knows he's just prodding, poking at her, like he does.

My mother twists her lips a little and for a second I think she might do it, might go over there with her tending ways like she tends to Dr. Aiken, ministering to his lonely-husband heart. But she and Mr. Verver never really talk much, and my mother, if she was feeling neighborly at all, always chose Mrs. Verver, the two sighing together about how long the soccer games were, when either of them went, which was hardly ever.

"Lizzie," she says, curling one hand over my shoulder, "he likes you. You go."

She says it as if he's the kid at school with the stutter or the harelip. Go make friends. Doesn't she see that all I want is to go, to have him shine himself on me like he could always do? But he can't. He's captive to this horror. I know things, I know them in a sneaking way, but I don't know how I can make him know them too.

"Hi," I say, standing before him, itching the back of one leg with the toe of the other.

"Hi," he says, nearly smiling. Forcing a smile, just for me.

"I remembered something," I say. "I remember Mr. Shaw here last summer. Do you remember? He was talking to you. Evie and I, we were doing cartwheels."

He winces when I say it. It's a wretched thing to see, but I go on.

"I remember something in his hand," I say. "I remember he had a cigarette lighter. Do you remember?"

He squints hard. "I . . . I don't think so," he says, and the defeat on him overwhelms me. "Lizzie, our heads, they can do funny things. Believe me, all I do is replay everything in my head, all the time. Everything reminds me of everything."

The words echo in me, they hurt.

I drop down into the lawn chair beside him.

I want to tell him about what I saw in the alley, but I know it won't matter. It won't matter because no one believes me now.

Sitting there, so helpless, I feel such desperation. All I can do is try to show him the knowing feeling I have, try to make him feel it too, at least a sliver of it.

"It's not true," I say, and I can't believe I've said it, and Mr. Verver looks at me like he can't believe either. "What that old lady said she saw. It's not true."

He pauses and he's considering his words carefully, or else the hurt is too great for the words to come out clean, steady. Either way, the look on his face makes me want to sink into the wormy earth and lose myself forever.

"Lizzie," he says, and there is only the slightest tremble in his voice, which mostly sounds very deep and very grave, "I wish I knew anything anymore."

"Mr. Verver," I say, pitching up in my chair, "that old lady is wrong."

He looks at me as though maybe, just maybe I have some kind of secret wisdom, and don't I?

"Mr. Verver," I say, and I find myself placing my stubby girl hands on his arm, and it sparks on me. "I know, I do."

I fill my face with weighty meaning, I make him lock eyes with me. He must believe, he must believe.

He looks back at me.

What a tortured wisp of hope to cling to — instead of drowning, his daughter has been secreted away by a lurching man three times her age, but it's there. It's the strand we've got and we clutch at it madly.

It is after midnight, one, two o'clock, I don't know, but the storm must have come, the winds pitching high, and there's this sound from outside, the metallic squeak of the chaise, scraping along the patio.

Heavy with a nightmared sleep, I stumble from my bed and I guess I mean to go out back and drag the chair inside. I can't shake my thoughts straight enough to be scared, careening through the dark house, wind thudding on the roof. My body nearly flings itself down the carpeted stairs to the kitchen.

I'm almost to the patio door, fingers reaching out for the clicking vertical blinds, when the voice barks out.

"Don't do it."

I nearly jump.

It's Ted, that flat, rough tone, his boy's sullen grunt. "Don't," he says, like when he tells me not to throw my cleats on the creamy vinyl of his car's backseat.

I turn to see him, or at least the crest of his blond hair, the two pale streaks of his long ballplayer shins. He's leaning against the kitchen counter, and looks, as always, a hundred feet tall.

I'm about to ask him why, but the words just hover in the back of my mouth. I wonder what he's seen. I think about burglars in black knit caps or packs of wild dogs, teeth clattering against the glass patio doors. What has he seen?

And then, of course, I think of Evie.

Is something coming for me, too? Something come to pull me down into the sumpy core, the hidden center where Evie hides, big-eyed and lost?

He ducks his head forward and I can see him now in the light banding across the kitchen from the Ververs' porch lamp. Ted's face, colorless, his lips pulled back. It's not his face at all. For a second, it is my dad's.

Watching him, I forget about the noise, the squeaking and dragging, but it's stopped and I turn and place my hand on a thatch of blinds, looking at my brother, as if asking permission.

I don't wait for it, though. Instead, I peek out into the dreamy green-black of the backyard. The patio itself is tucked deep in the shadow of the house, but I angle my head against the glass door, and there it is, shot through with the captured brightness of a streetlamp, a stray bedroom window.

I see all of it. I see the hard flash of a bare leg, my mother lifting herself upright from the chaise, her hair tumbling, a hand tucking a bare breast back into her open blouse.

And him, too. His back to me, I see him rise, his hand digging through his hair. I want him to turn around, to face her. I want him to look at her.

Instead, Dr. Aiken seems struck motionless by the sight of the strutting sports car in the Darltons' driveway next door.

He tilts his head, as if very tired. For a second, I can see my mother's face as she looks over at him. Her face, there's something sparking and sad in it at the same time. It seems like it couldn't be both at the same time, but it is.

I don't go back to bed. There's a sense of wicked license to everything. What did any of it matter when it's like this?

Head filled to the brim, mind racing, I grapple for my tennis shoes and sneak out, traipsing darkly through backyards, one after the next, houses trapped in quiet, all the way, all seven blocks to the Shaw house.

I don't know what I mean to do but feel it could be anything.

Before I know it, I am standing in front of the Shaw house, fingers tapping on the streetlamp post.

It seems there could be no darker house, its eaves drooping like batted lashes. The quiet in there, why, it's sealed tight, there's no breaking it. Watching it earlier that week, doors flung open, police officers in and out with cardboard boxes, notepads swinging like tails from back pockets, it seemed laid bare. Now it seems sealed over, plastered shut.

I picture Mrs. Shaw and their son, Pete — that dark-haired junior who got in the paper for winning the state robotics prize — huddled high in the house, the sloping storybook house with the steeply pitched gables that overhang so thickly as to hide within them things monstrous and beautiful. I picture bats folded in on themselves, bleating possums under the porch.

But maybe too something magical, something from a bedtime story, a glittery raven tucked under the eaves, a prickling briar rose.

I think if I look hard enough, I'll understand something. It will become clear to me.

What is there to see, to know?

The wind lifts and I stand, goose pimples rising on my skin, my eyes doing crazy things, like when I was a kid and thought I could see through walls if I tried just so.

But the house offers up no reward.

The minutes slink by and I've nearly surrendered, when I think what I might do.

I creep around to the backyard. Did the police even look here?

If he smokes in the Verver yard, isn't it possible he smokes in his own?

It's too dark to see anything, and so I'm bending over, then kneeling, feeling for things, rolling my palms over clumps of grass, flagstones, the thick gnarl of an old tree stump. The more I clutch my hands over everything, the more I think there's a kind of madness in it, scrounging, burrowing, on all fours on the Shaws' nighttime grass, like I might throw my head back next, howl at the moon, scream bloody murder.

I crawl on the Shaws' lawn for a very long time, corner to corner, but I find nothing, not one stub, not even a stray, curling match.

But I'm not done. Dirt under my nails, I feel bold and daring and walk freely along the driveway, up against the house itself, even laying my hands on it. The outer walls are cold to the touch, my fingers scuffing along the brick and stucco, the timber slats that, higher up, spoke through every gable.

The garage looks horror-housey to me. The place people said he hid the porn and the snuff film and all manner of things that it turned out weren't there at all. I press my face to one cloudy window, though all I see is my own face, a smeary negative, eyes wide and blinking.

I think of it maybe as Mr. Shaw's own private space, a space where he could sit or maybe even lie on cold concrete and smoke and imagine things.

Just past the garage, I rest my hands on the house again. This time, my fingers touching something colder still, like metal, and I see it's one of those two-way milk chutes from olden times, just like we have at our house, only ours has a broken hinge my dad never fixed. When we were younger Evie and I passed each other notes there and sometimes she'd still leave things—a painted barrette, a soccer ball key chain—there for me, and it'd take me months to find them, to think to look.

The chute at our house is painted bright green, but this one is brown, and half covered with creeper ivy. You could miss it entirely. I wonder if the police missed it.

Slipping my fingers under the spiny tendrils, I grab for the hinge, which is not broken and I don't even have to pull hard and it opens.

Not even stopping to think, I dart my hand inside. Whirling my fingers around, I don't feel a thing but tickly ivy stems on my wrist.

But then, as I start to pull my hand back out, I hear the faintest crackle of something just under my retreating knuckles.

It's something wedged in the lip of the chute.

Grasping eagerly, I feel something plasticky and soft, and something else, too, something cool and nubby. Tugging now, I claw my hand over everything and topple it into both hands, running to the streetlamp to see if I have found what I think I have found.

I have.

A pack of Parliaments, five left. And, rubber-banded to it, a silver lighter with a flip top. It's not like a drugstore lighter. It's special and feels old and heavy in my hands. I press my finger against the engraving, a seal that looks like a Kennedy half-dollar, like the kind my grandfather collected in a tall green-glass canister on his desk when I was a kid.

It's the one. It is. I am right, I am right. I know everything.

Don't you *know?* Dusty said. *You were always smart. I was sure* you *knew.*

I did know. I do. And somehow Dusty does too.

It was Shaw. It was always Shaw. Shaw out there every night.

And the police, what do they know? Missing this, missing everything.

I run my finger around and around the lighter's seal.

I feel myself standing like Mr. Shaw did, dangling it between my fingers, standing beside Mr. Verver watching Evie turn cartwheels, one after another.

The cigarettes, the lighter, seeing them, it is such redemption. I feel the pull of the thing, the full force of everything that's happened. These objects, cool in my hot hands, give me a hard yank back to the center of things.

Standing there, touching everything, I think of fingerprints and evidence and assorted TV show wisdom so hastily discarded. But it's too late now, so I press that pack to my chest with abandon.

Kneeling down on the plush grass beneath the streetlamp, I shake the cigarettes from the pack. Somehow I want to look at them, be with them.

But as I do something else flutters forth, from between the tumbling cigarettes.

It lands on the grass and I pick it up, handle it tenderly.

It is a photo clipped from a newspaper, coiled like a pointing finger.

I recognize it. It's just a tiny clipping, a smudge two inches long and two inches wide. It is from the article about last year's middle school soccer tournament.

The picture, I know it so well, because the same one is pinned with fat, sparkly thumbtacks to my own bedroom corkboard.

It's Evie, and, next to her, half torn through, me.

★   ★   ★

A year ago, that picture, the two of us knowing each other so bone-deep. But now parts of me feel Evie skittering away. The slips of Evie that I can't quite touch, the girl whose eyes drifted down to her backyard and beheld that man, that man older than her father, and saw him brooding in the dark, like an errant knight, standing in the backyard, heart in his outstretched hand.

What did she think would happen? Did she think he would just look forever? And why didn't she tell me? And what would I have done?

It's a lonely thought, and I push it away.

That night, I sleep with my plunder under my pillow. The cigarettes, the lighter, the clipping.

I knew I would use them. I knew already, even if I didn't know how.

I think of Mr. Verver, how it will be when I cast my spell of release. *Then Evie too will be released, stumbling, wing-wounded, from her steely trap.*

These are my strange nighttime thoughts.

And then the dream comes, and it is Evie:

In the dream, I'm in bed, and the sound starts. It is a slow scratching, so faint that each time I hear it, I shake it away. But then it starts to get faster, and it seems to be both inside and outside at once, and I think it must be like when my dad found those squirrels in the attic and had to smoke them out.

But the scratching keeps getting louder and louder, like claws on metal or steel, and I am walking through the hallways, my palms spread on the walls, trying to feel it, to follow it.

And then I'm outside, the wind kicking up and my nightgown flapping against my legs, the house so dark and it is so late that my feet sink wetly into the spongy ground and everything looks blue and tortured.

Not scratching now, but a sound more like clawing, and I want to slap my hands over my ears. But then my hands hit the painted metal door of the milk chute and the sound surges through me like an electric current.

Slowly, slowly, bending at my knees to see, I twist the knob and open the chute door and instead of looking through to see the dark of the kitchen, hear the shudder of our refrigerator, it's all blackness. I think the door has opened to the center of the earth itself, and it smells like loamy death.

I duck my whole head in, because this is a dream, I'm sure it's a dream, and I have nothing to lose, nothing at all.

I reach my hand in deep as it will go, and that's when I feel her.

I feel Evie before I see her, I feel the soft skin of her forearm, and then I see the white of her eye.

And then I see her face, and she is saying something to me.

I wriggle and she seems to loom closer and it's as if we're in some other place altogether, and I wonder if I will ever get out again, but I push farther, and there we are, and there's her face. And she is saying something to me.

Evie, Evie, Evie...

The crackle of the morning news wakes me.

"*Divers have been deployed to Green Hollow Lake...drag bars to search for the body of the girl identified by at least one witness as resembling thirteen-year-old Eveline Verver, missing for more than a week...*"

Lying in bed, I don't know if I can do it. I don't know if I can pull it off. But then I think of the dooms of sorrow that must've quaked through the Verver house last night, a day and night of imagining Evie slipping fast into the murky churn of Green Hollow Lake, the thought of her body dragged up by grappling hooks, her face worn away. Isn't that what happens? I remember reading it somewhere. The water takes their faces. Thinking of it, I wonder what despairing journeys Mr. Verver's mind has made in the last twelve hours and I cannot bear it.

Not when I *know*, I know.

She doesn't lie at the lake's swampy bottom.

She lies with him.

And so I must save her, save them all.

"Is that you out there, Lizzie?" Mr. Verver asks, and he opens the screen door. A weariness hangs heavy on him, heavier than I've ever seen. His face. It's his face that looks worn away.

"I'm sorry, Mr. Verver," I say, and I'm practically jumping from foot to foot. "I'm just waiting for my brother to wake up. I need his help."

"What is it?" he says, his morning coffee in hand. He does that eyebrow crinkle thing. "Are you okay? Is there something—"

"Oh, it's nothing," I say, shaking my head. "It's stupid. It's so stupid."

I point wildly to the side of my house. "It's the old milk chute. I keep hearing scratching sounds at night, and I think it's coming from there. Some animal or something trying to get in, or"— I flash my eyes wide—"out."

He walks over to the chute just like that.

As if my wispy problem must be attended to, despite everything else that matters so much more.

"The hinge is broken," I say quickly, and I feel like I might lose my nerve. "I'm afraid to—I just want it sealed up. So nothing can get in."

He looks at me and I can see all the kindness in him. He's happiest when he gets to be kind.

"Sure, honey," he says, his hand on the latch, fingers softly cradled about it. "It was probably just a raccoon."

There's all manner of unaccountable things happening in my body, including something looping through me, head to toe.

Even though I know what's in the chute, even though *it was me who put it there two hours ago, at sunup,* I suddenly feel like I'm in a spook movie and *what might jump out?*

And, one hand pressed against the side so the chute door won't fall, he tugs it open.

My heart jabbers in my chest and I put my hand across it.

And it's open.

And I watch as he sees the magic I have fairy-dusted there for him.

"Oh," he says, and his face springs to life again, his features reassembling before my eyes.

He lets the door toggle on its sole hinge because, transfixed, he cannot help himself, and his hands hover above the gleaming lighter, the white sheen of the Parliament pack.

But he does not touch.

He sees already. He knows.

The glory in my heart, it nearly shatters me.

Te n

We wait for the police to come, and Mr. Verver can't stop pacing up and down the driveway. He keeps running in the kitchen and calling up the stairs to Mrs. Verver. Sometimes I think she never leaves her bedroom.

Mr. Verver keeps looking at the open chute, but from a distance, from two yards away, like to go any closer might make the things inside disappear.

We wait and it's only five, seven minutes, but it seems forever.

At first, there is a jumpy thrill to it, that I gave him *this thing,* that he knows it because of me. He knows Mr. Shaw was here.

But then I think what a messy thing it is for him to know. How much better is it to imagine Evie with Mr. Shaw? If she's with him then at least she's not lost to dank depths. Or at least not those kind of dank depths. These are our choices.

And behind it, something else, something we don't say, which is this: how does knowing Mr. Shaw prowled out here, loved her with such secret longing, help find Evie?

The thought vaulting through me, I have a moment where she feels more lost than ever, sunk down into some earth-deep wormhole.

But Mr. Verver's mind is moving fast, and suddenly something seems to come to him. He takes my arms in his hands and looks me in the face with fresh terror, saying, "Lizzie, this is very important. When did you hear those sounds coming from the milk chute? Did you hear them last night?"

That's when I realize my mistake. I'd been so careful. Wiped everything clean. Thought it all through. Except this.

"What?" I say.

"If you heard the sounds last night, or even this week..." and his voice stutters off and I see what he's thinking: *if Mr. Shaw prowled out here last night, if he were here at all in the last week, where was Evie?*

Suddenly Dusty appears behind the screen door and I give a silent prayer of thanks, as it gives me time to think, think, a million thoughts and calculations click-clacking in my head.

"Dad," Dusty is saying through the screen, and it looks funny, the mesh across her face, breaking all that prettiness up into a thousand wiry pieces.

"No," I blurt. "It wasn't last night. It was a while ago. A couple weeks maybe. But I forgot about it until last night. With everything happening, I guess I just got scared last night. And I started to think about the chute."

"Of course," he says, and the dread that had been grinding through his face slows down.

I put my hand over my chest to stop my heart from rocketing through it.

"I just got spooked," I say. "And then I remembered about the noise."

"Of course. And thank God you did. It's all been very scary. Oh, poor Lizzie," he says, and I feel him leaning toward me and I think he might hug me, but the screen door screeches at us, and Dusty is saying "Dad" and her voice is like a shiver. It echoes in my head, a million times, Dusty calling from somewhere, anywhere, calling for Dad.

And so he goes to her.

Standing in the driveway, waiting for the police, I see them in the kitchen. Through the screen door, I see Mr. Verver holding Dusty, and she is crying and she is clinging to his shirtfront and she will not let go.

They're standing in the kitchen and his arms enclose her and I can barely even see Dusty, just the crush of her hair, her bare feet half set upon his shoes, her shoulders curling into him, trembling against his chest.

It reminds me of something way back. That time when Dusty was so sick, so sick she whittled down to ninety pounds. Mr. Verver had to quit coaching our soccer team after only three weeks, someone needed to stay with her, she was wasting away. She was never any good at being sick, we all said. But he was our favorite coach ever and we all loved him. Mrs. Verver worked evenings at the VA and who else but him could stay with Dusty, Dusty with that roiling sickness in her gut that had ravaged her almost overnight. She couldn't eat anything. And he'd come home, and Dusty, lolled across that sofa, oh, how she clung to him and said she felt like she might die. She looked like she might.

He could fix everything, couldn't he? His hands like some healer, and soon enough, she was well.

It goes on for some time, with the police. I'm talking with Detective Thernstrom when they find the newspaper clipping. One of them has the cigarette pack pinched in these long blue tweezers and he's turning it around in his upraised gloved hand when the clipping falls to the ground. He won't find any prints on it, which is too bad, but I had to wipe myself from the pack and lighter with the satiny edge of my comforter, wipe me, and so Mr. Shaw, away.

Mrs. Verver is finally outside, pale and ghostly, wrapped in a big sweater and her arms wrenched around herself.

I watch her watching them as they look at the clipping, the photo of Evie in her nylon uniform, hair in tight braids.

Mr. Verver is looking at the photo too. He has his hand over his mouth, and there is something awful on his face that feels like it will be in my head forever.

The next few hours whir and there's never any talk of me going to school and there are so many conversations, and my mother is there, and I can barely look at her because I keep picturing her on our back patio, all flesh and ickiness, tattooed from the slats on the chaise, where I will never sit again. She stays with Mrs. Verver, who is back in her bedroom. She brings her tea and stays with her all afternoon. I wonder what they talk about, hiding up there, burdened women huddled together behind closed doors.

I'm sitting in the kitchen when Dusty comes in, all her tears shaken free, her face scrubbed back to that tight, bright beauty of hers.

"You saved the day again," she says, tugging open the refrigerator door.

It's sort of coachlike, the way she says it, but you never know with Dusty, so I just shrug.

She pulls out a jug of juice, shaking it slowly and looking at me.

"It's kind of weird, though, don't you think?" she says.

"What?"

"That broken hinge. I mean, it's been broken forever. I remember when your brother busted it, swung at it with his baseball bat."

"Yeah," I say, remembering it too.

"Well, I was thinking about it," she says, unscrewing the cap. "It must've been a real hassle for Mr. Shaw, hiding those cigarettes there. When you open it, you have to hold the door with the other hand, just to stop it from falling off."

"Right," I say, keeping my voice as even as I can.

"... when there's plenty of other perfectly good places to hide things, like his car—"

"He probably didn't want his wife to know he smoked," I jump in. "She might have found them if he hid them in his car."

"How about a flowerpot?" she says, taking a sip from the juice, slanting her head, as if pondering. "One of those big old empty planters your mom has all over the place."

"I guess it could get wet there. It—"

"It just doesn't make much sense." She pauses, then taps the jug against her chest. "To me, at least."

"No," I say, my head hot and tingling. "I guess it doesn't."

I sit up straighter in my seat. I can shake her off, I can. But the jolt on me, it's like a coldness on the teeth. It's no surprise that she knows I'm lying. She reads me here, like on the field, like everywhere. She sees it all.

"I guess none of what he's done makes sense," I try.

She nods, but the stare she gives me, I know I'll feel it all day long.

★ ★ ★

Later, Mr. Verver pulls me aside to update me on everything. He stops and pulls me aside just to tell me.

"The police showed the lighter to Mrs. Shaw and her son," he says, "and the son recognized it. He said his dad kept it as a memento, that it'd been his own father's lighter, and Shaw used it to light the Christmas candles or birthday cakes."

"What about Mrs. Shaw?"

Mr. Verver shakes his head. "She said she couldn't be sure. She couldn't remember anything," he says. "But, here's the thing, Lizzie, Mr. Shaw's office assistant also identified it, said she'd see him spinning it around on his desk sometimes, called it his lucky piece."

Oh, to see him so animated, so enlivened. And I did that. Savoring it, I try to put Dusty out of my head. If she doesn't believe me, what does it matter? I keep telling myself that. Over and over.

Then it's on the news that night.

A college student comes forward, identifying herself as the girl the old lady saw jumping into Green Hollow Lake, the one she thought was Evie.

"I was just collecting samples for Geology class," the girl tells the reporter. Her hair's long and dark like Evie's, but she's nothing like Evie. I wonder how anyone could think this college girl with her big dorm-fed shoulders and cork sandals could be Evie.

All my mother can talk about, though, is the milk chute, as if it linked us to everything.

"I can't believe it," she says, standing in front of the refrigerator, trying to imagine dinner. Ted is nowhere to be seen. "The idea of that man skulking in our driveway. Hiding his things here, creeping around our house at night."

This is what she says.

In my head, Dr. Aiken stumbles through our back hedges.
I nearly laugh, I nearly do.

Sometimes, though, it's like I believe it myself. Sometimes I forget my own lie and I think of Mr. Shaw jerking open our milk
chute door, fumbling his hands inside, hiding his secrets. He gave
his secrets to me anyway, didn't he? Or I took them from him. It
was me who took them from him, my hands reaching, grasping.

Eleven

Tuesday, the school froths with revelations. Tara Leary stalks the halls with her growing pack, girls eager for her gruesome knowledge.

"It's a big manhunt now," she says. "My dad always said it was a sex crime. They're looking everywhere, across the state, and they have the best leads in Ontario. They're working with police up there. The wife says he was always talking about how he wanted to go live up there, get some cabin by himself. What a freak."

A cabin on a lake, like some romantic getaway, like some lovers' retreat...

"But my dad says it's probably a suicide at this point," Tara goes on. "Because now there's nowhere he can hide."

"But I heard they're going to do another search in the woods behind the school," Joannie says.

"They think they might be hiding in the woods?" I ask, picturing a pup tent and propane stove.

Joannie, now as worldwise as Tara, looks at me and shakes her head. "They're looking for the body," she says. "They're wondering where he might have buried the body."

★　　★　　★

We're in Health class and we're learning about menstrual flow again and Kelli Hough is playing Mrs. Miller like a carnival gawker, asking her why the blood "down there" comes so thick, and is it wrong that she feels "tingly" down there when it happens?

I am spinning my pencil in fast circles and clock-watching and it happens like this first: a buzzing, hot in my ear. Poking with my finger, I try to stop it. No one else seems to hear it, rapt as they are by Kelli and the "tuggy" way it feels when her period comes, "like a thread, you know, pulling down inside me."

But the buzzing sound has a heat to it and my head feels hot too and the room is so white, so glaring white, it hurts my eyes and I dig my hands between my legs and try to shut it out, try to think of other things. But I'm thinking of Mr. Shaw and Evie and how I know it seems to me he'd never hurt her, he just loves her so and why can't anyone understand?

And then I start to think of all these days that have passed— eleven days and counting—and what might have gone on by now, and if Evie finds his love beautiful and if it's turned to things done under covers and Evie's eyes rolling back.

I am sick with it, and sick with myself. And my mind jumps and it's that time last summer, waiting for my brother. I'm with his friend Matt Nettle, who just fixed my bike, and we're behind his house, by the garage.

I'm tired, he says, *let's sit down a minute,* and I do because he's sixteen and I just turned thirteen, and there is a trembly leg thing happening to me and sitting down seems right.

We're leaning against the heat-curled shingles of the garage and I can feel paint dust hot on my neck.

We're not saying anything. Then Matt starts talking about the things that guys need and he bets I understand because I have a brother.

I tuck my knees to my chest and pull at one of the tongues on my grass-stained Keds. He's talking and talking and I don't know that he will ever stop. He reminds me of my dad when he wants to explain his reasons for things, when he wants to say he's sorry.

I squeeze my fingers on that shoe tongue, my cheeks going hot and hotter. I don't look at him, or even hear him anymore, but then I feel his big callusy hand on my wrist and my stomach somersaults and my breath rushes back into my mouth.

Next I feel his fingers around my arm and he's moving my hand and then I feel my hand settle on soft fabric and I know it's Matt Nettle's shorts. My hand pulls away fast and goes back to the tongue on my Keds.

And he's saying, *Please, please, Lizzie, don't be a baby,* and yanking at me with his big basketball player hands. And then he says, *What if you just help me out? You don't have to touch. You just have to pull your shirt up and let me look. Just let me look.*

This is what he says, as if it'd be granting a favor, giving him a gift.

It somehow happens that I'm unwrapping my knees from my chest and his hands are there so fast, underneath my blue T-shirt, hot and dusty, they move like this, right to my small white bra, and I don't look at his face and he moves his hands and I hear him unzip and I don't look.

His voice all weird and breathless, he says, *Just let me see,* and I don't know what to say and he says, *C'mon, c'mon,* and I know what he's doing, I just know.

How is it that I pull my arms out of my sleeves and slide my bra down and let him see? But I do. My skin quills up, and he stops talking, he finally stops talking.

When he's done, he makes a little sound, and I feel his hand sticky on my chest and he pinches them and my eyelids flutter and—

I pull my shirt down and get up and grab my bike and run with it, the pedals cutting into my legs. I run through the Middleton yard, twisting my ankle on an old watering can and running still and finally jumping on the bike seat and it's not until I'm riding fast down the street that I realize, under my shirt, my bra is still down around my lower rib cage, straps so tight across my arms I can't ride and have to stop and hope no one's looking while I pull it up, back into place.

When I told Evie about it, in the quiet of our sleeping bags, she didn't say anything for the longest time, but I could hear her breathing. Then she said sometimes the ways boys need things so badly, like they could never stop needing, it almost scared her.

But, she said, *sometimes I feel like that too.*

She said, *Lizzie, do you ever find yourself wanting* so much *you feel like you might disappear? Like all that you are is the wanting, and the rest of you just burns away?*

This is what I'm thinking of and I'm so deep in the thinking of it that it's like I'm not in Health class at all, listening to Kelli and hearing her rapping her pencil against her barrette and her voice going up and down about the blood, the blood and the way it feels between her legs.

No, I'm with Evie, and we're clasped close together and she's about to tell me something, she's about to tell me everything, all the things she knows, all the things she's learned, the secret knowledge gained from a week and a half sunk deep into a place I can only see dark glimmers of.

I can really see her, she's really there, and she's going to tell me, her mouth opening, her teeth and tongue —

"Evie," I say, but no words come and the sound on the floor, my head hitting it, is loud enough to wake the whole world.

★ ★ ★

I don't tell Mrs. Miller or Nurse Stang anything. I say I feel dizzy and they ask me if I skipped breakfast and I did. I skipped breakfast and dinner last night too, except for the box of soft licorice coins I found in my room, which I finished in one sitting, a raw taste silting my mouth's inside all night.

.

The next night, Mr. Verver walks out to the backyard with a few cans of beer hanging from a six-pack's plastic rings.

He's taken a leave of absence from his job. He's spending his days driving, with the police, with volunteers, with anyone who will go. They drive all day. Because, everyone keeps saying, it just takes one lucky break, one eagle-eyed stranger. A known man with a known girl in a known car, they can't just disappear.

He beckons me over, pats the lawn chair beside him.

He says he wants to show me something and spreads a large map on the grass in front of us, a map spanning this county, the next, all the way up to the border and across into Ontario.

"It's this area," he says, leaning down and spreading his hand across a creased section at the top. "His wife says he always talked about scouting around here for cottages to buy. That he had these fantasies of a summer place up there."

I'm listening, and I'm looking at the map, the way he's marked all over it, Sharpied circles, lines, and stars. The map is thick with it, the inked pocks and streaks and wavering lines obscuring everything in some corners, like our corner.

"She told the FBI that she thought he had a college friend up here somewhere," he says, rolling the beer can between his palms. "Jim somebody, she said. The police can't find anyone else who knows who she might mean. But they've been driving from town to town, anyplace that rents or sells cabins around this area."

He's looking very closely at the map, and then at me.

"They're going through security tapes of the border crossing," he says. "There's been all these sightings. It just takes so long, tracking them all down. The manpower. But Canada—that's meant more support from the state and the FBI."

It goes on like this, and he shows me all the places he's driven to, in our county, the next. All the places the police are looking. All the leads, hundreds of them. The more he shows me, the more it starts to seem like the world is so big, and we are so small, that nothing could ever be found, anywhere.

Later, Mrs. Verver comes out and it's the first time I've seen her up close since Evie's been gone. Her face looks scrubbed across. Her hair—that hair that was always as smooth as shaved lemon ice—now has a strange texture, like the rubbed-raw hair on an old doll.

She stands behind us, a glass of iced tea in her hand, and she doesn't say anything, and Mr. Verver reaches behind to touch her arm, but he doesn't quite make it and she doesn't move toward it.

I would.

I watch her gazing into that same green tangle in the far corner of the backyard, the one we look into. It's not like my mom says. We don't expect Evie to shimmer forth, the tree branches releasing her. It's just the way the chairs face.

If they faced each other, if Mr. Verver faced me, I don't think I could sit there with him.

It hurts sometimes to look at him. It's all right there upon him.

Mrs. Verver stands there for such a short time, and later I wonder if she was ever there at all, or if she was just a ghost.

Evie, gone twelve days, feels more here than ever.

I'm surprised, though, that Dusty never comes outside on any of those nights. I think about how this is the seat she always took, her long legs tucked beneath her, her laugh so mean and delicious. That was how it always was between them.

It seems like she should be out here with him more than ever, now when he needs her the most.

One time, the summer before middle school, Evie and I were in my yard long past bedtime, sneaking into a purloined bag of foamy marshmallows and giggling wonderful silent giggles so no one would hear.

Dusty and Mr. Verver were back there and they had the radio perched on the windowsill and Mr. Verver heard an old song he liked and he started singing to it, and it was that kind of singing where you pretend to be making fun of yourself, but you're really loving it. His voice was always like that. Like he just might start laughing at any minute.

When the chorus came — "You don't have to say you love me, just be close at hand" — Dusty started singing too, and her voice was so delicate, like tinkly bells, but she gave it everything and they were having so much fun, stumbling over the words, and we started to know the chorus too, we heard it so many times.

I knew Evie would like to sing along. I wanted to too. But you didn't feel like you could. It felt like when you're opening those heavy church doors right in the middle of service, and everyone inside that hushed, perfumed, sacred space turns around and says, without saying, No, no, it's not for you.

Not for you.

These nights, though, sitting in the Verver backyard, Dusty never comes outside, even though sometimes, if I turn around, I can see her passing by the kitchen window, I can just catch the gold frill of her hair.

Twelve

The next night is the junior prom. Ted is rolling his neck around under his tuxedo collar. His date is Mindy Phipps, a deep-voiced wild girl who was thrown off the field hockey team when the assistant coach found a bottle of blackberry brandy in her locker. They will be one short in the limousine because Dusty isn't going, there's no question of her going.

"Tom could've asked someone else. I don't know why he wastes his time with Dusty anyway. At least I wasted only four days on her."

I'm watching my brother watch himself in the standing mirror in my mother's room. He looks like a man on a TV commercial, like the one with the dark sweep of hair who whirls the woman around a shimmering rooftop after he gives her the big diamond. Ted scowls, scratching at his neck.

"She's had lots of boyfriends," I say, even though I know it isn't really true. Not in the way he means.

There are always boys around Dusty, different boys, and sometimes there's one boy, but you never see her get too excited about one of them. The only one who stuck for a while was Joe Richmond, the summer before he went to college. He used to come over and play one-on-one basketball with Mr. Verver, who beat him every time.

"Boys love Dusty," I say louder, rubbing hard at the scabs on my knee.

"They like looking at her," he says. "But how long can you just look at that?"

This feels like a window into another world, the teen-boy world, a world of sweat socks and thumping bass and torn-out magazine photos of bulbous tan breasts and white rabbity teeth and yellow flossy hair, those girls always posed bending over or crawling or poking things in their mouth or twining them between their legs.

I wonder what a boy could want if Dusty wasn't it.

Eye to the keyhole, seeing Dusty through Ted's restless eyes, it makes me feel strange and unmoored and I stay in my mother's room long after he has left. I stay there while my mother, giddy and high, parades him around the house taking photographs and oohing and aahing.

I have this sense, suddenly, of Dusty, arms rigid at her sides, bored and harassed by the jabbing, prodding elbows of boys, boys trying to unwrap her, unfurl her, to unbend her from herself. And what was for her in that? These awkward boys wanting things all the time but not knowing what that means or why it matters.

In Dusty's eyes, regal and severe, there's the sense that she knows so much more than they do, and they could never glimmer for her, so why should she grant them her rough magic? Had they earned it?

And so there I am, trying to unsnarl it all, lying on my mother's bed, on the mauve bedspread she bought after the divorce, which is when she bought all those pillows, a hundred different sizes, mounding her bed so high you couldn't find a corner to sit on.

The pillows are gone now, migrated to the TV room and other places.

When you lie on the bed, you can see yourself in that long mirror, the one my brother was standing in front of. I fight off thoughts of my mother and Dr. Aiken and that mirror, the way it's tilted and the way, if I lie here, I can see up my soccer shorts.

I wonder how many times Dr. Aiken has been in this bed and what he does here, and what he says to my mother, and if she believes it.

"She didn't feel up to going," Mr. Verver says. "We tried to get her to go, but she said she just couldn't. But it's hard to miss that kind of stuff too. Proms, you don't forget them."

"Yes," I say. I remember how, a month ago, we were with Dusty when she bought her dress, long, sleek, and red, like a curling tongue.

"She's been holed up in her room for hours," Mr. Verver says, his brow doing that curlicue thing, like when Evie would show him her injuries, or tell him about a bad grade.

I picture Dusty up there on that cherry-top bed, entwined in her covers in gloom and frustration.

I picture her up there and I wonder what she thinks about Evie now. About what's happened and how they all must suspend everything, and it's like the whole world thuds to a halt.

I try to think of ways I could talk to her about Evie, to see what she thinks happened to her, but Dusty seems as remote to me as she does to those backseat boys, a high-tower girl and me on the far-flung ground, ankle-deep in the tendriled tails of her princess hair.

"I remember," I say, "when we were little and Dusty put on Mrs. Verver's old dresses, like her prom dress. The one with all the lace."

It had been a boring summer day and we were all in swimsuits but the rain wouldn't stop and we couldn't go to the pool. Mrs. Verver pulled out these big dress boxes from the top of her closet, and the prom dress was a long, gauzy yellow thing, with butterfly sleeves and organza flounces, like a princess would wear. It seemed impossible that Mrs. Verver had ever worn it, but Dusty, all of ten years old, tugged it on over her bathing suit and posed like a fashion model and strutted around, and she even put on the wedding dress, with the fluffy sleeves.

Mrs. Verver—I'd forgotten she used to do things like that, back when Mr. Verver was traveling a lot for work and always on planes and she wasn't so separate from everything all the time, up in her room, her head in a book, a slow retreat that has lasted for years.

But back then, she was different. Like that day, the way she got out a camera and took pictures of Dusty tiptoeing around, emoting glamorously, her hair spilling over her shoulders, her tiny tanned ankles tottering in her mother's heels.

Later, Mr. Verver came home. Dusty was so pleased she put on the dress again.

Mr. Verver, he told her she looked just like her mother, the spitting image, and Dusty burst into tears and wouldn't come out of her room for hours. Oh, did he ever have to entice her out, putting on all his charms.

Later, Evie and I pretended we were Dusty, fashioning gowns with our beach towels, draping the corners over our shoulders or around our six-year-old waists, puckering our lips and doing runway poses.

"I remember those pictures," Mr. Verver says now, smiling, and then the smile is wider, and I see a gleam there.

"Lizzie," he says, "I need you."

It's like a twang in my chest. "Yes, Mr. Verver," I say.

"I need your help," he says, which is not the same thing, and I feel embarrassed.

"Okay." I nod.

"How would you like to be a part of a very exclusive event?" he says, and there's such mischief in his eyes. It's the Mr. Verver from before.

"I want to, yes," I say.

"Then come with me," he says, and he puts his arm out. I take it, take his arm, and curl my hands around it and it's iron-strong and filled with heat.

We're in the basement, and Mr. Verver is pulling out boxes of holiday decorations and the big punch bowl Mrs. Verver used to fill with 7-UP and sherbet at kid parties.

"What's happening?" I say, my feet nearly bouncing.

"We're setting up for the gala of the season," he says, rolling up his sleeves. "Some of the city's lesser citizens are attending some sad little high school dance. But that stuff's for kids."

And soon enough, I am unfurling the string of red paper lanterns from the "summer" box, the same ones Mr. Verver hung across the backyard trees for last year's Fourth of July party. There's a few leftover balloons and silver crepe streamers and a fan-fold mirror ball to hang from the ceiling.

I remember when we were little, and Evie said she wanted to see a burning cabin like in the Little House book she read and Mr. Verver bought an old dollhouse at a yard sale and stuffed it full of newspaper and set it afire on the patio for us. We screamed with pleasure when the flames curled up its chimney and the shingled roof gave way. Oh, Mrs. Verver never stopped yelling, but we didn't care and he didn't either.

Smiling at me now, as if he's remembering it too, Mr. Verver loops winking Christmas lights across the bar. Music is playing, old songs I don't know, but Mr. Verver seems to know all the words to them, and he sings lightly, happily, and it's like we've fallen out of time.

"What if she won't come down?" I ask.

"She'll come," he says.

He's up in her room for a half hour and I make the punch, but there is no sherbet so I use glunks of butter pecan ice cream and everything swirls in lovely gold-curl patterns. I want to dip my fingers in, but I don't, and I try to listen to what's happening upstairs and I can't hear. I even find myself creeping, mouselike, halfway up the steps, but I just hear the low lilting of Mr. Verver's voice and first some broken, wailing sounds that must be Dusty.

Part of me thinks I don't want to see her. I'm still remembering the things she said, or nearly said, to me. Did she think I lied about the cigarettes? I feel a fresh anger before I remember she's right.

And part of me thinks, If she doesn't come, maybe this will be mine, this evening, all mine.

But soon, I hear her talking and finally I think I hear her laugh, for the first time in weeks. I run back down the stairs, grabbing the punch bowl from the counter and nearly slipping down every basement step.

He comes down first and says the guest of honor will be arriving presently.

We both grin and wait, the CONGRATULATIONS sign from a forgotten occasion hitting the top of his head.

★   ★   ★

What she must see as she slips down those carpeted steps: such holy enchantment, red and white lit, the crush of flowers tugged from the garden, the creamy white gold of the punch bowl. The tinkling music vibrating from the posts and steam pipes. The glowing face of Mr. Verver, as always, in his T-shirt and jeans, bowing slightly at the waist.

First I think she'll see me and she won't like it.

But she doesn't even notice me. I'm not even there.

Her face is wonderstruck.

She's wearing the dress, that long slash of crimson. He got her to wear the dress. She is barefoot, and the hem skims her red toenails.

Touching her fingertips to her hair, piled high on her head, a bobby pin poking from its knotty center, she minces so delicately down the last step.

Then I see her face, so hesitant, so guarded, and I realize how much it matters to me that she embrace it. I look at Mr. Verver, the way he's watching her, so expectant. I think, *Please, Dusty, please.*

She pauses just a second, then she lets everything rush through her face, all the feeling bursting there like little fireworks, and it's so lovely. It's a Dusty I've never seen, letting everything show there. Showing everything.

I look at him, that look on his face, his eyes creased and laughing, and it reminds me of how he was before all this. I realize how different he's become. I'd forgotten how he was.

I'd thought this was for her, but when I look at him, his arm around her, making her so happy, I see it's really for him.

And I love Dusty at this moment because it's a gift to her dad, it's a gift to him, and I almost love her just for giving it to him.

★   ★   ★

Mr. Verver dances with her, and I stir punch, skating the ladle in countless foamy figure eights. It's that moonlight drive song, and I wonder when Mr. Verver found it and if he looked for hours so he could play it for me.

Unless he's playing it for her. It strikes me, he must be playing it for her. *But don't I deserve it more?*

It's a strange song of echoes and mysteries.

Dusty pirouettes, and he dips her so low her hair tumbles loose, its edges skittering along the tiled floor.

The two of them, they are magic, and there's no talk of Evie.

She's just gone.

Thirteen

Eighth-grade graduation comes and there'd been talk of canceling it, but they don't.

The day before, after another anonymous tip, five hundred volunteers fanned out in the woods behind the school. No one finds anything, nothing real. Abandoned campfires, used condoms, a dead cat.

Tara tells me the police are all on overtime, their days spent fielding "nut calls." And some that they can't necessarily tell are nuts, like the man who'd been at the insurance convention and says he may have seen Shaw that week, looking confused and wandering through the bushes behind the convention hotel.

Today everyone is trying to forget. A lot of people seem to really have forgotten. My mother and Ted sit in the stands while I get my diploma, and she looks very happy in what we call her pretty-lady dress, the purple one with the rosettes for buttons. She smiles the whole time, all her teeth glaring at me. She can't stop herself.

Standing there, the sun so hot on my new dress, the rose print searing into me, I press my hand to it and it feels like it might singe.

My hands are sweat-curled around my diploma, and I'm looking somehow for the Ververs, even though they'd never be there. My head goes to murky places and I keep thinking of Mr. Shaw and what his love might be doing to Evie, and what it's already done.

Here I am, back stiff in strict formation, and what is happening to Evie, what beating love is beating down on her?

I don't want to think it, I don't want it to be so beautiful. But what if it is?

If we look at it from eye corners, or from places other than the center of our head, isn't there a kind of terrible beauty in it?

That night, and the next one, and the one after that, I sit for hours with Mr. Verver and they are mystical and uncanny hours. Somehow, with the sound of katydids and the creaking of lawn chairs and the echoey way of our voices in that space, it all feels a little better, a little separate, a little safe from everything else.

Even that spot in the yard, the place under the pear tree, it's no longer his, it's no longer Mr. Shaw's. There's some kind of divine transport and everything else glides away. I think these are the only hours that he is free from it, and I can make him forget, I can. Or I can help him remember in a way that does not ravage him.

Mrs. Verver, she is ravaged. She is worse and worse, he tells me. She can't sleep and it makes her crazy. She tells him, It's making me crazy.

She sits at her bedroom window for hours, like a widow on her widow's walk. One night she took Evie's room apart top to bottom, sure the police had missed something, left some clue behind.

"But she knew there was nothing to find," he says.

Then he says, "I think she might have called Mrs. Shaw. I don't know, but I think she may have called her house."

This seems gruesome, and I imagine the call, Mrs. Verver's raspy voice scratching into the answering machine, *I know he took* her. *I know he took her. Where did he take her, what did he do?* And Mrs. Shaw, huddled in some corner of her house, hands clasped over her ears, begging for it to end.

Everyone thinks it will never end.

Everyone is dying for it to end.

"She just feels like she has to do something," he says. "We all do. I can't seem to do anything else."

I start to talk about other things.

I talk about how I have been listening to all the different songs he's been telling me about.

And I tell him how my brother broke up with his girlfriend the day after the prom and how she kicked in his locker door and wrote things about him in permanent marker on the mirror of the girls' bathroom.

And I tell him how I remember when I was little and slid my bare foot hard on the slippery carpet in the hallway outside Evie's room and it dragged along the wood floor.

But you made it all better, I say. You propped me up on the bathroom vanity and spent fifteen minutes teasing the splinter out with tweezers and a burnt-tip needle.

I still remember, or at least it feels like it as I tell him, the smooth pressure of the heel of his hand, while I sat rapt, hearing about the time he learned to play piano at fifteen, listening to Ray Charles's "What'd I Say" over and over again, all to impress a girl named Eleanor Tipton, who told him, with a twitch of the nose, that she dated only guitarists, and preferred Roy Orbison to Ray Charles, who was overrated anyway.

"I told you that?" he says, grinning. "I don't remember that at all."

"You did."

"Eleanor Tipton," he says, and it's such a loose, careless smile.

"I thought my heart would break. I thought I'd never love again."

"But you did," I say.

"A hundred times," he says, winking, "before I hit eighteen."

When I head home, just before the eleven o'clock news, my mother is so pleased with me. She says I'm growing up into a good and thoughtful person. Her silky new kimono tied tight at her waist, she feeds me doughy cinnamon rolls from the oven like when I was a kid, the kind that come with the plastic disk filled with frosting.

She sits with me at the kitchen table and I know she'd like me to tell her things, to tell her what's going on with the investigation and how Mr. Verver is doing. But I don't feel like telling her. I wouldn't know how to make her understand.

She leans toward me, her chin tucked in her hands, and I feel it like a breathless tug.

She wants me to confide, and then she will confide too.

Oh, how it must twist in her that I sit there and I lick that icing, and lick it off all my fingertips.

I just look at her and take another bite, my hand sinking over the softly wheezing roll.

I just look and look and look and my face gives her nothing.

I give her nothing.

It's just past midnight, and I'm sitting on the front porch, which I know would make her crazy. But I can't sleep and the air conditioner was thundering at me and I felt all closed up. Out here, it's still a heavy June heat, but the air moves a little, it stirs.

And I have something to watch. It seems like I always do.

A car is in front of the Ververs' house, a lonely blue car.

I recognize it right away. Bobby Thornhill. Bobby Thornhill is back. Everyone else—neighbors and the slinking mailman and even the slow guy who delivers the church circulars—have all hunkered away since everything happened. All keeping a safe distance, not wanting to push, to touch, to graze against, to get too close.

But not Bobby Thornhill, and there's a funny warming in my chest. I'm somehow grateful for it. Despite everything, there's still *this*. *This* still lives and breathes and gasps and stutters. This doesn't change. This doesn't stop.

Bobby Thornhill still inches his car along the streetlit curb, lights off, shoulders slouched, neck craning, peering at the Verver house.

Bobby Thornhill still gazes yearningly up at Dusty's window, that window beaming with promise, a faintly curtained invitation.

"How long can you just look?" my brother once said. But what boy ever really put hands to Dusty, tongue to her teeth, her pearly ear, searching for ways in, and found what he'd been promised by that curving smile of hers, that golden girl-face? I know it must have happened, but I can't remember it. I can't even picture it.

"I see Dusty with college fellas," Mr. Verver once teased, lying back on the pillow balanced on Dusty's tanned lap.

Evie and I perked our heads up, so eager to know what he meant, what he knew about Dusty and what she should and would have.

"Graduate students. Wire-frame glasses and bottles of Scotch. They'll recite odes to her, write songs about her on battered acoustic guitars, and promise to take her away from all this suburban dread."

Dusty rolled her eyes magnificently and pretended to snore

and tugged at Mr. Verver's dark hair, twisted it between her dainty fingers.

Bobby Thornhill, though, I am glad for you. You remind me of before, just when "before" seemed gone forever.

I slink along the driveway and I think maybe I'll get closer and maybe I'll see something. Something I might want to see, with his head jerking, his eyes glazed, and such magic behind them, visions of Dusty stretched out before him, reclined, fine-spun curls twirled in her own twirling hands.

I think I might see Bobby seeing that and I don't mind whatever I see, not even that.

I'm so close, and suddenly his car door pops open, and I jump back, feet on the curb. Startled, Bobby looks at me.

"What're you doing?" he says, leaning out, eyes on me.

"Nothing," I say.

There's a half-empty six-pack of beer on the seat next to him, the cardboard sweating. I can smell gusts of it when he talks.

"You're not calling the cops, are you?" he says. "Or her dad?"

"No," I say.

"He seems like a cool guy," Bobby says. "Everyone says he is. I feel bad for all of them."

I nod, not knowing what else to do.

"She came out here two nights ago," he says. "Maybe you don't believe me. You're just a kid. But she came out."

I don't know if I do believe it. But I can't guess why he'd lie.

Then I think again how she's never out there in the backyard with Mr. Verver anymore. Is his heartache so great she can't bear it, just like I almost can't, seeing it on him, wanting to fix it?

I think about her up in her puffed pink room, restless and bored. She doesn't know what to do with herself, I think. She doesn't know what to do if she's not under his bright lights.

"She came out and she stood right here." He points to where I'm standing. I look down at myself, my knobby legs and bare feet.

"She asked me what I wanted, but I didn't know what to say," he says. "And then she just got in the car with me. I couldn't believe it.

"And I couldn't believe it when she let me kiss her."

I pictured it, the kiss, his hands grasping at her, at Dusty's clean, tight pureness. Would she let it unbend, unfurl for him?

I imagine him trying so hard, his mouth on her, on her cheek, the side of her mouth, her neck. Trying to animate her, to share all that want, show her what it means, and what it can do.

No, no. It was all so wrong. I didn't know why, but I couldn't see it. Dusty's eyes glassy with want, with surrender. There was no picturing it, not like this.

"It was like she was giving me my shot," he tells me. "To see what I'd do."

He looks at me and his eyes are sad, helpless.

"But it turned out I didn't know what to do," he says, and he's not even embarrassed to tell me. Maybe I don't count enough to be embarrassed. "Because she's not like other girls. That's why she's Dusty."

What made him think he could do this? What made him think he could touch, even with the most delicate fingertips, much less with those hapless, grabbing hands of his?

He looks up at the window, past my tugged-loose ponytail, his voice breaking softly.

"I never thought she'd come outside."

Fourteen

My head filled with thoughts of the yearnings of Bobby Thornhill, I slink back in through the patio door. The kitchen is pitch-black, and my bare feet skid hard on the linoleum. I stumble, and there is a feeling of softness, like I've slid into a basket of laundry, but I haven't, and I see the flash of eyeglasses, and it's Dr. Aiken, shirttail hanging out, arms holding me up, in our kitchen.

I feel the half scream from my mouth and I stop it fast with the heel of my hand.

"Lizzie," he whispers, loudly, and tries to keep me upright, hands on my jerking arms.

"I don't know you," I say, and the light flashing on his glasses, I can't see his eyes.

"I'm a friend of your mother's. I was just leaving—"

That's when the hall light streams across us and I see my mother whirl around the corner, tying her kimono fast around her.

"Lizzie," she hisses, and her eyes fix on the open patio door and my grass-stained feet.

"Lizzie, what were you doing outside?" Her hand claws over my wrist. "Were you out there? By yourself outside, with everything that's happened?"

Her hand on me so tight, and she has so much nerve, and I

raise my chin and the words jump from me. "I can do what I want," I bellow. "Don't you?"

Like that, her hand leaps to my face, a slap that sings.

"Diane," Dr. Aiken says, and he reaches out. "She wasn't outside. I was the one who opened the door. She must've heard something and come downstairs. We just surprised each other."

I look at him, my cheek throbbing. I look at him, listen to him save my lily-white skin, but all I can see is the light on his glasses and I don't say anything.

At breakfast, my mother wants to reach out to my face, I can see it on her. Ted's started his summer job at the country club and it's just the two of us. There's been no talking about anything, and I slept dreamlessly, waking to the sound of her on the phone, whispering plaintively, her voice rising once, saying, "I don't know what to say. I don't know what to say."

I scrape the black off my toast mercilessly. She tries to start conversations. She says pained, half-embarrassed things, all without saying anything.

There's something wobbling in her and her hands shake and all the heat and tingliness she usually has after he has been over are gone. She raps her knuckles on the newspaper and sighs and slathers a dishrag this way and that and swivels noisily around the kitchen.

And finally she leaves for work too.

I wander the house, lingering in the doorway to my mother's room. I don't go in, I just can't, but I see the bed's unmade and I can almost feel the pocketed warmth in the center.

Does she think, now that he's seen what he's seen, her doctor will be gone forever?

Fleeing, nights, late, the closeness of his house, the wifely claws snaring him. He runs from it and finds such ease, such leg-stretching, laughing ease here, and it's so wonderful, so warm and fun, and who wouldn't want that?

But then it just gets scissored through, doesn't it? The seams are torn and he sees all the misery he thought he left at home, well, it's here too.

All that misery's burst through and you might choke from it.

An hour later, maybe more, of ambling around the house, and I see the way time can nearly stop.

I can't imagine the stretch of summer days without Evie.

I can't imagine summer without Evie. I've never had summer without Evie.

It's pouring rain too, and I keep looking outside and it's almost noon when I see Mr. Verver out there with Detective Thernstrom. Mr. Verver's face is so white. It's the whitest face I've ever seen.

I inch toward the open window screen and try to hear, but I can't.

Mr. Verver has one hand on his hip and he's shaking his head, nodding, and looking down at the pavement. He's soaking wet, and Detective Thernstrom is trying to keep him under his umbrella, but Mr. Verver doesn't seem to notice, keeps drifting away.

I feel a churning in my stomach and before I know it, I've pushed myself out the screen door and into their driveway.

Mr. Verver turns and looks at me, and his face, the rain glittering on it, I can't read it. It's like an assembly of the parts of his face with nothing behind them.

But suddenly I know it, I just know.

It's because of that look on his face, all that blood and life and feeling wiped clean.

The rain keeps pelting at him, pelting him so hard, like when ancient statues are worn away.

It happens just like that.

I suddenly feel Evie's fingers slip through mine, feel her falling into the earth itself.

How could I have missed it, the way I knew her, the way I could put my hands on my own face, body, throat, heart, and know it was hers, how could I have let it go by? She slipped from me while I, while I...

"Lizzie," Mr. Verver says. And Detective Thernstrom continues to look at me, the rain slanting from the black umbrella.

"What happened?" I say, and I feel the wet hanging on me, and I can't move, my sneakers filling with water.

Detective Thernstrom walks toward me.

"We thought we found her," he says. "But it wasn't her."

"Found her," I say.

"They found a body, Lizzie," Mr. Verver says, and he puts his hands on my shoulders, and his hands are wet and heavy and I feel myself sinking. "They called me a few hours ago to tell me they found the body of a girl down in Preston Hollow. We thought it might be her."

His hands loosen, his wrists turned up, resting on my shoulders. "But it wasn't. It wasn't her."

Detective Thernstrom slopes the umbrella so it cocoons me. The rain on the dark canvas throbs.

"Everything's the same," he says. "We're back where we were."

But it isn't true, is it. Because in that minute—a minute that had been hours for Mr. Verver—everything changed forever.

In that minute, I felt Evie dead and now I knew she could be.

★   ★   ★

Mr. Verver is drinking beer from a green bottle. We're in the paneled basement. It's three o'clock in the afternoon now, still raining. We've been here for hours.

I know I should be home, I know my mother's probably called to check on me, but there is no way for me to leave. And I can't think of leaving. We have been here for hours, hearing the rain tick-tick-ticking. We have eaten potato chips and played darts and backgammon.

I'm wearing one of Evie's shirts and a pair of her shorts. Mr. Verver didn't say the clothes were Evie's when he handed them to me, but I know they are. I've worn Evie's clothes dozens of times, even worn this blue T-shirt before, soft and pilling and smelling somehow of Evie, of pencil shavings and soccer cleats and shampoo. The shorts feel tight on me, on my thighs. Listening to my own clothes tumbling in the booming dryer, I find myself tugging at Evie's and the strangeness of it all grieves me and I put it out of my head.

Mrs. Verver and Dusty are at her grandparents.' They spent the night there. When the police called at six a.m., Mr. Verver was alone. He spent those hours of waiting all alone. He would not call them.

"I'll never tell them," he says. "If I can help it, they'll never hear about it."

He carries the world for them. Do they even know?

They've just abandoned him. Even Dusty, his shining star, his partner in crime. She, a fair-weather daughter, forsaking him.

But here I am.

And now we share this, this secret knowledge, it binds us.

Let's look at it: Evie died for both of us, for a second, a minute, hours. She died for us, and that knowledge heavy in our hands changes everything.

Also this: For me at least, I let her. I let her. The tight knot of my hand over hers went slack, my fingers springing up and touching air. I let her go.

I hate myself for it.

I wonder, did he feel it too?

Old vinyl records fan across the floor. Mr. Verver is remembering when he was my age. There's a story for each album. He says he doesn't have his turntable anymore, but he likes to show me the covers.

Then he suddenly thinks of something and rustles around in the laundry room until he finds an old record player with torn cords in a box that says DAD'S STUFF. For twenty minutes, I help him, tearing masking tape and handing him pieces as he strips and cuts wires and hooks everything up to the speakers.

When the music burrs through, popping and scratching soft nothings into my ear, it is a wondrous thing. We smile at each other, feeling triumphant.

The records all speak to him of memories, but they are old memories, older than me, older than Evie. They are about his father and his old girlfriends and the pals he used to go on road trips with, to see concerts, big outdoor concerts that lasted all day, tattooing themselves into you with sense memories so strong.

Sitting there, he runs his hand over an album cover balanced on his lap.

I have my eyes on his worn deck shoes, large and soft, and I almost want to touch them, squeeze them, they look so soft. I somehow think I could touch them, I really could, and he wouldn't say a word. Not a word.

We're listening to one of his own father's country-western albums, which is sad and woeful. The cover is cracked and peeling with the sticky shreds of an old price tag, and I put my fingers to it. I feel helpless and ruined. The songs, they speak to me.

Evie is not the dead girl they found on the roadside in Preston Hollow, the dead girl who is just another thirteen-year-old, run over by a car, a tire track across the center of her, splitting her in two.

Evie is not the dead girl, but she might have been.

How did I not know this?

Mr. Verver runs the heel of his hand over his stippled jaw.

I am sitting next to him on the swirl of the braided rug, my arms wrapped around the album sleeve, holding it to my chest.

We haven't talked in a while when Mr. Verver suddenly says, "You talk to your dad much, Lizzie?"

I look at him, feeling like a finger has just been dragged up my spine.

"Sure," I say, resting my chin on the sharp cardboard edge of the album cover. No one really asks about him anymore. But no one ever asked much before the divorce either. Sunday dinners, driving me to school on the coldest days. There wasn't much to know. Now there's less.

He isn't looking at me. He's looking at something else, some invisible thing glinting in the dark of the laundry room.

"You know...do you want to know something about being a dad, Lizzie?"

I look at him, waiting.

"What?" I say. I think I say it twice.

"It's the greatest thing in the world," he says, and he turns and faces me. Looking at me, eyes blinking, waiting for this to register.

Not knowing what to do, I nod. I nod and nod and nod.

He smiles, his eyes glassy and haunted.

The music booms and suddenly I feel like bursting into hysterical tears with it. Not because I'm sad but everything's happening all at once and I can't even say what it is.

Mr. Verver finishes off his beer with one last foamy gulp.

I can see it on his face: he is saying, *All I know, all the clues you've given me. Can't you give me more? You've shown me who, but can you show me where? Where is she, Lizzie?* He doesn't say it, but I can hear it, I can hear it thrumming through me. *Give me more, Lizzie.*

The phone rings and Mr. Verver runs upstairs. It's the police again. I know they've been doing a new round of interviews with Shaw acquaintances, and Mr. Verver is on the phone a long time, frantically taking notes on scraps of paper.

I wave a good-bye, but he doesn't see.

"Dusty," I say with a start, my hand on the Ververs' kitchen door.

She has a duffel bag slung over one arm, her book bag on the other, and all that whorling hair is pulled tight atop her head.

"Hey," she says, "you scared me." But she doesn't look scared.

Everything seems backward, her standing there, waiting for me to let her in.

"You're back," I say, because I can't think what else to say.

Looking at her, a million thoughts, *Getting into Bobby Thornhill's car, trying to make him show her what it means to—*

She pushes past me into the kitchen.

"I'm back," she replies, and she sees her father, phone pressed to his face in the hallway, hears his *Uh-huh, uh-huh, do you think that might—do you think we could—what if he—okay, okay. . . . But what did they think about the tip from Iron River?*

She watches him for a second.

Then she swivels to lift her book bag from the floor.

"Can I help?" I say.

"That's what you do," she says. "Isn't that what you do?"

The book bag comes smacking at my outstretched arms. I take it, even though I'm not sure what I'm supposed to do with it.

"You came back without your mom," I say.

"She's staying there a while. With my grandparents," she says, pulling the rubber band from her hair, letting it all tumble down. "She can't be here now."

"It's so hard," I say, floundering. "Not knowing."

She fans herself a little with her hand, lifting her damp hair off her neck.

"You're just here all the time now," she finally says, twirling a long strand through her fingers.

"I don't know," I say, my chin nudged against her book bag, weighing down my arms.

All our life, it was Dusty. Evie and I whispering about her, speculating, spinning ideas, imagining. Listening to her through walls, from upstairs, from downstairs. It must be so different for her now. Who's listening for her now?

"What would he do without you," she says. "What would we do."

There's that steeliness to her voice that always puts the shake in me. I start thinking she's going to ask me about the milk chute again. *There's plenty of other perfectly good places to hide things . . .*

The way she looks at me, I feel like she can see every lie on me, even the ones that aren't lies.

"You're never out there anymore," I say, very fast, before I lose my nerve. "I'm so used to seeing you out in the yard, like always. With your dad."

She knows what I'm saying. She knows I'm saying: *You've abandoned him, but I won't.*

She looks at me, those slitted eyes. My skin raises up, cold and briary. If we were on the field, I'd be bracing myself for her, eyes shut.

At last, she says, "Why don't you just go home?" And she snaps the rubber band over her hair. "I think I hear your mother calling you."

That night, late, there's something building up in me, like blood rushing to my face, my chest, like iron in my veins, my heart.

It's the day spent in that basement with Mr. Verver, the things I knew he was asking of me, even if he didn't ask them out loud, even if he doesn't know in the front part of his head what he wants me to do. And it's Dusty, it's Dusty, and she's circling me, and she knows things and it feels like time is running out.

These are the things tearing around in my head.

I'm in bed with my clothes on.

I'm waiting for the quiet of the house.

There is no Dr. Aiken that night, and I knew there wouldn't be. My mother makes herself a margarita from an old powdered mix she finds in the back of the kitchen cabinet.

Later, I hear her on the phone and I think she's called my father and I don't want to think about what they might be saying to each other.

I turn the radio as loud as I can and wish I had a turntable and wish I had that record Mr. Verver had, the one about swimming to the moon and how, if we got real close and real tight, we could make it through the tide.

There's a feeling of needing to make something happen, make something break, stop the pressure, the diresome pressure that makes me feel like I am lost forever, an iron weight across my chest.

I can feel Evie nearly wiped clean from me. It'd happened twice that day. Once, watching them in the driveway, the umbrella bending down, and once more with Dusty, the things she said and the way I maybe almost believed them.

I can feel her nearly wiped clean from me.

Fifteen

My hands are on one of the back window ledges, bowed over the molding. I've run my hands around all four sides of the house. I've laid my hands on it like maybe a healer might, or a fairy-tale witch.

Standing now, on tippy-toes, I can feel the house sounds humming under my fingertips. A floor squeak, a pipe running.

I'm standing outside the Shaw house just past midnight and I'm going to get in. I'm going to get in that house.

Where are you? Where are you? Some creaking cabin high up in Canada, or right here in town, hiding before our very eyes? Are you at the bottom of the lake, or deep in some far-off woods, and wherever you are, is Evie tucked under your arm, your sleeping princess? Is she anywhere at all?

The thing is roiling in me, I can't breathe. I feel like I'm very nearly clawing the walls, begging them to turn the house inside out, to give up its hiddenness and show me everything. I'm ready now to see everything.

(But what if there's nothing to see? There's that thought too. What if there's nothing? What if I know all there is that can be known and the rest is lost to me forever? I can't ponder that. I can't.)

Somehow I think if they're asleep, they will not hear me. I

will not be heard. From where this crazy confidence comes, I can't guess.

When I'm sure the house has fallen lifeless, when I can't see a light on or feel anything moving or flittering by windows curtained tight, I tug hard on the old hinged pane and my face hits the screen and I take the penknife from my pocket, the one I brought just for this, and I run its tip along the mesh, tearing it until I can squeeze through.

It's so fast, like I was born to it.

My feet hit a carpeted floor, and I'm in.

There is no thought of the craziness of all this.

I guess part of me sees it like the way dreams work: *Somehow, I'm just there, I'm in his house. And I'm not scared at all. Because somehow I'm supposed to be there.*

It's very dark, and I'm standing in some kind of family room, because I can see the porch light's glow reflected in the gray face of a television set.

My first move and I nearly fall, my foot sliding over something smooth, a slick magazine cover spread open on the floor. I pull out my key-chain flashlight and wave it helplessly around the room: bookshelves, a shiny-topped coffee table, a set of Civil War books, what is there to see?

But I begin. It seems to take hours, it's probably minutes, but it seems forever because I slip, so soundless, from room to room on the first floor: kitchen towels, standing lamps, a hard plastic vacuum cleaner, a bathroom night-light shaped like a teapot.

Finally, I stumble into the living room, eyeing the staircase with menace. The dark at the top of it. Do I dare? I do not. I cannot.

I can't guess what I expected to find that the police missed. But they'd missed other things, hadn't they?

I just know that night I'd stood out there on the bristled tip of that lawn I felt it. Like a little girl slid between the folds of window drapes, between the folds of her mother's skirt, I stood there and felt small and unwise, like the wisdom of the world lay just above me, lay right out there, lay through this keyhole, past this doorframe, behind these window blinds.

And now I am inside that space. I am right in there. And where is my hard-won wisdom? Where are the secrets of the world laid bare?

Instead, nothing. A house like any house. Like my house. The Verver house.

The unfairness of it all nearly defeats me.

I have to think, I tell myself, there must be something. I'm in the house and there must be *something*.

I let my eyes go in and out of focus and I scan the room, wedging my flashlight under my chin, turning this way and that, scattering the little pock of light.

I think about how burglars must feel. There is so much in a house, how can we ever unearth its treasures in five minutes or even five hours? I remember on TV, the ex-thief who walked around an average person's house showing the spots where people always hide valuable things—the bedside table, under the mattress, in the bureau drawer, nestled between underwear and socks.

But I don't even know what I'm looking for and my head feels jammed with circuits, like I can't stop the thoughts from hissing, sizzling, popping in my ears.

Mr. Shaw's house, Mr. Shaw's house. His family room, his dining room, his study. Somehow it doesn't seem like him at all. Somehow the outside, that gabled house pulled tight upon itself—well, it felt more like him than anything inside.

Trying to slow myself, I sink fast into an armchair, a tall-backed man's chair, deep and leathery, and press my face against it. Bowing my legs beneath myself, I hunch into the chair as deep as I can, ducking my head low, pushing my fingers between the arm and the cushion, curling around myself and feeling like I've reached the end of the world and found nothing.

I try to focus and calm myself.

Breathing deeply, I gaze up at the mantelpiece just above my head, inches from my face.

Flashing the light across the family photographs, I see Mrs. Shaw in tidy little outfits, boatneck shirts with jaunty stripes, denim skirts with smocked pockets, matching baseball caps, with Pete Shaw, who tentatively holds a bat in his hands like it's a stick of dynamite passed to him by a cruel enemy.

Mr. Shaw, with a full head of dark hair in one old picture, his face half hidden behind a Christmas tree garland he is hanging with care.

Behind it, a faded photo of Mr. Shaw in front of grassy water. It's so familiar and I realize that it's Green Hollow Lake. Mr. Shaw's kneeling beside Pete, who looks all of seven years old, water wings wedged up his scrawny arms.

Behind him, swimmers float, a big yellow raft bobs. There is such peace. Something flickers in me and I move closer, squirming up in the chair, and I'm sure. It's my old Hawaiian Punch raft, and that's me, ruddy little-girl cheeks, my hands holding tight to the raft's meaty white rope as my brother tows me along.

It's all so funny I nearly laugh, my fingers tug at my lips and a funny sound comes from my mouth.

There I am, with Mr. Shaw.

I slink back down in the chair, feeling dizzy, twiddling my flashlight between my fingers and breathing fast.

I feel like I've been caught somehow. Caught in Mr. Shaw's gloomy, love-haunted world, trapped under glass and pressed together, without either of us ever knowing.

Just like, somewhere, somehow, he sits with Evie now—he does, I know—and I sit in his chair, my hands on his things, his hands on mine.

Something mournful has caught me, and I have to go, and I can't unfurl my feet fast enough.

That's when I hear his voice, a throat clearing, hear it before I see him, or anything.

A floor lamp snaps on.

My heart catches.

I have to turn, and I do, one leg still resting on the seat cushion, one foot on the floor.

There's an electric crackling in my chest, a burning, tingling thing.

I turn and there he is.

His hair sleep-tousled, he looks at me, long spindle fingers scratching his chest through a T-shirt with a drawing of a large stapler on it.

Pete Shaw, standing there on the living room carpet.

He's staring at me, and he's so tall in that stretchy high-school-boy way. I don't know what to say, but I feel my arm go across my chest.

"I saw you here before," he says. "Outside."

I feel my goose-pimply arms. *Mr. Shaw's son. Mr. Shaw's son.*

"I was hoping you'd come back," he says, his head bobbing. "I was waiting for you to come back."

I drop my other foot to the floor and try to stand as straight as possible.

"I have to show you something," he says, pointing upstairs,

his eyes starting to take on a glitter, like he really has been up there, waiting for me, waiting for the night I'd come.

I don't know what to think. It's all like a dream—how in a dream people say things like they'd never say in real life, do things they'd never do.

"Don't worry," he says, and he takes a step toward me. "She can't hear anything."

I look into the dark at the top of the stairs.

"She'd sleep through the end of the world, with all the stuff she's taking," he says, his voice speeding up. "Each night, the rattle from those pill bottles lasts through most of the eleven o'clock news. She has to fill her water glass three times."

I look at him, the strange energy that seems to be coiling up in him as he looks at me, and I don't know what to do. Pete Shaw. That dreamness makes it seem like there are no rules. But aren't there rules?

He reaches his hand out toward me, not near enough to touch.

Something fumbles in my chest and I have this sudden thought of Mr. Verver, head craned over the record player, smiling sadly at me, tapping his fingers on his leg in time.

"I just want to show you something," he says, and though he's seventeen and a boy and he's in what he wears to bed and so am I and I feel my heart bucking, I don't feel scared, not exactly. He just seems so sure, like this is all as it's meant to be, has to be.

I tell myself: this is Mr. Shaw's son, *and here I am, right in his world and now it's not a sleeping world but an alive one and this is my chance and, and, and—*

"First," I say, my voice splintery, hurting my own ears. "Is she okay? Evie. What is he doing with her? Do you think...is she okay?"

He tilts his head, teeth dragging into his lip. A darkness spreading through his eyes. "I don't know," he says.

He looks sorry to say it. But that doesn't help at all.

I follow him up the carpeted steps, eyes on the faded red of his T-shirt.

Walking down the hallway to his room, though, I feel twisty things in my stomach, like I might at a haunted house but one you somehow know, and that knowing is the creepiest thing of all.

I think somehow I can hear Mrs. Shaw sleeping, the deep sleep like Mrs. Verver's, the buffered sleep of mourning mothers everywhere.

Once we're in his room, though, it's different. All the lavender darkness, the eerie quiet of the hall, is gone.

Here, everything buzzes with electronics. Red blips, orange, green, glowing like a big control room. Stereo, computer, consoles, hulking black speakers, who knows what. The other kind of boy from my brother. In Ted's room everything is stale, sweaty, but here, it's like the whole room is alive, humming and breathing in my ears.

Pete wheels a desk chair toward me and I sit down on it.

Looking at him, his head ducking under wires, under the glittering silver wing of a model airplane dangling from the ceiling, I think suddenly about how I have nothing on under my T-shirt, and then I remember it's Evie's T-shirt, the one Mr. Verver gave me to wear.

I have sudden weird, skittish thoughts of Pete as some kind of deranged killer, a bunch of girls and his parents, too, dead in the basement.

But then I look at him, the lights blinking Christmas-like on the wall behind him, flickering and flashing in gentle pulses and it's like they are Pete's own breaths and I start to feel them pulse in me.

Finally, he fixes on me and it's like he's gathering himself, color flushing up his face, his skin hot and bothered, so much he wants to say. It's all blazing in him, you can see it, and he's trying to figure out how to tell, how to make it understood.

When he starts, it's in the middle of things, and I see it's a conversation he has with himself all day long, all night long. This is what he does, up here in his room, waiting for me. And now, at last, I'm here.

"He used to take these walks at night. My dad. And drives. He'd say, 'I'm going for a drive,' and we never knew where he went," he says. "We didn't care. He lives here, sure, but sometimes it's like he was never here at all. Just this shadow moving through our house. At the head of the dinner table. And then in his chair, the TV on, news and some game—your name's Lizzie, right?"

The question jolts me, and I nearly jump in my seat. "Yeah," I say.

"Lizzie," he says, and he swivels his chair right in front of me, his knees brushing mine, my skin prickling. His breath is nearly on me, and I feel my legs tremble, but it's not scary, it's not. He just, he just—

"I mean, now that he's gone, is it really that different?" he says. "People keep asking, the counselor at school and stuff, if I'm okay. But it was always me and her. Not him. Sometimes it's like I forgot him before he even left. He was like a ghost who haunted our house my whole life."

I look down at him, feeling my skin under my shirt, and he

has his hands on the arms of the chair I'm sitting in, he's telling me such private things, and everything's glittering around us, all the lights from all the buzzing electronics. My face burns from it, and the way his eyes, black and swampy, fix on me, and I can't even think.

"Except here's the thing: now that he's gone, he's suddenly taken over everything," he says. "He never gave us anything, and now he leaves us with this."

So quick, he grabs my legs, my thighs in his hands, and I think, *Is this happening,* and *Too much is happening at once.*

"Lizzie, I've been hoping you'd come back because I want to tell you. I saw you out there and you're the one I can tell," he says, his knuckles white on my legs, veins cording at his neck.

"You saw me here, before?" I say, and a fear barbs up in me. I think of him watching me from this window, overlooking the darksome backyard. What did he see, a hedgehog, a burrowing thing with twigs in her hair, knees grass-slicked? Or did he see more than that?

"Later, I heard about how you found the cigarettes," he says.

I look at him, my mouth dry.

"Can you believe the cops missed them?" he asks, shaking his head.

I don't say anything.

"Don't worry," he says. "I won't tell. I'm glad you took them. You made everything happen. It gave me this idea."

"What...," I say, fumbling.

"He calls her," Pete says, then pauses, letting it settle on me for a second. But I'm too jangled for settling.

"It's like suddenly, after twenty years," he says, "he's alive and actually wants to speak to her. Now he wants to tell her about himself and make her see. Because now he needs her help."

My whole body drum-tight, I try not to move. I know something is coming for me, that he's going to give me something, *oh he is, isn't he.*

"He's sure they're tapping our phone," he says, his fingers pressing into me. "Maybe they are. I hope they are. So he calls her at the place she volunteers. The senior center. And she won't tell the police. She lies to the police. That stuff about him wanting to move to Canada, that's all made up. She has them running to all the wrong places."

My fingers grip the armrests. I'm here to receive something. He's been waiting, the pincers tight on his heart. *I know that feeling, I do.*

It's coming, it's coming. All brimful revelation. I feel an exhilaration that shames me.

"She came in here yesterday," he says, his hands finally releasing my legs. I can feel his hands there still, though, the place each finger pressed hotly.

"She asked me how much money I'd saved up," he says, pointing to his dresser. I twist my head around and spot a scoop of bottle green glass there. The bottom rind of an old-fashioned piggy bank, like the kind you see at the rummage sales they have at the church.

"I'd been saving all year for this used car," he says. "I'd saved eight hundred and thirty-five dollars."

He looks at me, his hands curling at his sides. The room seems to be getting hotter and hotter and the one burning lightbulb above his desk radiates mercilessly. I feel my shirt sticking to me.

"That didn't matter, though. That wasn't it. And she stood there," he says, pointing to the doorway. "She kept talking and talking and talking, and I was sitting here, and I didn't say a word. She kept talking until I thought she'd never stop."

And the more he talks, the more I feel, neck tingling, like if I turn around and look at the doorway, I'll see her there. What did she matter to me a month ago, a minute ago, but in his telling, she now looms forty stories high to me. Mrs. Shaw, Mrs. Shaw whom I've never heard speak, never thought of, only passed by, glimpsed through a car window, from my whirring bike. Her ponytail and her crisp white tennis shoes and her face all ruined, like all their faces have been ruined, like Mrs. Verver's face, shell-shocked to ruin.

"She said she couldn't touch the bank accounts. She said the state police, the feds, are watching everything."

He walks over to the dresser and picks up the piece of green glass, a gleaming shard.

Then he tells me how she took the piggy bank and slammed it hard against the metal edge of the desk until it shattered, pocking her hands red, and green glints scattering.

"It all flew up over her face," he says. "Like confetti."

Sitting there, I can feel the ghostly crunch of pieces under my feet.

He pauses a second, breathing deeply, settling himself.

"She said it had to be me," he says. "She was sure they were watching her, and I was his only chance."

So she made him drive to Hunts Wood, forty miles away.

"I had to find a place to send a money order. I went to this convenience store. I had this baseball hat pulled low, like one of those robbers on a surveillance camera. She had me double back, do all this stuff to avoid toll roads. It took me two hours each way. I was sure the cops spotted me. I kept waiting to get caught. It would've been okay to get caught."

He lifts his head up fast. "But I did it. I sent him all my money, like she asked."

I don't know what to say, and see I'm meant to say nothing. I'm looking at the rug, and I slide my foot into its center, swirling it around.

"He asked her for it," he says, and he's looking at me, so I lift my head up, and he's holding that piece of green glass so tight I can see the way his skin goes white, and the way the blood comes, almost black, streaking narrowly through his fingers. What a thing to see.

But I have to ask again. I have to ask. He's slipping away into his misery and this feels like my only chance.

"Pete," I say, and my whole body feels tight and concentrated. "Would he hurt her? Would your dad hurt Evie?"

He drops his arms to his sides and squeezes his hands together. He's looking at the door, the dark in the hallway.

"He hurts everybody."

There's so much bundled up into him as he says it, but he's not answering me, not like I need.

"Has he hurt her?" I say. *"Do you think he's hurt her?"*

He stirs from his gloomy stare and looks at me.

"I don't know," he says quickly, simply, like it never crossed his mind. Something in it, the briskness, the resignation, reminds me of Dusty.

He shakes his head and turns from me, his voice suddenly breaking high. "My mom, she...I hate her."

"You hate her," I say back, because I know he wants me to. Because it's the saying of it that calms, consoles, subdues, and I know it means: *I love her, I love her, I love her, and he's ruined us all.*

The bolting despair in him, I feel it howling through me too. I think I might touch him, but it seems impossible to touch him. It seems like he could never be touched.

But then I touch him anyway, on the hot inside of his arm. I put my fingers on him, feel the ribs under his T-shirt, feel the shudder.

I hate her, I hate her, he murmurs, over and over again, and you can't ever know anyone's private darknesses.

"Where did you send the money?" I whisper, fingertips touching, moving. And his voice lifts, high and trembly, and my hands are there, and he says it, he gives it up, he tells me.

I can see all the sorrow veining through him, but I can't know where it comes from or how to stop it. I don't know that I'd even want to stop it because I've come to feel that deep sorrow and the longing for lost things is the most beautiful thing ever.

Sixteen

"It's Evie," I say. "It's Evie. She called me."

I practice the words over and over again. I say them into the dawn hours, fully dressed under my sheets, waiting for light to come.

I have it in my hand, the answer, the key, the way to end everything. Pete Shaw gave it to me. I just have to figure out how to use it. I have to figure out if I want to protect him, or if he even wants me to.

I choose to protect him.

In those minutes, that half hour after he gifted me in this way, well, I gave him what I could and I don't regret it.

It was just my hands on him and it was nothing but a kind of healing, a try at the laying on of hands.

Hearing the catch in his throat, the tight gasp, my hands there, I'd given him something, hadn't I?

I know I could not heal it—the wound torn across him will always gape hollow, deathless, but I tried, I tried. Or maybe I tried for other reasons.

Whatever the reason, I did it and I'm not sorry.

And now, my mother off to work, I'm standing in the driveway, Mr. Verver has his arm propping the screen door open, open for me. He's saying good morning and he has a cup of coffee in his hand, and he's wearing a maroon T-shirt with a picture of a sunset on it and it says, I know I will remember this always, "Paradise Is Yours."

I open my mouth.

The lie is immense, and I don't hesitate.

"It's Evie," I say. "It's Evie. She just called me."

In my bedroom, practicing into the pillow, in the bathroom, saying it to the mirror, it had sounded grave and real.

Now it sounds like a quavering string, a girl's sputtered nothing.

But that doesn't matter. That doesn't matter because all he hears are the words. The words are magic.

He's looking at me, and he's not saying anything at all.

I feel a shaking in me, and it's the ground. It's like the ground is shaking and I will slip through.

Then, in a flash, his hands reach out and, like in a movie, really, the coffee cup falls to the cement steps with a sharp crack and he grabs my arms and his face is filled with everything that is urgent and loving and meaningful in the world.

I feel so powerful, like a god, thunderbolt in hand.

And my thunderbolt hit.

Seventeen

We're sitting on the living room couch, but I'm still feeling that feeling, standing in the doorframe, my face pressed against Mr. Verver's T-shirt, the way he held me and it was so hard, his arm against me, pressing against my neck so I thought it might break. Like he'd forgotten I was just a girl and he just might crush me from holding me so tight.

I'm thinking of the smell of his T-shirt up against me, the smell of him. The way he always was, that strong, warm scent of cut grass and fresh air and limes and Christmas morning all at once. So many things, and all these things, and I'm feeling them all so much and I need to concentrate, and I have to focus, but I can't focus at all.

"It was right after my mom left for work," I say. "The phone rang and I answered and she said, 'Lizzie, it's Evie. Can you help me?' And it was hard to hear her, like she was whispering, and all I could get was the Five of Diamonds Motel. And then she hung up."

Keep it short, I tell myself. It's the only way to keep it straight, to keep straight about it.

For a minute, I'm sure he is going to get in the car and go, even though, riffling through the phone book, which keeps slipping from him, sprawling to the floor, he has no idea where the motel is. He tries to find it, the pages nearly tearing in his hand, as the questions fly from him and he can't seem to stop.

"You're sure it was her?"

"What did she sound like?"

"Did she say she was alone?"

"Did she sound scared?"

It takes him a few minutes to call the police and I think it's because he really is contemplating tearing out of the driveway and going himself.

All of this worries me, not the least of which is this: I know that just because Pete Shaw wired money to the Five of Diamonds Motel two days ago doesn't mean they're still there.

But what if they are?

I'm sure they are.

Waiting, going places in my head, I picture myself tapping on a big motel window, the brown-tinted glass. I'm tapping there, and peering in, peering through curtains tugged shut with a plastic stick. Let me in, let me in. Oh, Evie, you are so close, it's like we are six and playing tag and I am chasing, heart booming, and you are so close and I reach out and I can feel the ends of your dark hair on my fingertips. I can feel them tickling my fingertips.

Oh, Evie, gone so long, near gone to nothingness, do you see? I will deliver you...

The police are harder. Their questions are better and they are listening with cooler heads. They ask me over and over about what I did or did not hear, what I said, and most of all why I think she called me and not her own family.

I say I don't know.

I am cool, stone-cold perfection.

I have passing fears of phone records. Can they track calls to our house? Will they know? On TV, they know everything. *But, Lizzie, they might say, there's no record of any calls to your house this morning.* But I push it to the side. I have to.

Mrs. Verver is back home, having driven from her parents' house, her hair now spreading gray at the roots, like she's turned middle-aged in just a few weeks. Her tan gone, her skin stretched tight across her bones, she walks like the school librarian, shuffling endlessly to find you your book, turning pages slowly with licked fingers.

She says over and over again, "How can we be sure? How can we be sure it's not a prank? Kids at school. Kids are so cruel. Kids are the cruelest things."

One of the officers tries to comfort her, Mr. Verver too manic to help, huddling with the officers like the football star ready for the big play.

Detective Thernstrom tells us they have found a Five of Diamonds Motel in Indian Wood, twenty-three miles away. He's sending officers. He's going too.

Mr. Verver says he's going with them and no one stops him.

"Shouldn't Lizzie go?" he says, his arm lunging out to me, pulling me close, tucking me under his shoulder. "If she called Lizzie, Lizzie should be there."

I am buried beneath his arm and there is a discussion and even raised voices and I don't hear any of it, my head hot, my stomach doing zithery things, but they will not let me go. They will not let me go.

"She has to come. She's the one Evie reached out to. She can stay in the car, but she has to come." That is what Mr. Verver is saying, in the sternest voice I've known from him.

I spot Mrs. Verver standing by the door, her purse over her shoulder, and she's not even looking at any of us, and that's when I realize I don't even know where Dusty is and I wonder if anyone else does either.

"She has to come," Mr. Verver says. "I need her to come."

The diamond is so large, and it spins and I bet at night it glows. You can see it from the highway, a big metal sign, far bigger and more beautiful than the motel, which looks like a flattened shoe box.

The police have called my mother and she made them put me on the phone before she'd give permission. She made them promise I wouldn't leave the car, that an officer would be with me at all times.

It went on and on and by the time she said yes, Mr. Verver was already ahead of us, miles ahead, with Mrs. Verver and two detectives.

Now they're inside the registration office and I'm in the car with two other officers, and one of them, with a bright-white crew cut, keeps singing about a girl who had diamonds from the mines for eyes.

We are waiting in the parking lot, the officers and me. We sit there under the FREE CABLE AND HOTTUB sign and he hums for a while and then we play I Spy, which I am too old for but it was my idea. It was my idea because I can't stand the feeling anymore.

"I have a good feeling about this," the crew-cut one is saying to the other one, like I can't even hear. "But if it doesn't pan out, we go to the phone company, see if we can get a log of incoming calls to her"—he nods back at me—"house. Get a number for where the Verver girl did call from."

I try not to think about what might happen if they find that log. If they find no phone call at all came that morning.

Evie. Evie. Evie. Are you fifty feet from me now, behind one of those red doors, each one painted with one crooked black diamond, the seeing-eye hole in the very center, glittering in the sun? Are you there?

Because, Evie, truly, I haven't felt you alive in the longest time.

I see them walking across the parking lot toward us, Mrs. Verver slumped against Mr. Verver, and I feel myself tighten inside.

"You stay here, little miss," the crew-cut officer says, and he steps out of the car. All the men are helping Mrs. Verver, whose face looks flat, like a white sack.

I watch as they put her in the other car. They fold her into it like she has no bones to hold her up.

Mr. Verver goes around the other side and gets in too, to help her.

It is not until the officer comes back that I find out what's happened. He and the other officer talk about it the whole way home, as if they've forgotten I'm there.

The motel manager looked at the picture of Mr. Shaw and said he sure looked like Mr. Curtis.

Mr. Curtis had been staying in Room 202, had been there for nearly a week with his young daughter.

He said the daughter looked about thirteen, yes, but he thought she had blond hair, not dark brown. He looked closely at the picture they handed him and said that it could be her. He said he'd seen the missing child reports, like everyone else. He said if she'd had dark hair, he'd definitely have called the police. He was a Good Samaritan.

No, they haven't checked out, the manager said, so he couldn't explain why their car—yes, a maroon Skylark—was gone and why their room was empty, except half a six-pack of Dr Pepper.

They must've left in a hurry, he guessed. But he couldn't understand why, since Mr. Curtis had come by the night before to settle his bill and pay ahead, cash.

Oh, and he almost forgot. A money order came for Mr. Curtis while he was here. No, he didn't bother to check ID, he rarely did, but he did tell Mr. Curtis that he would have to wait forty-eight hours for the money. Motel policy. Mr. Curtis did seem concerned about that.

He seemed a pleasant enough fellow, the manager said. And he took good care of his daughter. He went into town to get her pizza every night.

We are halfway home when I tell the officers they need to pull over. I jump out of the car and am sick for a long time, the one with the crew cut holding me by the waist.

From the corner of my eye, I see them looking at each other.

The last ten miles, I hunker in the corner of the backseat, covering my face.

Mr. Verver spends the afternoon at the police station. My mother comes home from work hours early. She asks me to tell her everything two, three times. She stands at my bedroom door, even as I pull the itchy sheets over my head.

I don't want to talk about any of it.

I don't know what I feel.

My mother keeps saying what I should focus on is that this is all good news. It seems to mean Evie is alive and now the police have a hot trail. That's what she calls it: a hot trail.

I don't say anything. I open and close my lips under the sheets, letting the worn cotton sink into my mouth.

I can't wait for her to leave.

She says she's going to see Mrs. Verver.

"Annie's all by herself," my mother says. "Like always."

Sometime in the lost hours of the afternoon I spend in my bed, half sleeping, half breaking to pieces, the phone rings.

"Lizzie?" It's Pete Shaw, his voice like a flare.

Hearing him in my ear, in daylight like this and after everything.

(What did it mean, sitting in that motel parking lot, waiting to see? What did it mean to know she'd been there, maybe just minutes before, she'd been there, so close you could maybe still feel her, hear the squeak of her tennis shoes on the doormat, smell her baby-soft hair. They'd been there, been there behind one of those clotty red doors, and done such things...and now gone. And now gone. And every night they stayed there when he left to get her food, did he lock her in—did he lock her in? How could he? But he would leave there and she would be there, and would she wait, ready for her dinner, ready for him to click open the door and provide her with her dinner, like a jailer with no keys, with no locks, with no prisoner at all.)

"Did you do it, Lizzie?" Pete is asking me, and I feel my throat close up.

"I...I..."

"The cops were just here," he says.

"Pete," I start, and in my head I'm saying: But you wanted me to tell, you wanted me to tell, you were practically begging me to tell.

"Lizzie, you should've seen her face when I told her that it was me," he says, his voice high and excited and strange. "When I told her what I'd done."

It takes me a second to realize he's talking about his mother.

"You told her?"

There's a ragged laugh, and I'm trying to understand. I think I do understand, but I can't quite believe it.

"She was making breakfast," he says, and I can hear his mouth nearly press against the phone, like a whispered confidence. "She said she felt so bad about taking the money I'd saved up. She was going to make my favorite, pancakes. She was wearing—it was so weird—her special Christmas morning robe. The red one with the white tufts, like Mrs. Claus."

I am listening, gathering my bedsheet, piece by piece, into my fist.

"She was stirring the batter," he says. "I said, 'Mom, guess what I did last night? You'll never guess.'"

"Pete," I say, but my voice trails off. He feels so far away. Everything does.

"She kept stirring, not even looking at me," he says, a strange giddiness to him. "I said I'd told someone what we'd done. I'd told about the phone calls, the money order, the motel."

"You told her about me?" I imagine all kinds of terrible things. I imagine Mr. Verver finding out. I imagine him finding out everything, even my hands on Pete, his tingly skin.

"I didn't need to say who," he says. "She didn't care. She was standing there, and the pan was burning, it was smoking every-where. And I told her I'd torn the whole house down overnight and what did she think of that?" he says, his voice splitting, cracking in my ear. "I told her I'd burned it all to ash, and there was nothing she could do."

There was nothing she could do.

"But she *did* do something, didn't she?" I say, realizing it now.

"She—she," he stutters. "Well, yeah. She drove to the pay phone, the one in the church parking lot. She called him. Warned him. But that was later. That was later. First—"

"Pete," I say, and lights go off in my head, all of a sudden.

"Lizzie, you should've seen it when I told her about what I'd done," he says, his voice dropping to a whisper. "We were both just standing there in the kitchen. She wouldn't look up at me. Smoke from the griddle was everywhere. And she's stirring and stirring and her face . . . I'm sorry, Lizzie. I'm sorry."

"I know," I say. Of course I know. *But couldn't you have waited,* I want to say but don't. *Couldn't you have waited a day, ten hours? Then we might have found them, Pete. We might have found them in time.*

"Lizzie," he says, his voice splitting like struck wood, "I watched her for so long, the stove so hot, all that heat on her face. Like she was shimmering. She just couldn't say anything to me, Lizzie."

I put my hand over the mouthpiece for a second and breathe deep three times. I can hear him talking. He keeps talking. But I can't listen anymore.

Eighteen

Nine o'clock at night on the longest day I can remember. Was it really only twelve hours before that I stood outside the Verver door, epic lie at the ready?

The music comes first, and it's almost ghostly, and I think I'm dreaming.

The music has this echo like when you're in a museum or the big library downtown and the voices blend and dip and flutter up.

It's like those stories we read in school, the bird women who sing those songs and lure the sailors to the rocks.

Soon enough, I'm tripping my way downstairs and out the patio door.

There's a throb in my chest when I see him. Mr. Verver is back and he is pulling the nozzle trigger on the garden hose, spraying the dry thatch of flowers, the frail brown shrubs. There's a beer bottle by his feet, foamed to the top, and two more empty ones, shuddering slightly on the windowsill next to a small speaker gushing restless tales of lost love and the loneliness of the road.

Then he turns his head and sees me...

And it's all the wonderful things in the world at once.

I feel my feet caught in the tangled hose, and nearly trip into him. He steadies me and smiles, but it's not really smiling.

You don't need to do that for me, I think. *You don't need to smile or do anything because I feel it too. The awful slipping feeling inside of something go-go-going. I don't know what it means, but it's there.*

He tells me a few things, not much. How the police feel strongly that they will find them, and fast. How the FBI has put even more men on the case and the car will surely be spotted. How they're going to put something called a trap and trace on our phone, in case Evie calls again. How, with Mr. Shaw's funds so low and his wife under threat of prosecution, well...

"They seem very confident," he says, the water pouring down onto the marigolds in big gulps. "I don't think they would say it if they didn't believe it."

"No," I agree.

I look at him, and he looks at me.

"What would I do without you, Lizzie?" he says, and the look he gives does rough things to me inside.

He sits down and takes a sip from his beer. I ask him if I can have a taste and he says absolutely not, like I knew he would.

"Hey, look at me here," he says. "I'm such a bad host. Get yourself a soda." He points to the foam cooler on the patio.

I turn, and as soon as I do, I feel a cool jet of water slather over me with a sharp plash.

It catches me so unawares, I nearly gasp, and he almost laughs, dropping the hose.

I start laughing for real, so loudly it nearly hurts, my throat raw in an instant.

"Dusty hates it when I do that," he says, trying to bolster his voice, get some heft behind it. "Says I mess up her hair."

I feel myself smiling all over and finally sit down.

My shirt wet from the hose, the water beads prick me. I yank at my sopping T-shirt and when I let go, the cotton sticks fast to my chest. You can see everything. I look down and there's no hiding it. Mr. Verver catches me and looks away.

Tilting my head back, I see Evie's window and something moving. It doesn't startle me, so dreamy-headed am I, until I see the gold shiver of Dusty's hair. Dusty up there watching.

But then I squint and I can't see anything but Evie's soccer ball mobile, twisting in the nighttime breeze.

A new song comes upon us moodily and yet it's not a sad thing. It's thicker. It's a feeling of abandon, like the ragged chaos of the last day of school, the building nearly emptied out, the derelict textbooks flapping open, the rooms empty, the locker doors flung wide, the smell of firecrackers and menace.

I don't know what to do with it.

I'm glad when it ends and a new one begins, and it's loud with thrumming fiddles and a whirligig sound that makes you feel like you're spinning.

Mr. Verver leans forward, craning his ear toward the speaker, his eyes bright with recognition.

"I forgot about this song," Mr. Verver says, his voice speeding up, his fingers tapping hard on the metal armrests.

The chorus kicks in and he jumps to his feet.

I get terribly excited, in a flash.

"Oh, Lizzie, I haven't heard this in years. Years. Since you were just a glimmer in your father's eye. Lizzie, listen to this."

And I do. It's one of all those songs he plays that I don't know at all. It had just been something clanging in the background, that's all any of them ever were for me, so distracted by everything else humming in my head. But he changes it all. It's just sound, and then he hurls his magic at me and suddenly I realize that, whatever song it is, it's the perfect song for such nights, such feelings.

Before I know it — *but didn't I know it, hadn't I been waiting for it for my whole life, or at least since my earliest memories of the Verver family, me toddling, glitter-haloed, at the Easter pageant, age four*—he extends his hand before me.

That hand, extended.

And there's such desolation in his face, and I catch all the beer and grief and loneliness on him. I see how much this matters to him. That how much it matters to me is a balm to him.

"May I have this dance, Thin Lizzie?"

It is the thing I'd've died for.

In the murk of my head, it's like I have.

My hand slips into his, and I feel it to my toes.

It's not a song to dance to, not with hand in hand, hand on back like this, but who could stop us?

One hand swooping around my waist, he lifts the other high, our palms touching fast upon each other and my heart crashing from corner to corner.

Don't let it ever end, I say to myself. *Let it go on forever.*

My bare feet scraping the patio, then sinking into soft grass, I can't look at him and feel my eyes waver drunkenly to one side, to the wire diamonds of the fence.

He's saying things, his copper face burning hot in laughter, and I'm laughing too, and he spins me and my foot knocks the beer bottle, frothing warmly over my right foot.

"Clodhopper," he says with a laugh and he twirls me fast, his hand pressed hard and the way it feels, I can't see how I can go on, my breath caught in my throat. If it goes on, I will pass out, faint, fall to his feet.

But what if the song ends?

And then it does, in a sharp thrumming punch, and all the air tugged out of me, and Mr. Verver drops back into his lawn chair, so I do too.

I'm thinking about how fast it all happened, and how the sadness is sinking into him again, and to me too, and how now it is over, and how I might never get to dance with him again.

The emptiness at the center of me, it's a new thing I've never felt before.

Walking, dazedly, to the Ververs' bathroom, I hear my name and I know it's Dusty. I know that whispered snake curl of hers, the one that's made me stand up straight since I was four years old.

And there she is, running shoes on, her shirt damp with sweat. No more nights lounging on the patio with her father. She spends them running in mad circles, doesn't she?

She's breathing hard, her cheeks flushed and a heat coming off her that seems to pulse in the air between us. I can feel it under my eyelids.

"Do you ever go home?" she says, chin raised.

"I just...your dad...," I mumble, flailing, backing up against the bathroom doorframe.

Before I know it, her hand clenches my arm, and the pain is fast and knocks my breath away.

It happens in a blur and she's dragging me up the stairs and down the hall.

She nearly flings me into her room and slams the door behind her.

That delectable room, all foamy pink curves and curlicues.

Released from her grip, I stumble back against her bureau and stay there, my feet digging into the mint green fluff of the carpet.

I try to get my balance back. Rub feeling back into my arm.

"So she called you?" she says. "My sister just called you up."

"Yes," I say, tight and quick, ignoring, as best I can, the tremor in my chest. Somehow it was easier to pass the story off to Mr. Verver, even to the police.

"How is it you keep ending up in the middle of everything?" she asks, holding that panting breath in, slowing herself down. Slowing her words down. For the first time, I can feel the effort on her to keep that cool intact. For the first time, I can see how hard it must be for her.

It makes me feel stronger.

"She called me," I say, jutting my jaw out like she does.

She pauses a second, then sighs heavily, as if bored, and pulls her sweaty shirt over her head, tossing it so it hits my ankles, damply. It's all in one quick, tidy gesture and there she is, in a frilled bra, yellow gingham.

My eyes go straight to the soft swell of her breasts, before she twists around and grabs for the pearly pink T-shirt draped over her desk chair, slipping it on, all of it happening so fast I almost miss it.

I can't even believe those breasts. I feel like I am seven years old, or a boy.

I'm so distracted by the thought, I've forgotten my mounting dread, but it returns.

She slumps down onto the bed and leans back, resting on her elbows. I see thin cuts up both arms and know she's been practicing again, taking the scraping glances of the stick. She looks at me, like she's ready to get back down to business.

"She just calls you up," she says, twisting a little, her elbows nestling in her pillows, "just like you just happen to find those cigarettes. You just happen to have suddenly remembered the car. The cigarette butts under the tree."

"I'm helping," I say, and even saying it aloud, as true as it is, as much as I know it, feels like a lie.

The lie isn't in what I'm saying, though. The lie is somewhere else and I won't look for it. But I'm so aware, all of a sudden, that all I do is lie.

She just looks at me, but I can see a sneer in it, I can. In that Dusty way, like when we'd underhit a short pass, or use our foot on the ball.

"What are *you* doing?" I jump at her. The only way to fend off Dusty — Evie always said it, even if she could hardly ever do it — is to strike back. To take the bigger shot, the harder hit. It's the only way. "You aren't doing anything. You don't even help your dad."

I think she's going to jump to her feet, but she doesn't. She just watches me. The stillness, it throws me. I don't know what to do with it.

"If you think I'm lying," I say, trying to keep my nerve up, "how come you haven't said anything? How come you haven't told your parents what you think?" I can't believe I'm saying it. The thought of her telling her father, making him doubt me, is unbearable.

"Lizzie," she says, the words slipping slowly from her and with such coolness. "You don't know anything. You don't know anything about Evie. About him."

And something, the thing that's been clicking around in me, tapping odd corners of my head, springs to the center.

Weeks ago, that conversation with Dusty, about Mr. Shaw. *You were always smart,* she'd said to me. *I was sure you* knew.

"What do you mean?"

"What I mean is this," Dusty says, singsongy, like a bored teacher. "She knew he was watching. You get it? She *knew.*"

Like when you're in the basement and you find the old book with the golden-foil spine, the frizzle-haired doll with the painted freckles, a dozen things you didn't know you remembered until suddenly you do, and it fills you with all kinds of crazy aches inside and you don't know why.

"That's not true," my voice sputters. "You're making it up."

"I'm not," she says quietly, calmly. "We'd see him out there. Evie and me. We'd see him under the tree, at night, the glow of the cigarette. Looking up at her window. We'd see him out there all the time."

I feel my teeth clicking against one another.

Because hadn't Evie said it to me, crouching over those cigarette stubs?

Sometimes, at night, he's out here.

Almost sighing, Dusty flips a shoe off with her other foot and it lands on the floor in front of me.

The casualness of it flares something in me. The way she is reclining there, so regal and assured.

"Why didn't you tell?" I nearly shout. "If you knew he was out there, why didn't you tell?"

She shakes her head slowly, like she's not sure about me, like if I'm dumb enough to ask that question, I'm too dumb to deserve an answer.

"Why didn't *you?*" she says. "She told you, didn't she? Why didn't you tell?"

"I didn't know," I stutter. "I only knew a little bit."

She looks at me with those slitted eyes of hers.

The feeling in the room, it all starts to pile on top of me. The smell of bubble gum and pink sugared perfume and cloudy face powders. My head feels light and I'm thinking of all the Dr Peppers I drank in the backyard with Mr. Verver and the thick carpet catching under my feet.

Why didn't *I* tell? *Sometimes, at night, he's out here.* I never told.

I never even thought to tell. It was mine, and I held it close to my chest.

It was mine, and I didn't want to share it.

"What are you saying?" I ask, almost moan. "So she might have known he was watching her." Even saying it out loud, had I ever said such things out loud? "But she couldn't have known he would take her away. That he would take her away from all of us."

The look Dusty gives me is a long one, those green-gold eyes prickling on me, prickling along my skin.

Oh, she knows even more, doesn't she? She knows so much. Why won't she say, why won't she say?

"Can't you figure it out?" Dusty says, her voice low now, a throaty whisper. "Can't you now?"

"Figure out what?" I say, my voice breaking, my hands flailing at my sides.

I feel that Dusty is on the cusp, I feel it so close, a truth so tantalizing I have only to let my eyelashes bristle against it, my lids shutting fast.

She lolls her head back slowly. "Oh, Lizzie, she knew. She knew he was coming for her. She knew."

"You don't know that," I say. Because she couldn't.

But she's not even listening. She's someplace else entirely, her face going soft, like when she'd lose a game, years ago, when she still lost games.

"Isn't it rotten," she says, "the way everything is happening, all this stuff everyone has to feel, and nothing can be like it was? And it's all because of her. She's so selfish."

Everything is so close in the room, powders clogging me, heavy smells and choking cotton balls, and I wonder if this is what it always feels like to Dusty.

"She thinks she can just do whatever she wants," Dusty says. "She can get whatever she wants. Why does she get to have whatever she wants?"

That's not how it is, I think. That's not how it is. And how can she talk about Evie this way? Except Dusty's not Dusty right now and you can't believe her, metal scraping sidewalk, sparking ruin on herself.

"Look at what she's done to him," Dusty says, and for a second I think she means Mr. Shaw. But she means Mr. Verver. I know because her voice goes high suddenly, and it starts to shatter into tinkly pieces. She shakes her head back and forth, back and forth. She can't seem to stop. "You see why I can't tell. I can't tell him that. What his daughter's done to him. What she's brought down on all of us. How she destroyed everything for all of us. I can't tell him any of this."

I can feel my breath catch. I do see it: *Evie can break his heart,* she is saying, *but I won't.*

"Don't you want to save her?" I say finally.

"Lizzie," she says, her eyes lifting up to me, "what makes you think she wants to be saved?"

I sit on our back patio for a long time, my thoughts jumping on one another.

I already knew, in part, the things Dusty said, but it still felt like an explosion in my head. There was a world of difference between knowing something on some sneaking level in your own fevered head and hearing it banked into hard little syllables by Dusty.

Sometimes, at night, he's out here. She'd said that to me. I had never told about that. Why had I never told?

What was there to tell? Evie herself said she guessed it was a dream, all confused, like a dream.

And it didn't seem like something you could tell.

It was something Evie showed me and, after learning about Mr. Shaw, the way he loved her in such secret and powerful ways, why *wouldn't* Evie be moved by that? Why should she be afraid? It didn't seem strange that she might have known and said nothing. Kept to herself, a most private feeling. Evie who never had boys buzzing, swarming. Never had many things.

But the idea of night after night the two sisters seeing him. And sharing it. There is a hurt in there. Evie sharing things with Dusty, but not with me. Dusty, who always stood apart, yet Evie shared it with her.

But, thinking about everything Dusty said, in some way I'm not surprised by any of it, am I? Are there any more surprises?

In bed later, I hear Dr. Aiken's voice from down the hall, low and even. I can't make out what he's saying, but there's a calmness in it, a stillness. Somehow I am glad for it. I hope he'll keep talking on and on, and he does. It's the sound that sends me, finally, to sleep.

In the dream that follows, the phone rings next to me. *"Lizzie,"* the voice tingles in my ear.

And I know it's Evie, in that dream-way of knowing things, even if it doesn't sound like Evie at all, her voice, high and trembly, like a pull-string doll.

"I don't know where I am," she says, *"and there's so much blood."*

"Evie," I say, and it's a whisper, like a secret no one can know. *"Where are you? Tell me. Tell me."*

"I don't know," she says, and she sounds so small, like when she has to talk in Algebra, standing at the chalkboard.

"Where are you?" I say again, and there's a pounding in my ears. "Is it far?"

"Lizzie, I couldn't get the blood to stop. I used three towels."

"Evie, please," I cry out, "where are you?"

"I don't know," she says, and I can hear her breathing go faster and faster. "How do I find out?"

"Evie, are you far away? Are you far?" And suddenly the tingling feeling on the back of my neck, the uncanny feeling suddenly of Evie right there, right there.

"Are you close?" I whisper. "Evie, can you see me?"

"Lizzie," comes the whisper, now a sizzle in my ear. "What did you do? What did you do?"

It is four o'clock, maybe five o'clock in the morning. I can't see the glowing numbers on my clock, and then I feel a cord twisted in my legs. Yanking it up, I see I've dragged the clock into the bed with me, its plug hanging loose, its face black and hopeless.

I don't know what woke me, but then I hear the squeaking of a screen door and I peek out the window into the darkness.

Craning, I can see the front door of the Verver house is wide open.

I tumble down the front stairs and hover there a moment.

What did you do? What did you do? Evie's dream-voice still blazing in my ear.

I feel a twitch under my eye. That happens right before the noise comes. The noise is loud, it's a scream, the screeching sound of something, some animal caught under a car and crushed from tire to tire. It's the worst sound I've ever heard.

I run out the front door and that's when I see Mrs. Verver standing in her doorway, her hands over her open mouth.

She's looking down the street, and my eyes follow.

There's an eeriness about it, the thick of predawn and the streetlamps with the shimmery moths and bugs, and, my eyes adjusting, I can't see what Mrs. Verver sees, what she's screaming about, until suddenly I can.

Until the ghostly thing limps under one of the streetlamps.

The ghost with the pale white legs, the sear of bright green soccer shorts.

I am running now, my summer-hard feet pounding into the sparkly asphalt, and suddenly it seems like that game we used to play when we were kids.

It's like I can hear that chanting, *Ten o'clock, eleven o'clock, twelve o'clock, MIDNIGHT! Bloody murder!*

And I want to scream out, my lungs exploding, *Home base, Evie! It's here, Evie. It's here, you just need to touch the door, the lawn, the curb. I promise you, it's here!*

I hear myself screaming.

I am screaming and I can't stop.

Running, running, my arms swinging wide.

I'm nearly there, nearly there, just a few feet away from that candescent circle under the streetlamp, when I feel something hoist me back and it's Mrs. Verver, her arms on me hard, pushing me to the side.

I nearly stumble backward but catch myself.

Hand to my chest, I watch Mrs. Verver hurl her arms around the ghostly thing in front of us.

And I watch the blankness on the ghost's face.

A blankness that makes me start.

Why, that's not Evie, I say to myself, and I think: *This is a dream, and that's a ghost, a phantom. A trick.*

It's not a dream, but it can't be Evie.

I'm looking at the bright yellow hair hanging in hanks around her face. I'm looking at the funny texture of it, like flossy batting.

The strange sweatshirt, gray fleece, torn at the wrists.

The odd flush to her face, the way her arms hang stiffly.

Her fingers, the nails torn and red-rimmed.

Mrs. Verver, she is sobbing and on her knees and she is holding the girl, arms wrapped around her waist, and the girl looks startled, unsure. She turns and looks at me, her head bobbling slightly, like a doll.

She looks at me, and I look at her.

The eyes, the eyes like an oil-slick rain puddle. The eyes I know better than my own. The eyes that hook onto me and dig in fast.

Oh, Evie.

Oh, Evie.

Warm things rise up in me.

I smile.

I touch my hands to my face, I feel my cheeks, and it is a smile.

I guess it's probably the strangest smile in the world, but it goes on and on and on, and I am shaking my head and smiling and I can't stop.

And she looks at me and something rustles there, a slip of a grin, and I reach for it.

I actually reach my hand out for it, her flushed face under my fingers.

"Evie," I say. I say, "Evie."

★   ★   ★

Mrs. Verver picks her up even though Evie is nearly as tall as she is. She lifts her and starts carrying her, and that's when I see Mr. Verver running up to us.

I stop and cover my eyes.

I don't know why, but I can't watch.

When I look again, Mr. Verver is twenty yards ahead of me and he has her now, he has Evie in his arms like when she was six and Dusty shoved too hard and knocked her from the top of the jungle gym.

He carries her and I follow far behind and Mrs. Verver is jogging alongside, trying to keep up. She is reaching out, scrabbling at his arm, touching her fingers to that strange blond hair.

I follow them back down the street and I stand on the sidewalk out front.

Dusty is on the front porch, her face hidden behind that whorling hair of hers.

I watch it happen.

I watch Evie's wobbling blond head, the pale legs dangling like shorn twigs. I watch Dusty stumble back and Mr. Verver push past her, push past everything, carrying Evie like a bride over a threshold.

I watch them all disappear into the dark of their front hallway.

I watch Dusty whip around and, face red and ruined, shut the front door behind them.

I think I stand there for a very long time, waiting for my heart to slow down, waiting for my breath to come back. Waiting for something else, but that thing never comes.

★　★　★

"I'll take you to the hospital in a few hours," my mother says. "They need some time."

We are standing on the front porch, my feet dew-damp.

The sleeplessness so light on me, I feel more awake than ever, and the mistiness of early dawn is just right.

"Okay," I say, but I don't intend to wait. I intend to hop on my bike and pedal the three miles as soon as she goes upstairs and turns on the shower.

"Lizzie," she says, and I can feel her hand fasten on my shoulder. "I..." Her voice goes soft and wilting. "I guess I didn't believe it would happen."

I brush my foot back and forth on the concrete, feeling the delicious burn, bringing me to life.

"I guess, deep down, I thought she was never coming back," my mother says, and she curls her arm across my shoulders and presses into me.

"I know you did," I say. Why should I admit that I ever thought so too?

"I guess," she starts, her words falling strangely, like she is still half asleep, like she is saying things she'd never say out loud, "I guess it always seemed like something like this might happen to them. The Ververs."

"What do you mean?" I say roughly.

"I don't know," she says. "There's always just been something about them..." There's almost a blush on her, like she's been caught without her clothes. She can't quite look at me.

"I don't know," she says. "Like something had to break. It could only go on for so long, before something had to break."

"That doesn't make any sense at all," I say, shaking off a flinch deep inside. "You're not making any sense at all."

My legs pump as fast as they can. The bike ride to the hospital is a breathless blur, my lungs choked and pained.

I keep conjuring the silvery sight of blonded Evie, eyes startled and knowing.

Was it her, even?

Was it Evie who returned?

Or did I dream it all, conjure it from wishes and longing?

The weird, unwholesome emptiness of the damp streets and the metal smell of early morning, it all conspires to make me feel forgotten, swabbed off the world.

Part of me thinks, as I walk through the sliding doors of the hospital, that no one will even recognize me. That I will move through the halls, past every Verver, as though invisible, a slippery shadow.

But it is only seconds before Mr. Verver, begrimed and fumbling with forms and a clambering Dusty, hands in her hair, spots me.

His face is filled with such light, it nearly blinds me.

The heavy stubble, ribbons of dirt across his pant legs, the look of heat and flush on him, none of it matters, he shrugs it all off.

He is restored.

We have restored him, I think, and then wonder at the "we."

It's me, me, me.

"There's Lizzie," he is saying, clipboard now against his chest, across his heart, like a knightly shield, and Dusty whips her head around to me, and the look on her face, like all her looks, is unreadable.

Thoughts flit through my head about everything she must feel, but I don't have time for them. I don't have time.

I am rushing for Mr. Verver, who outstretches his arms, who tows me in for a half hug, his right hand still clasping the clipboard, which bangs against my head.

"Oh, Lizzie," he says. "Lizzie, she's here. She's here and she's okay."

I think that's what he says, I don't know. The next few minutes jumble together and he's telling me things and saying that Mrs. Verver won't leave Evie's side and they're doing some exams but everything is good, that Evie is strong and that Evie is well.

"She's fine," Dusty pipes up. "She's great and everything's over. It's all done. She's back, and it's over."

She says it briskly, as Dusty says most things to me, to her mother, to everyone but Mr. Verver.

But it seems off, and all I can think of are the things she told me, the things Dusty knows, or thinks she does.

Oh, Lizzie, she knew. She knew he was coming for her.

Mr. Verver puts down the clipboard, his pen, all his things, and rests his hands on Dusty's shoulders.

He lets his fingers wiggle in her hair.

She looks up at him, waiting. I can feel her toes curling in her shoes, waiting for that gift, any gift, the gifts he hands out so freely.

Oh, I can see it on her. She's thinking, *Now maybe it will go back, now it will be as before.*

The way she stands there, that open expression she gives only to him — suddenly I feel like I should turn away. I feel like I've seen something no one's supposed to see.

She waits for him, bouncing in her shoes, but this is what he gives her: "Maybe you should go home," he says.

All the lovely expectation on her face disappears.

He glances over at me for a second, and she sees it.

A baton passed, from her to me, even as she hadn't meant to pass it. Even as she still felt it in her tight, clawed hands.

She looks at me with those hawk eyes, and I feel, in a flash, like she can see right through my clothes, my skin, my everything.

She sees right into the center of me. I can't unravel it all now, but it's like she sees things in me, in him, that I can't even see yet.

"I'm going back to Nana's," she murmurs, her hand reaching for her bag.

"Dus'," he says, furrowed brow, his fingers resting on her neck.

"Don't," she says, so hard, jumping back, her arm flipping up as if to fend him off, as if they were out on the field and he'd high-sticked her.

She picks up the clipboard. For a crazy second, I think she's going to throw it.

He steps forward.

"Don't, don't, don't," she says, her head whipping back and forth.

Stunned, Mr. Verver raises his hands high, like in a stickup.

"I don't want to see her," Dusty says. "I don't want to be here. I can't be here."

She shoves the clipboard into my hands, reels around, and in an instant she is gone.

Mr. Verver is shaking his head. He is shaking his head, and looking at me.

My fingers fumbling on the clipboard, I don't know what to say.

He swivels around on his foot, looking up at the ceiling. Then he says, "Until these last few weeks, she never wanted to spend more than an hour there, in her life."

It takes me a second to realize he's talking about the grandparents. It seems funny to me that he's thinking about where she wants to go and not everything else she just showed him. The things she showed.

"She can't stand the rose perfume," he says, "and the vacuum cleaner going all day long."

I nod.

"But I guess all this, it's just too much," he says. "It's a lot to take."

He keeps looking at me.

He seems overwhelmed, by everything. I want to rescue him from it.

Detective Thernstrom and Mr. Verver are talking in the corner. The police are all around and everything seems to be crackling.

I wonder who will tell me what happened. How did she get back? Where did she come from? Where's Mr. Shaw? And I have even silly, furtive thoughts that now they'll uncover my lies, all of them.

Somehow I can't bring myself to ask Mr. Verver, who has shaken off everything with Dusty. Shaken it off so easily. Everything popping and sparking, his face is like an amusement park, all filled with fear and elation.

"She can't talk to anyone right now," Mr. Verver says, as soon as the detective leaves. "She's all drugged up. But she's great. She's great. Oh, Lizzie, you should see her."

I did see her, I want to say. *I saw everything.*

"The police—they...," I try.

"They haven't been able to figure everything out yet," he says.
"He's on the run again. You saw—he'd dyed her hair."

We both let that thought hover between us for a second. I feel
it teeter in my rib cage.

"He was in for the long haul," he adds quickly. "From what
we can figure out, she...got away from him. A waitress at the
doughnut shop out on Falls Road said she saw a girl get out of a
car and walk into the woods. So she must have gotten away somehow and walked home. Four miles."

My head is jumbled with questions. It all seems strange and
impossible.

"And they don't know where he is?"

"No," he says, so quickly, his face clouding over. "Not yet."
He pauses. "But she came home, Lizzie. She made it home. She
fought her way home."

The words sound big and movielike and I want to burrow
myself under them. But it doesn't feel right. None of it feels right.
And none of it feels over, at all.

Nineteen

There is nothing to do and Mr. Verver is in with Evie and I know I should go home, but there's a funny and hollow clang in me, and I just start wandering the hospital corridors, dragging my bike lock along the walls, gazing mournfully at all the fluorescence and disease.

It's so odd when it happens, the man looking at me as I make my way down yet another long hallway flapping with posted greeting cards tacked to bulletin boards.

Leaning on the nurses' station counter, it's like he's waiting for me.

I wonder if I'm in trouble somehow, so I slow down and when I see a bank of worn pastel chairs I slip into one, like I'm there for a reason.

That's when the man starts walking toward me and I feel a ripple of panic until I see it's Dr. Aiken, with a white coat on and everything.

I remember his calm voice through the wall from the night before, how it soothed me. There's something calm about him, or something in him that calms me. For all his chaos, his stumbling through bushes and sliding on our kitchen floor, there's something that seems still about him. Comfortable.

"Lizzie," he says. "I thought you might be here."

"You work here?" I say, because I thought he had an office, that he was that kind of doctor.

"I work here too, yes."

"Oh," I say, and I see he has new glasses, with pencil-thin wire frames, like the ones my mother used to pick out for my dad. "I'm here because of Evie."

"Yes," he says, with care. "She's going to be fine."

"What happened to her?" I say, my voice going high, like I might cry. I can't believe how it sounds. "What did he... what is she..."

There are too many words and none seems right, none seems to contain it all.

"She's going to be okay," he says. "Don't worry."

And he turns quickly, and looks up at the clock.

"I think they'll release her later today," he says, and he's still looking at the clock. I think he's nervous to look at me. I think he doesn't know what to say to me. It strikes me too that, for any number of reasons, he feels sorry for me.

My mother drives me home, my bike in the trunk. She's wide awake now, not like earlier, and is filled with scoldings, but how worried could she have been? Where else would I have gone?

"I saw your boyfriend," I say.

"My boyfriend," she repeats, eyes on the road.

I wait and wait, but that's all she says, like she's stuck on the word and she's trying to unstick it.

The phone is ringing when we walk in the house. It's Tara Leary, and I know she's ready to swap information. She says I have to meet her and Kelli at Joannie's house. They're already there and she knows everything.

"I don't think so," I say, though of course I want to know. But

I don't want to know from Tara. I don't want to hear any of it from Tara's candy-twist mouth.

"Go on," my mother says, slumping down at the kitchen table. "Go relax a little. Be with your friends."

She insists on driving me over, even though it's only six blocks.

"Call me when you're done," she says. "Have fun."

I wonder if she knows anything at all.

"Did you hear?" Tara says, filled with gritty energy. She can barely contain herself. We're bundled tight on the big sofa in the den, with cold cans of orange pop we drink from straws. "He dumped her on the roadside."

"She escaped," I say. "She got away. She jumped from the car."

"Like hell she did," Tara says. "The waitress at Dawn Donuts saw the car in the parking lot. They sat there for ten minutes before Evie got out. Then he peeled off like a bank robber."

"No," I say, shaking my head. "Why would he just leave her there, after everything?"

I feel my head go back to the lustrous places of the first few days after Evie disappeared. Those days when the heaviness and beauty of the love first hit me square. A love like that, like Mr. Shaw's for Evie, a love so big it took him over, it swallowed them both whole.

"Because he was done with her, Lizzie," Joannie says, her voice fast and impatient. "He was done with her, and that was that. He'd used her up."

"I don't think so," I say. "It doesn't just stop."

All three of them look at me, their summer tans perfectly matched. They look at me and they think they know everything in the world.

"What'd you think," Joannie says, "he wanted to make her his child bride?"

"Romeo and Juliet," Kelli pipes up.

"Do you want to hear the rest or not?" Tara says, nearly jumping in her spot.

I know what's coming. I know because Tara's lips have a shine on them, her body nearly rocking.

It's the part I've been waiting for with all kinds of dread and fervor:

"They gave her a pelvic," Tara says, leaning back against the sofa cushion, watching our faces.

Kelli squirms a little.

"They did all these tests," Tara says, and it's like she's reading a report. "For gonorrhea, syphilis, herpes, and pregnancy. I bet even AIDS."

Like on the poster on the wall in Health class. The one with the big red letters, tall and menacing: ANYONE CAN GET AIDS. PROTECT YOURSELF.

I picture Evie on a white sheet, a set of probes, like some steel claw, poised between her legs. I start to feel sick.

Tara takes a long sip from her pop, then says, "She's clean."

Leaning against the wall, Joannie seems to slump a little.

"But, confidentially, girlies," Tara says, her mouth twisting over her straw, "he did it. He did it all."

"What did he do?" I ask, my jaw aching with it.

"He tore her in two," she says, with a knowing tilt of her head that makes me want to smack her.

"Tore her...," Kelli says, her voice tiny, her mouth hanging open. "Tore her..."

"Probably did it to her five times a day," Tara says. "Ripped her all up down there."

She leans backward and jiggles her fingers in front of her hips. I feel my skin go to tingly ice.

"But she's okay," I say, wondering how Tara could know all this. Could she?

Tara rolls her eyes. "How okay could she be? He ruined her."

When she says it, it sounds old-fashioned, like something from an old book, one of those big hardcover ones my grandma would read with blooming roses and silvery script on the cover, or a black-and-white movie where all the women speak in high, elegant voices and the piano music sweeps up every time a scene ends.

But it also sounds true. It sounds true.

Evie's in the hospital two days. Much longer than they'd first said.

My mother says it's probably to deal with "emotional conse-quences," but time seems to inch.

I'm not supposed to leave the house, and no one seems to know what the rules are. Should parents be afraid of Mr. Shaw, on the loose? Is there something to be afraid of? The second day, my mother makes Ted take me to his job, and I sit in the air-conditioned clubhouse, watching him cut tree branches in the hot sun.

We have lunch together in the staff cafeteria, peeling plastic wrap from gluey tuna sandwiches.

I can't eat anything, but Ted eats both sandwiches, a carton of milk, and two bananas.

I ask him why he thinks Evie's still in the hospital.

He shrugs, then stretches his golden arms wide. They are thatched with little twig cuts, like those pictures of saints. It makes me think of something.

"She's probably getting sewn up," he says, eyes wandering past me, watching the girls in the pool, on the other side of the glass.

They all have string bikinis this summer, with beads on the tassels. They click-click when they walk.

He's watching them, but all I can think of is Evie and a long needle, like with Nurse Stang. But down there. Down there.

"Sewn up," I say, barely a whisper.

"Yeah," Ted says, eyes back on me. He picks up a piece of plastic wrap, still slick with mayonnaise, and stretches it taut.

"Hold it tight," he says.

I reach my hand out and stretch the plastic, pinched between my fingers.

"It's like this," he says, and he pokes his finger through the plastic. A vicious hole clean through.

"So she's probably getting all healed up," he says, pulling small clots of plastic from his finger. "And then she'll be fine."

But they're all wrong, aren't they? It couldn't be like that. Because I know. Because Dusty said it too, even if she can't understand it.

Mr. Shaw waited, hoped, dreamed his way into Evie's night-lit room and he couldn't have done all that just to hurt her, but instead to take all the hurt in the world away.

At the window night after night, Evie's hand pressed against the screen, eyes on the pear tree, glowing greenly in the dark. Seeing him there.

Evie felt Mr. Shaw's love, and what girl wouldn't eventually sink into that love, its dreamy promise? He, a man three times her age who's seen the world and known things and knows most that she is the most special girl of all? She is everything and he would tear down his life for her. He would tear it down because just one downward glance from her would heal him, save him. She has that power. What girl wouldn't want that power?

★   ★   ★

It's seven o'clock at night and the Ververs are finally home. Mr. Verver calls my mother and says if I'd like to come see Evie, he'd appreciate it.

My mother makes me wait while she bakes a batch of brownies from a mix that's been sitting on top of the refrigerator since Halloween.

I carry them in the heavy glass casserole dish. Mrs. Verver answers the front door, holding it open for me with her foot.

"Hi, Lizzie," she says, her voice a scrape.

It's so unusual to see her, and I can't think of a thing to say.

"Hi," I sputter, handing her the dish.

She takes it in her bony fingers, and we both look down at the brownies, crackled on top like a peeling ceiling.

"How is...," I say, and then it just goes away.

My eyes drift to the staircase behind her, that furred blue carpet I know so well. Two doors down to Evie's room.

When I turn back to Mrs. Verver, she's already halfway down the hall to the kitchen.

We're grateful for you, I think I hear her say, her voice half swallowed by the quiet of the house.

I place my foot on the bottom step. The house is so still. I hear Mrs. Verver drop the casserole dish on the counter with a clunk.

I wonder where Mr. Verver is, and I bet he's with the police again.

I take a breath, then creep up the steps.

All the doors are closed and I stand in front of Evie's.

I stand there, my foot slipping from my flip-flop, my toes kneading the carpet. I stand there and I stand there and I stand there, my heart like a cannon. I feel it shaking the walls of the house. I feel it might tear the whole house down.

I knock.

"Come in," a voice says, and, my God, it's like a thousand other times, and it's like no other time.

This is the part that can't be imagined. If I pause at all, I won't be able to do it, the moment too large, the largest of my life.

I open the door.

I open the door, and as I do, all kinds of hectic pictures flash through my head, and I somehow expect to see a scene like those from the center pages of one of those true-crime books at the drugstore. I expect to see Evie splayed there, bloody sheets and thermometers and sanitary napkins and cotton balls and the stench of girl-ruin in the air.

But I open the door, and all I see is the tidy room I know so well, the soccer mobile swaying in the breeze, the bed made tightly, hospital corners, the swing-arm lamp craned over the desk.

And Evie.

No longer the specter, the haunted vision.

Evie, leaning over her desk, pencil in hand, pink eraser top bouncing as she writes.

If it weren't for the strangeness of the hair, those glaring wheat-colored tufts yanked into a high ponytail, it would be like nothing had happened at all.

"I'm so behind," she says, and then looks over at me. She's wearing her old jeans from elementary school, now too small, and one of Dusty's jerseys, which hangs down nearly to her knees. "I think they'll still graduate me if I just take the final tests. When did we get to polynomials?"

For a second, I think I've lost my mind, or she has.

But then something clicks and shutters in me, and everything big and momentous—I shove it all aside. I feel like she wants me to, and suddenly I want it too.

"Oh, I don't know," I say, and I sink down onto her bed, trying to make it like any day, any day Evie missed school on account of the flu, a stomachache.

"It's hard to concentrate," she says, rubbing the eraser tip back and forth on her lower lip. "They gave me these pills."

"Does it hurt?" I say, my eyes on her neck, the faint yellow smudges there, like she'd run a highlighter across her throat.

She twirls the pencil. "Nothing hurts," she says, and there's a wince in her eyes and I want to stop it, I want to keep us going.

"You look good," I say. "For a feeb."

She grins and I grin back. I can feel myself relaxing, I can feel time itself swiveling back.

"I bet you can eat whatever you want," I say. "And watch TV all night."

She nods, smiling. "Everyone's afraid to say boo," she says. "And no chores, no practice, no nothing. Like I got mono."

"Give me a kiss, then," I say, reaching out with my foot to kick her leg, "so I can lie around all day too."

She looks at me, and everything changes. Her knuckles go white around the pencil.

"I feel like I want to die," she says. "I want to die."

We're lying on her bed, staring at the ceiling.

The crickets are so loud, like they're in the room with us, but I can tell she's glad to hear them.

"You'll sleep over," she says, and I say yes.

She slips her hand in mine, our fingers braided tight.

I keep waiting for her to tell me.

I wait and I wait.

But she just lies there, breath uneven, legs jerking, and says nothing.

★   ★   ★

I wake up very early, but Evie's already gone.

I have that split second of sureness that she's gone forever.

Then, lying there, looking up at her mobile, the familiar water crack in the ceiling corner, I start to feel like I've dreamed myself into Evie, that she's gone because I'm here, and if I look in the mirror, I'll see her stony face.

But then I hear the churning of water, and the din of feminine voices. Tugging on my shorts, I make my way down the hall.

Through the flush of steam from the half-open bathroom door, I see Mrs. Verver with kitchen gloves on, brown slicked, the Clairol box torn open on the floor.

Evie's on her knees, curled over the bathtub, that pale hair covering her face, like a thatch of birch bark.

I stand there, so quiet, one palm on the wall, and watch as, water rushing from the tub spout, Mrs. Verver, on her knees now too, plastic bottle in hand, sluices the brown dye into Evie's hair. Evie's hands covering her face, her eyes, Mrs. Verver curls herself behind Evie, pressed against her back.

Mrs. Verver's body is shuddering and I can't see her face, hidden by Evie's wet wall of hair, but I know she is crying. She is holding Evie's back, her browned gloves splayed, and crying.

The water gurgling endlessly, I see Evie turn her head, and she looks at me, she does.

She looks at me and I see her face, and all the weariness there. The weariness of someone who's lived a century or more in a few weeks, who's seen everything and has already stopped being surprised by any of it.

Evie's face, it's filled with words, and I see what it's saying: *Make her stop. Make her stop. Why won't she stop?*

Twenty

We spend the whole day together, Evie and I. I put her hair in long braids. The color is brown, but it's not really Evie's brown, and the texture is still funny, soft and pilly like doll's hair. But with the braids in, she looks more like Evie and she starts to feel like Evie.

Mr. Verver takes us to the pool. He keeps saying how he's not supposed to, that he's supposed to take Evie back to the therapist, but that we need some rest, some fun—don't we? We nod, both of us, in unison.

He can't stop talking in the car, and Evie smiles at him, even shows him her teeth. It's almost like he can't believe it's her, the way his head keeps darting over to look at her, to check on her. She's smiling so much it starts to hurt my face. I know that smile, it's the school portrait smile, the team photo smile. And I know Mr. Verver must see that too.

He says he'd rather we didn't go through the women's bath-house to get to the pool. That he'd rather we just skip the shower, even though it's against the rules.

It's just as well. Enough people are looking already, out by the pool. Not everyone, I'm sure. They can't all know Evie, recognize her from among the other girls there, cocoa butter slicked. But it feels like they do.

We don't care, though. We float on our rafts, our hair filled with chlorine, our skin sweating it. My face presses against the plastic, cool water gathering in small puddles where my head dips into the raft. Reaching behind, I stretch my green shiny one-piece farther over my bottom, skin clammy beneath my suit.

I look over at Evie, whose eyes are hidden behind large zebra-frame sunglasses. Her lips are slightly parted. Her white two-piece glares. She's lying on her stomach and floating, floating. I can't tell if she's looking at me, or is asleep, or is just thinking.

My eyes flutter, time and again, to Mr. Verver, who sits on a pool chair and never takes his eyes off us, not even to look at the newspaper in his hand.

He watches us and I bet he thinks we're talking. I bet he thinks Evie's telling me things. But Evie tells me nothing.

I want to let her know it's okay. That she can tell me anything and I'll understand. But it's the kind of thing, if you say it, it no longer seems true.

It's only an hour and we have to leave. Mr. Verver is on the pay phone by the bathhouse and he keeps saying, "I know, I know. We're leaving now. I just—I just—"

Mom, Evie mouths at me.

She asks Mr. Verver if we can shower in the bathhouse first. He looks at her a long time and I know he wants to say no, but he says yes.

In the showers, we stand under one of the communal spouts and frothy shampoo skates over our bathing suits and collects in our jelly sandals.

We still have our sunglasses on because we like how we look in them, we like how everything looks, tinted pink.

We stand there quietly and let the water run across us. Evie sighs, looking down at her feet, down at the brownish swirl at her feet, some of the dye still slipping off.

She's looking down, staring so hard into the drain at our feet. She has those sunglasses on, so I can't guess what she's thinking.

In the car on the way home, we're in the backseat and Mr. Verver's talking again, like before. Talking about summer plans and neighbors who are painting their house salmon pink and field hockey tryouts. He can't stop.

It starts to hurt to listen.

Then, suddenly, Evie leans forward, sunglasses still on, and presses her chin next to his headrest, nestling against his cheek.

"I'm sorry, Dad," she says, her voice scratchy and rushed. "I'm sorry."

"Evie, I—" he says, startled. He tries to turn and look at her, but the light changes and cars honk and the car surges forward.

"I'm sorry," she keeps saying, and did you ever know what someone meant even if you couldn't explain it, even name it?

"Evie," he says thickly, reaching his hand back to touch her, and the car feels so small. My hand over my mouth, I turn my head away, press it against the back window and, this time, try not to hear.

"Will you stay again tonight, Lizzie?" Evie asks. "Will you?"

And I say I will. My mother, on the phone, says, "Okay, just one more night."

But I think, how will I ever say no?

I think, I will stay and stay and stay until she tells me everything. And she has to.

★   ★   ★

The feeling at night, with the windows all shut, the air-conditioning rumbling, the clicking from the motion detectors every time you pass them, it feels like we are in a high tower, armored and moated and immaculate.

The alarm company people had been there all day, installing a system, drilling holes in the walls, running tests with beeps and sirens and lights.

Dusty is still at the grandparents'. I want to ask Evie about it, ask her what she thinks, in the old way we always speculated about Dusty, rendering delirious guesses. But it seems like I can't. I think maybe Evie feels the crackling anger from Dusty, and it might hurt, a lot.

Evie stares out the window, her fingers pressed on the glass, the shiny new security emblem stuck there.

I wonder what she thinks.

I have this idea in my head of her thinking this: *As if an alarm could stop him. As if anything could, that love so strong. If he wants me back, nothing will stop it.*

But it's all a guess. She turns and faces me, a sphinx.

Tucked close in bed that night, I trace letters on her back like we used to do when we were kids. Somehow we feel like kids again, small enough to fold ourselves into soft pockets.

First, S-U-M-M-E-R.

Then, A-L-E-X, the boy at school Evie used to love in sixth grade, the one with the bottle-opener belt buckle.

Then I trace the S, the H, the A, and I feel her breath draw in tight when I draw the W.

"No," she whispers. "Lizzie, no."

"You can tell me anything," I say. It's something I never said to her before. But now that I have to, it seems like a lie.

I look at the window, think of Mr. Shaw out there. Wonder about all the nights he stood out there even while I was here, laughing with Evie, tickling her ribs, talking about boys, untangling her hair, her hands in my hair, braiding tightly. Mr. Shaw. *Oh, Evie, just tell me. Tell me so I can tell you. So I can show you I understand.*

"Evie, I know he loves you," I say, the words rushing from me helplessly. "He loves you."

"But he thinks I'm different now, doesn't he?" she says, tapping her fingers on my open palm.

I stop for a second, puzzled, and then I realize she thought I was talking about Mr. Verver.

"No," I fumble. "He doesn't think you're different. He's so happy. He was so lost without you. He just wants to know you're okay."

I hear myself and I know what I sound like. A spy. An informant. I guess I am. I want to deliver her to her father all over again. It twists in me. But I wouldn't, I tell myself, tell him anything she wouldn't want me to. Anything I wouldn't want him to hear.

"Are you thinking about Mr. Shaw out there?" I ask, trying again.

It's a crazy thing to say, but I say it.

"No," Evie says, her body stiffening so fast it startles me. "Why would you say that?"

"I don't know," I say. "I'm sorry."

"He's not coming back, Lizzie," she says so quickly. I swear I can hear her teeth chatter. "He's not coming back. Why would you ever say that? He's not."

"Okay," I say, hurried, "okay." I put my fingers on her arm, and it's goosefleshed.

"Lizzie," she says, shaking her head. "I wish I could explain."

"Don't worry," I say, but there's a quiver under my skin now. It's something in her face, all her features jumping, her eyes like two pinpoints.

I lay my hands on her, I try to lay them on her like when I was very little, my mother pulling me into her lap, hand in my hair.

"It's all over," I say, "Everything's going to be like before."

There's a love so big it can break you, that's what she is saying to me, even if she can't say it and I can't make the words come.

How do boys matter in the face of his colossal love, like a pressure on the heart?

How do boys with their loud hallway taunts and their jockstraps and greasy foreheads, legs sprawling under desks, how do they matter one bit? They are big bulging Adam's apples and pitching voices and they tug at their pockets and punch one another in the hallway and put ice cubes down your collar and shove their hands up your shirt, and what could any of that possibly mean in the face of the big, bone-breaking, chest-bursting love from this man whose heart cannot hold itself together? Whose heart batters itself for you every night?

Isn't that what she's saying to me?

It has to be. I feel it. She must feel it too.

She's asleep at last, but I'm not, and I can hear Mr. Verver down in the basement. I can hear faintly, through the vents, the tinny sound from the record player.

I slip myself from Evie, her right leg draped across me, and dash silently down the steps and to the basement door.

The music is pacing gently, a slow, crawly song filled with tiptoeing guitar sounds and mewling voices.

I stand at the top of the stairs and whisper, almost losing my nerve, though I'm not sure why, "Mr. Verver?"

He pokes his head around the corner and looks up at me, a green beer bottle in his hand, his face flushed and caught up in itself.

He looks surprised, and not surprised at all. And he smiles and waves me down.

Suddenly I feel conscious of my bare legs and tennis socks, but I scramble down the stairs and he makes "quiet, quiet" motions with his hands and mouth and we both grin at it.

I settle down on the hooked rug, spreading the stack of albums like a poker hand, looking at all their covers.

"Couldn't sleep?" he says, settling back into his chair.

"No," I say.

"Even with the alarms, the cops driving by all the time," he says, rapping his fingers fast on the table, "it's still hard for me to let her out of my sight."

"I know," I say.

"I'm sure I'll feel safer when she starts to...to share things. And there's the therapist. But...but she still hasn't told you anything? Talked about what...he did?"

"No," I have to say, and I can see the disappointment in him.

Tell me what I want to hear, he's saying. *Give me what I need, Lizzie.*

"Not yet," I add. "But she's so happy to be home. She feels so safe now. So happy and safe."

His smile, even if it's filled with doubts and wonderings, is immense, and my face goes very warm and, sitting on the floor at his feet, I find myself wanting to lean against his legs and bury myself there.

We're quiet for a while and Mr. Verver keeps switching records, and he's enjoying his beer, and still not letting me have even one sip.

"It's late," he says. "You should hit the sack."

I nod, but he keeps talking, and so I get up from the floor and settle into the chair next to him, and then a new song comes on, and it's jauntier, it's like a swagger and it hits me low and makes my stomach twist, riotous.

"Oh, Lizzie," he says. "Thin Lizzie, do you hear that bass line? Do you? You don't get that on your cassette tapes. I don't even think you get it on these *compact discs*. That sound is too huge to be *compacted*. You can feel it in your chest, can't you?"

I'm listening, but it's hard because the song that's playing, the lyrics are slow and loud, the singer talking about different kinds of girls and the things they do. It has lots of swearing and a slow, lingering beat and Mr. Verver doesn't seem to notice the lyrics at all until suddenly he pauses, and that's the exact moment the singer slurs about how black girls like to get fucked all night.

Mr. Verver looks over at me with a jolt, and I know he can see my red face, feel the blush radiating off me.

He laughs, and as he lifts his beer bottle from the floor, its coldness brushes up against my leg and makes me jump and suddenly I'm laughing too. We look at each other and laugh, strange, jangling laughs that make me feel hot and shaky.

We laugh so hard that I feel the chair scraping beneath me, and I look down and see my very own fingers curled around his wrist.

My fingers pressed against his pulse. *Oh, to feel it throbbing there, I do. It's fast, and my heart—*

I look down and see my fingers there.

His hand on the armrest, and there they are, my God, they are, *my fingers* curled around his wrist.

He looks down too.

The split second is endless and I can't breathe.

He pats my hand and smiles, turning all of it into something else, just for me. He makes it into something else, something light and meaningless.

The song ends, then a new song rises up, and Mr. Verver starts talking about how I'll be going to dances soon.

"You'll have boys circling you," he says. "Oh, will you ever."

"I don't know," I say, still trying to catch my breath, my voice funny and high. "There's no one at school I'd want to dance with."

And he grins and he starts to tell me about his first dance, and how he tried to get up the courage to ask a girl named Miranda Morton to dance, and she was so pretty, with hair up tight like a ballerina. But he didn't have the guts. So his friend Toby did it instead and she said yes.

Mr. Verver burned with jealousy, watching them dance under the strobing lights, pretending with all his heart that he was the one holding Miranda Morton in his arms, holding her wrist, like blown glass, in his hand.

Watching, pretending, he could feel his life unspool—that's what he said, unspool, his arm fanning out—a majestic life with Miranda Morton at his side. A life of beauty and warmth and golden days.

But then he spotted Miranda's friends coiled in a corner laughing and he realized that, through the whole dance, Miranda had been rolling her eyes at them over Toby's shoulder.

"I'll never forget that," he says, then prods me with his finger, right in the ribs. "The cruelty of women."

He scissors his finger into my ribs as he says it, and I can't help but laugh. But his finger there, it—

"So you see, Lizzie," he says, "you have to dance with them, those poor fellas. You have no idea how important it is, and what those dances mean. You have to make up for the Miranda Mortons of the world."

"I will," I say, meaning it with such fervor without even understanding it.

"You dance with them," he says, and takes a long sip from his beer, "and they'll dream about it for weeks after, months, years. Decades. They'll play it again and again in their feverish little heads." He looks at me. "Don't you want that?"

"Yes," I say. *Yes.*

"Lizzie," he says, eyes on me warmly, so warmly I can feel it in my toes. "You're going to leave a long trail of broken hearts— one for every finger and toe."

He knocks my foot with his, sending tingles through me so I can't breathe.

"But just remember," he says, eyes still on me, "I told you first. I was your first."

The words thrum in me, fierce and swiping. How could I ever forget that? As if I would ever forget that.

"You girls never know how hard it all is," he says, grinning lightly again. "The asking, the pursuing."

Just like that, everything slips away, and he's talking to me like I'm so small, like he thinks I'm a little Brownie in his basement, playing Chutes and Ladders.

I can't stop myself. The words come tumbling out.

"I know things about boys," I blurt.

He looks at me.

"I'm sure you do," he says.

"I know things," I say, and the minute I do, I want to crawl under the chair and hide.

"Well," he says, slowly, looking at me carefully, like he's trying to figure something out. "I guess it's different than when I was your age."

There's a pause.

"Now I sound like an old man." He laughs, but it's a funny kind of laugh and I feel him yanking the conversation into a far corner, far from where we are.

"You're not an old man," I say, fast and too loud. "And I don't know what I meant. I don't know anything about boys. Men. Nothing at all."

He smiles.

"You know more than you think," he says, and then he turns away from me quickly.

It's so fast I almost miss it.

But the look on his face, the look on his face... it was...

I feel a shudder tear through the whole of me.

And we sit, and we sit, and it gets so late and the music swallows everything and I'm glad for it.

It's hours later that I name it. In my sleep that night.

The look on his face.

He had all the sorries in the world on his face, filled brim-full with sorries and regret, and I hate myself for making him feel it.

There was something, and you weren't supposed to look at it, you weren't supposed to lean in, peer too close, and I did, and I made him do it too. And he did, and . . .

And now something's gone forever, and I feel its loss. It crushes me.

When I climb back in bed, Evie's eyelids twitch and she stirs.

The moonlight bleaches us both. I see her eyes, so wide and white they sear me.

"Oh, Lizzie," she says. "I want to tell you, I want to tell you, but I can't."

"Why not?"

She hunches up fast on her elbows, looking at me so hard.

"I don't know," she says, blinking slowly, watching, the looming whiteness of her eyes. And then, "You don't seem like Lizzie."

"What do you mean?" My mouth goes dry, I'm not sure why.

She doesn't say anything.

"It's me," I say. "Why can't you tell me?"

"Because of the way things are," she says. "Everything looks funny now. But I don't think it's really changed. I just never saw it before. The pieces just got switched around."

"What do you mean?" I say again, but something flashes in my head, me on the patio with Mr. Verver, laughing, warmed under his warming gaze. Looking up to Evie's darkened window, the shadow of the mobile, still and listless, and seeing Dusty up there where Evie should be.

I feel a crawling trespass inside me. I fight it off.

"I don't know what I mean," she says, her fingers clawing out at me, twisting tight on my hair.

I don't say anything at all, I can't say anything at all.

And she's looking at me like I'm the ghost.

Twenty-one

It had been a dreamless, lost sleep, like sinking down an end-less hole. I'd been grateful for it.

And then the noise, some noise, a firecracker pop.

I look at the clock flaring five forty.

I feel Evie stirring, jumping up, running to the window.

It's the tiniest gasp from her, and I wonder what she sees, but my head isn't working right and I can't unfurl the sheet from my ankle.

I stumble to the window, squeezing my eyes into focus.

It's the pear tree out back, there's something at the foot of it, something black at its knotty roots.

That's a dog, I think, *or a trash bag. What is that dark thing?*

At the same moment, elbows bumping each other, we lift up the heavy window, push our faces against the screen.

That's when I see.

It's a person.

It's a man, sprawled under the tree.

"Evie," I say. "Evie."

It's all happening, I think, *he's come here to reclaim his girl-queen.*

He's returned from the darkest depths to take her back again, in a titanic gesture, like a knight rescuing the princess from her high tower.

I feel myself running out her bedroom door and it's so fast and in my head her antic breaths are right behind me. In my head, she's right behind me.

Sliding across the kitchen floor, I land at the side door, hurling it open, the new security alarm wailing, crashing in my ears.

I'm pounding across the dewy grass of the backyard, my eyes flashing over the black mass under the tree and, ten feet away, my legs shudder to a stop.

I hold my aching chest and stop.

He's lying there, his arm flung to his side, like when you do snow angels. The black thing in his hand, the gun, looks so small.

I let myself look, I do. I can't stop myself.

I look down at Mr. Shaw, eyes struck open, and mouth too, the mouth like a black ragged hole.

Like something black inside him exploded, soot sprayed across his left cheek.

Like the thing inside him, the dark and helpless thing, had become so immense, he could no longer hold it. He could no longer contain it. It overtook him.

His eyes open like that, looking straight up into the branches of the pear tree, and I bet he wishes he was looking at her still, looking up at her window, stuck that way forever, arrested.

Then I remember: *Where's Evie? Where is she? This is for her, for her to wail and cry out his name and fall to her knees like in a movie, slow motion and music rising.*

Because he's waiting here for you, Evie, don't you see?

Wheeling around, I look up and see her. She's still at her bedroom window. She hasn't moved at all. She's looking down at me, watching me. And I want to see the horror on her face, the roaring grief and confusion. I want to see it all. I want her to show it to me, to him.

But there's nothing on her face at all. Stock-still and vacant-eyed, she's like an old wax doll, propped on a windowsill.

Where is it, Evie? Where's all that feeling?

Because I look at your face and all I see is nothing.

The blankness, it terrifies me.

What happened, Evie, that took your face away, that smeared it blank? What happened to Evie?

That's when I feel Mr. Verver's arms grabbing my waist, whirling me around.

He's trying to pull me away from Mr. Shaw, but I'm not done.

Mr. Verver's hands are on me, he is grabbing me so hard, but I am so much stronger, I am sliding through his arms back to Mr. Shaw.

Mr. Shaw, eyes wide open, and I never got the chance to have that heavy, heartsick gaze on me. And now here it is, eyes open forever, gazing in dreamy wonder.

All these days, these endless days, trying to crawl my way into him, trying to burrow through, I won't be stopped now.

I want to look at Mr. Shaw's face forever.

I feel myself drop to the grass, hands and knees, peering at him, my face so close the smells burn in my nose, smoke and sweat and unnamed things, lowering myself nearly to the damp dirt, inches from him.

His face.

I see no horror there, not the gun lacing through his splayed fingers. Not the blood webbed across the tree trunk.

Not even that dark tunnel in the center of his face.

That dark tunnel I stare down, like I might follow it, like it might swallow me whole and I would let it willingly, to see where it might take me, to see what secrets it might tell me, secrets Evie holds in her chest now so tight, inviolate.

She's holding it all fathoms deep, she hides it from her face even, pulls a mask across, but he won't. He can't. He will tell me.

Mr. Verver's arms across my chest, trying to drag me back, and I won't go, I won't.

Those eyes, lashed open, looking straight at me.

For the first time ever, those eyes looking straight at me, into my own black heart.

My heart.

I feel my body swing, flung by Mr. Verver, his hands across my eyes. My knees hit the grass again, my legs wilting beneath me, and I see nothing.

But it doesn't matter. It doesn't matter because it took only a second. It took only that second.

I know how it was for Evie now. She looked into his eyes and thought, Oh, what things he must know, what glistening treasures and wild terrors and white-bone regrets the likes of which we will not know for decades. He carried all this wisdom in him, and loss and feeling, and he carried it for her, he wanted to bring it to her, to press it onto her, a sealy emblem of his own regard, the imprint of his life and sorrows. Doing this, doing it here, he wanted to make her feel it forever, on her very own skin. And she will. And now I will too. I will.

Twenty-two

There are hours that go by, they are unmarked. What would the Verver house be like now without officers blueing every corner, their police radios crackling, those detectives in their blazers, latex gloves snapping. All their eyes, the way they move, their hard, blinkless eyes.

"Let's go home," my mother says, and it's nearly noon. "Let's go home."

I am thinking of how, an hour before, I crept stealthily by the Ververs' bedroom, saw Mrs. Verver and Evie on the bed, both cotton-stuffed with tranquilizers, buried under mounds of sheets, Mrs. Verver's arms swaddling Evie, encasing her.

I am thinking of Mr. Verver's face, white and vivid, his hands fisted as he walked, his voice loud and strong. His daughter's captor gone forever, I think he feels victorious.

I can't think of what to make of it.

I can't think of anything.

Back at home with my mother, I wonder how I will fill the rest of the day, all these hours, the weeks to come?

How will anything ever be still, aweless, again?

The alleged abductor of a local 13-year-old girl took his own life Tuesday outside the home of his purported victim, police say.

Dead from what police are calling a self-inflicted gunshot wound, Harold K. Shaw, 45, was found by the family of his alleged victim in their backyard early Tuesday morning.

Shaw was wanted in connection with allegations of abduction and child molestation. According to police, Shaw kidnapped the girl outside her school on May 28, embarking on a three-week run from the law.

No suicide note was found.

I read the article five, ten times, and there is nothing there. Nothing that means anything at all.

I keep circling it, wondering if I will ever find a way in. When Evie looked at Mr. Shaw, in those motel rooms, in those rooms as she sat on scratchy bedspreads, on bedspreads worn part through, sitting across from Mr. Shaw, did she look at him and see something so beautiful or so ugly that she couldn't stop looking, could never stop looking at him no matter what he did or wanted to do?

What did it feel like to her, seeing him there, trapped in his shadow, him leaning over as she sat on the bed?

Evie, she had a jaw that clicked when she opened her mouth wide or when she ate sometimes. When he kissed her, did he hear it click, like a cocked gun? Did she open her mouth wide, like an animal, for him and did he hear it click like the safety on a gun?

It's eight o'clock the following night when Mr. Verver spots me in the backyard, rolling a soccer ball up and down my legs as I lie on the lounger.

He rests his arms across the top of the wire fence.

"How you doing?" Everyone keeps asking that question, my mother, the family doctor, and the lady my mother made me see at the counseling center that day. I keep saying I didn't really see it happen. That I am not traumatized. I say it so many times it no longer seems true.

But when he asks, it's different. It just is. Something nuzzles inside me and I forget everything else and remember only private things, me-and-Mr.-Verver things, the wafting detergent smell in the basement, his face summer-burned, my fingers on his wrist, pressing pulse to pulse, feeling it in my toes. I want it back, I do.

"I'm okay," I say, walking over to the fence. The thought comes to me: What did he think when he had to pull me away from Mr. Shaw? What might he think? "I don't know what I am."

He smiles faintly. "I know what you are," he says, reaching across and putting his hand to my hair, curling a strand around my ear.

I let his hand sit there, I know I will feel it for days, lifetimes.

"Please come over, Lizzie," he says. "She wants you to come over."

I open the door to her room and Evie's sitting, cross-legged, on her bed, staring out the window.

"Mom wants to chop it down," she says, and we both look at the pear tree, its crisp, shiny leaves, its rambling lushness. Her face so still. Now I think that stillness, that blankness, it's a trick. She can't show me yet. She hides it all behind that mask. But she will show me, she will. For him, I will get it.

"Evie," I say, and she looks over at me, unblinking.

"It's all done," she says, almost a sigh. "It's all done."

We pull the sleeping bags outside, onto the whiskery grass.

It is so hot, and the house is tin-can cold, but Evie wants to be outside, so we sneak out, Evie punching the security code on the panel next to the door.

So wanton, so reckless, the whooshing thunk when the door opens, the stifling night air filling our throats.

Even so, even in that fulsome heat, the closeness of all things, there's a dizzy kind of freedom in our chests.

Besides, what could happen now? All the happenings gone forever.

In my head, the sight of that dark tunnel mouth, the chute of a mouth, the way you could sink down it forever and never reach the shimmering center.

We don't even think about going into the Verver backyard, that haunted spot in the center. We sneak across the driveway to my yard.

We are both wearing T-shirts and underwear and lying on top of our sleeping bags. Evie keeps pulling her hair off her sticky neck.

The air doesn't move at all. Everything is glowing from the new patio light, the biggest I've ever seen, its globe face like a milky moon.

The cicadas are everywhere, and twinkling lightning bugs. I stretch my toes, which feel dry and scratchy against the sleeping bag.

I'm trying to figure out Evie, her calmness. I'm still picturing her up there in that window, her face like wax.

"Evie," I venture, "remember when you showed me the cigarette stubs?"

I poke my fingertips into the grass, the cooling dirt.

She wriggles under her T-shirt, elbows poking, pulling its cotton fabric stickily from her damp chest.

"Yeah," she says. "You know, Lizzie, my dad told me how you helped. How you gave the police all that information."

"He did?" I say, and I feel my hot cheeks grow hotter and I put my hands to them.

I wish I had heard exactly what he said, and how he said it. I wonder what words he used and what his face looked like when he said it and if he said it big, like he says things sometimes.

"And about the phone call," she says. I'd been waiting for this. "That you told them I'd called you. From that motel. I said, yes, I guess I did. Call you."

I look at her. And she looks at me. The moment is long, and I surrender before her.

"Pete Shaw," I say. "He told me where you were."

She nods slowly, drawing it all together for herself. Then she lets it go.

"Dad says it's all thanks to you," she says, and I can feel her body tense, hear her voice twist a little. "My coming back. It's all because of you."

Her little fingers are on my arm, on the soft dimpled girly inside.

"Thank you, Lizzie," she says, the tiniest whisper, almost just a burr of hot breath in my ear.

And she's Evie again. And the feeling is all over both of us.

We huddle closely, huddle like we did centuries ago, Brownies at summer camp, racked through with midnight tales of horror and woe, the dreaded sound of lightning crackles and boys hiding in the woods.

It's very late, but the heat never lifts. I turn and look at Evie. Her eyes shut, but I know she's awake. We are in that in-between state and it seems like there are no rules other than the half rules of dreaminess and lost hours.

I think about Evie in that window, watching. Watching Mr. Shaw's body and doing nothing, showing nothing. Was she dying inside? Is she dead now?

And I think about Mr. Verver and what he wants. The things he needs to know, most of all that Evie is okay. That she is really okay and there is nothing lying in wait under her skin, behind her eyes. Nothing broken that he can't see and can't fix.

But truly it's me. I need to hear her tell it, to give it all to me, to drop it, a gleamy pearl, in my open palm.

He loved you, Evie. He died for you. You have to tell.

I feel it pressing so hard on me. I can't stop myself. So I say it.

"Evie, tell me," I say. "Tell me now. What happened with you and Mr. Shaw?"

I feel her gather her breath deep. "Lizzie," she says, shaking her head over and over again. "No."

"Are you going to tell Dusty?" The words pushing from me and surprising me.

"No," Evie says, stirring suddenly. "Why would I tell Dusty?"

It was a crazy thing for me to say. Dusty still at their grandparents, I haven't even seen them in the same room since Evie's been back. Something rustles in me when I think of it. Have I even seen them together? But I push it aside.

"It's just, she told me you'd see him out there," I say. "She said the two of you would watch him out there, by the tree," I say, my voice taking on a funny wobble. Something seems so wrong all of a sudden. Some hinge squeaking in me.

"Lizzie, we never saw him together," she says, her voice newly cold. Quiet. Pulled in, tucked tight. "We never did at all."

My head feeling soft and confused, all I can think is, *She's afraid, she's afraid to say.*

And then I do it: "She thinks you knew he was going to take you."

"What?" she says, sitting up abruptly, her hands leaping to her throat, her jaw, a few tendrils sweaty-stuck there.

"It's okay if it's true. I'd never tell," I promise with all the urgency I have. "Neither of us ever told."

She leans close to me.

"Lizzie, don't you listen to her," she says, a quiet pleading in her voice, like she's trying to make things plain, for a child. "You don't understand about that."

"What do you mean?" I say, flinching. "I understand."

"I mean about Dusty," she says, and she won't quite look at me. "She doesn't...Dusty doesn't understand things like that."

"But *I* do," I say, with such fancied wisdom. "I understand how you could look out that window night after night and see him there and never tell."

"Lizzie," she says, "he didn't take me at all."

There is such a quiet on us both, a sense of true hushness. *There's knowing and there's knowing and I knew this, innermost, didn't I?*

"I went," she says. "I went with him. I wanted to go. I asked him to take me away."

She says it and it seems like all the far-flung pieces jolt into place. I feel the jolt in me and I nearly shake.

Of course.

I knew it, didn't I?

It was no kidnapping at all.

"I understand, Evie," I say, firming my voice as much as I can, caught in the lusciousness of all things, and the wickedness too. "He loved you so much. It's okay if you loved him."

Because that was the real secret, wasn't it? Barely a secret at all.

You love him.

And you can tell me now and we can share again, such private, furtive things. Things we can tell no one else.

But she's shaking her head wearily, the oldest woman in the world.

"You're wrong, Lizzie," she says, and it's a sad, beaten smile. "You're wrong about everything."

It's such a sharp dismissal. I feel it cruelly.

"What do you mean?" I say, face burning. The youngest girl in the group, the baby everyone rolls their eyes at.

The smile drops away and she puts her hand on me. And I know she's going to do it. I know at last she's going to tell. But suddenly I don't know if I'm ready for it.

"I don't remember when it started," she says. "Just, one day, I knew."

"Knew he was watching," I almost stutter.

"Knew everything," she says. "I don't know how to say it. It was like this. I could see how it was in him and he couldn't fight it."

She turns on her side and faces me. She leans close to me and talks right into my ear, her mouth nearly touching my hair.

"He told me it was like a piercing thing in his chest. One day, it just happened. He saw me and it happened, and after that there was nothing else. A hole in his chest like you could stick your finger in.".

I feel a shudder right through me, quaking. I feel my thighs go loose and hot. Oh my, it's a sickness. A sickness. I swoon into it. She is telling, she is finally telling. It's like dipping your toe in a magical lake in some fairy tale.

The beauty of it, I wait for it.

She tells me how she saw him all the time, in the yard, on the street, outside the school. He would watch and never say a word. It was like her special secret and she had to admit, there was something in it that drew her close. There was something in him, always there, always looking at her. Why, it moved her. It did.

She tells me how she knew it would happen eventually. She'd known it for a while.

That day, walking with me, our clacking hockey sticks, she saw his car go by, twice. She couldn't think of a day in the last year when she hadn't seen his car. But today would be different. She knew it would. She knew somehow she'd end up in that car with him.

And when they were driving away, she thought, *This is it. This is it. It's all begun, and how could it stop now?*

As he drove, he told her how it had been. How he loved her, but the love grieved him, shamed him. It had begun last summer, but really long before that. He saw her at the pool, doing dives. Watching her, it all came back to him. How, nearly ten years ago, he'd seen her fall in the water at Green Hollow Lake. The most important moment of his life.

"He pulled me out," she tells me now. "No one saw me fall, but he saw, and he rescued me."

I put my fingers to my mouth, tapping them there. I am thinking of something, something far away, but I cannot hold onto it.

And then he told her when he saw her at the pool last summer, all those years later, it all came back to him.

He said it was like a hammer on his heart.

The words crackle in my head. To hear something like that, what would it mean? Would it change your life? How could it not?

They drove for hours, she says, but they never seemed to get anywhere. Sometimes they passed the same spots. Like he couldn't decide about something. She kept seeing the same motel. The big sign, like a deck of cards, and a swiveling diamond in each corner.

It seemed like he'd never stop driving. But finally he did. They sat in the car in the motel parking lot for an hour before he went inside to check in.

He said he'd thought many, many times of ending everything.

And he reached his arm in front of her, careful not to touch her, and clicked open the glove compartment.

He didn't take it out. He just pointed at it. The handgun there, so small, like a toy.

The shame, it was so heavy, he said. So many times, he thought he couldn't go on. But he was a coward, really. And he couldn't bear the thought that he'd never see her again, never see her in her summer shorts, dangling her legs. Never see her dive from the high board, her face in such concentration. Never see her flipping cartwheels on her front lawn.

He snapped the glove compartment shut and he looked at her, for the first time, really. She must have shown him something on her face, because that was when he got out of the car and walked, hands in his pockets so fast, to the registration office.

"The room was so small," she tells me, "and there was a picture of a leopard over the bed. He was so nervous. But I wasn't nervous at all."

I am waiting. I am waiting and my stomach is so tight, my hands clamped between my thighs.

"He sat on the bed," she says, "and I sat on a chair, and he talked for a long time about his life and how it was over for him now and he didn't care."

My heart beats, my heart beats.

"It was so late when I told him," she says. "I promised him it was okay. Because it was okay."

She can't say it, but I feel what she means. He loves her, he loves her and it's the biggest feeling she's ever known and she feels special in it, and she is. And who wouldn't?

She wriggles up on her elbows. "I told him he could," she says. "And then he did."

I feel like she's skipping things, I feel like she's moving too fast.

Slow down, slow down.

I shut my eyes tight, I shut them so tight.

"But, Lizzie, it wasn't okay after all," she says, her voice suddenly brimful, aching. "It wasn't okay, but then it was too late."

My eyes open and I see her face, moon-daubed.

"He should've seen," she says, her lip lifting, baring her teeth. "He did see. But he couldn't stop."

My eyelids flutter involuntarily.

"It burned like cigarettes. Like this." She pokes an imaginary cigarette into the soft flesh on the underside of her forearm.

"And it lasted forever. I kept squirming and the burning turned to tearing. He should've stopped, but he couldn't."

I feel my head nodding, my jaw creaking.

"And after," she says, "in the bathroom, little pieces of bloody guck came out of me, stuck to my legs. I couldn't move without more coming."

My hand over my mouth—why is she doing this? I feel suddenly like she's doing something to me. Something awful. And she is, isn't she?

"He kept knocking on the bathroom door," she says, relentless. "He was so sorry. He was so sorry. How could he have known? That's what he said.

"Then he was crying and I promised him it was okay. I promised every time."

Every time . . . every time.

"Because once he'd done it, it was like he couldn't stop," she says. "All those days . . ." Her voice drifting.

I can't listen. I can't.

"Lizzie," she whispers, her voice a needle in my ear, "he loved me so much in those nineteen days I thought I might die from it."

I cover my ears, I clamp my hands over them.

"One night, really late," she said, her hands on me, hot and relentless, "he cried after. He cried for so long. He went to get ice and when he came back he had the gun, from the glove compartment.

"He put it under his chin, standing there at the foot of the bed, and he said I should just tell him to do it and he would."

My hands on my ears, rocking, trying not to see Mr. Shaw, but seeing him.

"I told him to put the gun down. Would you believe it? It didn't seem strange at all. Not after everything. That's how different everything was.

"He crawled into the bed and cried like a baby. He said he never would, not now, because of what I'd taught him.

"He said I'd taught him how to love."

There they are, the words I've been waiting for, but not like this. None of it's right, it's not. I don't know how to make it stop.

"He told me he knew they would find us," she says. "And I told him I wasn't sorry, even though I was."

She looks at me. She's making sure I feel every bit of it. And I do.

"But maybe I'm not really sorry," she says carefully. "He saved me, so I gave him this thing. Even if he shouldn't have taken it, I guess I don't feel bad for giving it."

He saved me.

She slips her hand in my hair, tugging me toward her.

"And when he dropped me off, he said this thing."

My hands fisted over my ears, but nothing can stop her.

"He was so calm, like he never was. I had the car door open, and I was looking at him, and it was the longest minute.

"And then he said, *No one will ever love you like this again,* and I knew he was right."

You can never tell. Lizzie, you can never tell.

I won't. I won't.

But, Evie, I say after, when my voice returns from such dark reaches, I don't know where, *there's so much more. There's so much more you haven't said. There's a piece missing. Why did you go with him? What did he do to get you to go with him? Why did you finally go? Why that day?*

And, Evie, you said he saved you. What do you mean he saved you?

But she says nothing. She's through.

Twenty-three

It's the first Fourth of July celebration without the Ververs I can remember.

There are no tiki torches blazing in their backyard, no star-spangled streamers wound round their front lamppost. There are no lemon bars from Mrs. Verver, no watermelon punch.

There's no Dusty dancing under the lights in her summer dress.

No Mr. Verver to drive across the state line to the Fireworks Emporium, bringing back silver-tailed Roman candles, bottle rockets and their keening whistles, the triple bangers that make everyone jump, and the tall cones from last year that released swarming sparks like clustering bees.

None of that.

Instead, when it gets dark, the fathers gather and light up a few straggly comets and smoke balls, but it's all so different, none of that red-faced energy and that swelling feeling, like anything could happen, the sky itself could rip open. Mr. Verver, he could tear the sky open and rain light down on all of us.

There is no Evie and no one to run sparklers with, no one to light magic snakes on the driveway, fingers black with the soft ash, but maybe we wouldn't have done that this year anyway. Maybe this was going to be the year we stopped doing that. We'd been doing that long past anyone else, hadn't we?

The heat, and the kids laughing, and the speakers dragged into the street, the rolling beer bottles, the slick tug of fallen marshmallows under your feet, it's all happening, but none of it is.

The Ververs, they packed up a car and headed north two weeks ago, just a few days after Mr. Shaw, after everything.

And that time before, those nineteen days when life felt unhinged, wild and headlong, well, now it feels like a forlorn thing. A whistle in my head, a distant rumble.

When they left, I watched from an upstairs window. Watched Mrs. Verver huddle Evie into the car. Watched Mr. Verver lugging jammed suitcases, a duffel bag with a shirttail caught in its zipper. Watched Evie lean her head wearily against the car window, and I wondered, Will she now be weary for the rest of her life? I wondered about faces she used to wear—curious, wonderstruck—and if she will ever wear them again.

I thought of all the questions she'd never answered and wondered if I'd ever get to ask them. Somehow, somehow knowing that a key had turned, a lock had clicked, and that was it. That was all I'd ever get.

It felt like the end of everything.

And the last thing, I watched Mr. Verver, red and white cooler tensed between his arms, look up for a second, like he knew somehow. Like he knew I was there. He glanced up at me, and I can't tell you the expression on his face. I can't describe it. It was both broken and serene.

Dusty was the last one to come outside. I didn't even know she was back from her grandparents'. She stood at the car door, hand on the window. Evie, already inside, stared straight in front of her, like they were already driving. She didn't turn her head.

Dusty stood there for so long, and she wouldn't open the door till the very last minute. She kept looking all around, head darting everywhere. It was like she couldn't imagine how she would get in that car. There was something lonely about it, and something else too.

I never did see her get in. My mother said something, I turned my head, and when I looked back, she was gone. They all were.

After, my mother told me they went high into the woods, hours away. A cottage Detective Thernstrom had told them about, one he'd rented himself once. An A-frame on a lake.

I picture them all on paddleboats, with fishing tackle, around campfires, in horseshoe pits, doing family things.

I picture it all the time.

I picture it especially tonight, the Fourth, hiding on the back patio, hiding from everyone, I picture it all.

I think no one sees me, but then I hear a chair scrape and I nearly jump from my skin. It's Dr. Aiken.

He'd come to the house earlier that day, wearing madras shorts and the new glasses. The first time he's ever showed up in the daytime, not even four o'clock, and he came to the front door, holding a white box with red string, which he handed to me with a half smile, one of those smiles from someone who doesn't smile much and isn't sure what it's supposed to look like. But somehow it comes out all right.

When my mother walked in and saw him, her face steamed pink, she ran upstairs and changed from her T-shirt and shorts to a sundress I'd never seen, with little blue pindots. She moved in it with great care.

In the bakery box were hot cross buns, so strange for Fourth of July. He must have seen the look on my face because he said he wanted to bring Rice Krispies treats, but the bakery didn't make them.

"You're missing everything," Dr. Aiken says now, standing on the patio, extending a wilting paper plate toward me. "You mean to tell me you'd miss the limbo contest?"

I look down at the plate he's handed me and see it's one of his hot cross buns, the glaze melting onto the corners of the plate.

"I saved you one," he says.

I almost smile, even as I feel so far away, so far away from all this. Like I'm watching everything through glass.

"Actually," he says, "looks like I saved you all of them."

"I remember the song," I say suddenly, my voice surprising me.

"Of course." He nods. "'Hot cross buns, one a penny, two a penny.'"

"'If you haven't any daughters,'" I say, "'give them to your sons.'"

"Not much of a song," he says, shaking his head.

"Are you a dad?" I say, my hands on the plate, my fingers growing stickier.

"No," he says.

I look up at him and his glasses slip and I can see his eyes behind them.

"My wife—my ex-wife now—we wanted to, but we never did."

I don't say anything. I can feel him watching, delicately. Watching to see that I understand this. That I understand what he is saying. *Ex*-wife. And my mother twirling in her blue dress.

"Lizzie," he says, his voice shifting, "have you heard from the Ververs?"

"No," I say. "They'll be home soon."

"You know," he says, sitting down beside me on the back step, "I've seen those girls for years. Through broken arms, jammed fingers. Tough girls."

"Yes," I say.

"I saw Dusty just...must've been the end of May."

I look at him, and, just like that, I start to feel a pressure in the air, but I'm not sure why. Maybe because he is speaking with such care.

"Her parents brought her in for a stomachache. All the stress from her sister, I'm sure. This was just a few days after she'd been reported missing."

There's a flicker in my head. A flickering thing flickering from a hundred thoughts I've had over the past weeks. A hundred thoughts I've pushed aside, didn't want to pause long enough to ponder.

Dusty's flaring anger, as if saying, a thousand times in the last month, *How dare Evie do this to us, to all of us.*

"Did you help her?" I say. "Was she okay?"

"Yes," he says, and he takes off his glasses and looks at them, even though it's dark and what could he see?

"You're not supposed to talk about this stuff, are you? Doctors aren't, right?"

"No," he says. "I'm not."

I nod.

"The funny thing, though...," he starts, putting his glasses back on and turning to me.

"What?" I say, my voice sounding so small.

"Well, when she took off her sweatshirt she was covered with scratches."

"Field hockey," I say. "Field hockey."

"That's what she kept saying. Long scratches on her arms, on her neck." He's looking at me so intently and I feel the pressure in my chest now.

Something's happening, but I don't know what, and it's like a booming in my chest.

"From practice. From sticks, the cleats. From...," my voice scraping. What can he mean? I wonder. What does this mean?

"Well, I've seen a hundred field hockey injuries," he says. "I know what they look like. They don't look like that."

He looks at me, and I feel his eyes on me.

The pause is so long, and the pressure is in my head now, pounding.

"Things can get pretty rough out there," he says. "Can't they? For you girls? You're all a bunch of warriors, aren't you? Lionhearted."

"Yes," I say. "Yes."

In bed that night it comes to me: everything that was so raw and fleshy and gaping, everything that felt chaotic and blood-torn — it all might mean something after all. Something more than what it was, a man fighting a private affliction, until he couldn't fight it anymore. *Of course it was more than that . . .*

But to look at it, it's hard.

I think of Dusty, and everything seesaws and all the things that made her so remote, so far away . . . the things that made it seem like you couldn't touch her no matter what she said, or did. No matter if she took her stick to you, if she laid her own rough justice on you. She had a fire in her. She did. And . . . and . . .

All Dusty's misery, her preening rage, and Evie insisting, "We never saw him together. We never did at all."

They never shared anything. They were never sisters like that.

Long scratches, battle scars.

I have this picture in my head, Dusty, a sentry. Might she have tried to stand guard? Tried to stop it? *Don't you go with him, Evie, don't you dare go,* that's the imagined voice whirring in my head. Dusty.

I can't quite get at it. I'm circling, I'm circling, but I can't yet see the darkening center.

These last weeks, I replay, and replay it all the time. Everything Dusty and Evie shared with me, revelations on tongue tips. The center of things — or is it the bottom? — I haven't reached it yet.

"They're back," my mother says, waking me, her fingers tickling my face, and she leans down over me, her long hair pooling on my cheek, whispering in my ear.

It's the last week in July and the Verver car is in their driveway and my mother is making waffles, which has not happened since never.

Her face is warm, as though brushed soft with something gold and smooth. She is touching everything with light, dancing fingers, the backs of our chairs, the serving spoon, Ted's husk of yellow hair.

I can't take my eyes from the kitchen window, the Verver house, you can feel it jolting to life again.

"So, Mom," Ted says, shrugging from her tickling hand. "What's up? You bust out that old Harvey Wallbanger mix again?"

He's laughing, and I think he means for her to too, but it makes her look at herself and all the butter-softness leaves her face. He didn't mean to do it, but he did. He took it all away.

"No," she says, "nothing like that." She smiles a little and, bit by bit as she pours syrup onto our waffles, sliding the dewy tub of butter toward us, the gold comes back.

Dr. Aiken, could he really have such magic in him, could he cast spells and glimmers and make my mother shine like a piece of fine brass? A man like that, why, he has no glimmers. He has no magic. But there she is, shining.

It's all so fast. The car in the driveway, and by noon Evie and I are riding our bikes to the pool.

She tells me the trip was nice. She tells me everything is better. She says the school mailed her diploma and she'll start high school with me in September.

She tells me many things and it's like she's talking us into it, talking us into everything being back to the way it was. Like we're both secretly saying, *It's like before and we can talk forever, and we can spend every minute together.*

It's like all these things. It's the picture of these things. And Evie and I, it's as if we're standing there looking at the picture of how we once were and we're moving our arms the same way, turning our head this way and that. If it looks like the thing, maybe somehow it will become the thing.

Me and my shadow.

In everything she says, though, I hear the hollow knock behind it. I am knocking hollowly at Evie's hollowed heart.

It's over.

But here's the thing: in its overness there is a crazy freedom, and I watch Dusty, I watch her, and I am waiting for my moment, the clearing field. The things she might know. The things she might have tried to stop. The scratches on her arms, and suddenly I remember Evie's neck, the faded yellow marks still whispering on Evie's neck after she first came home. The faded yellow smudges there, like she'd run a highlighter across her throat.

And the way the two separated, never in the same room, seldom in the same house, since Evie's return. Like two boxers gone to their separate corners, spitting blood.

Don't you go with him, Evie. Don't you dare go. Was that it?

There's still knowledge to be had. If Evie won't give it to me, Dusty will dare me to take it.

Twenty-four

I wake up that morning with the words on my tongue already. The things I will say to Dusty.

The tryouts are at eight o'clock, before the heavy August heat sinks into the skin.

Evie won't be trying out with me.

She tells me she never liked field hockey that much anyway. She'll stick to soccer. She tells me this with her head turned, and I can't see her face.

Evie goes with her mother to special therapy sessions twice a week now. They go shopping after, to Reynold's for ice cream, to the movies. Some days I barely see Evie at all.

Sometimes it's like her head is always turned away, so I can never see her face.

The field is clogged with freshman girls, all with a bristle of fear on them as Dusty and her cocaptains stalk the sidelines. They look a hundred feet tall, even though Dusty probably doesn't break five feet four. They are tremendous. And she most of all, her purling gold hair, her nut-brown limbs, her kilt snapping as she strides back and forth, eyes hidden behind mirrored sunglasses, her face blank and inscrutable.

We all go through it, the ball control and push-pass drills, then the attack drills. Drive, push, slap, drive push slap. It goes on and on and she's thirty yards away, she's barely even watching me, but her voice thrums in all our ears, and then, at the very end, she takes the field with me, and I knew it was coming, but could anyone really be ready for her?

The ball on the end of my stick, I feel my blood roaring, and then there she is, the tackle so hard, our sticks like locked swords, and I bend double, all the air sucked from me.

It's a fair tackle, it's fair, but still, there's a thudding, charging feel in me and before I know it, my shoulder is vaulting against her chest, my elbow corkscrewing, knocking her chin sideways with a sickening clack.

The whistles are blowing at me and there is shouting, but we're in it now. I feel her turf shoes gnash against my face, my forehead going wet, my mouth guard nearly down my throat. But my arm clips her, swinging around, my foot wedging between hers, she losing her balance, crashing hard to the sparking grass.

Standing above her, I push my hair from my eyes and give her my whole face. I won't blink, I won't, we, squared off western outlaws.

Barely glancing at me, she raises her hand up to me, a bangle bracelet dangling there, the one that must've caught my eyebrow, tore a gash across it.

She reaches up for me, and I hook my hand around her forearm, lifting her to her feet.

We are walking down the empty school hallways, far away from the clattering locker room, the girlish sounds of breathless girls.

Dusty, her long, pearly ringlets drooping down her back, saunters ten paces in front of me, queenly.

I don't know where we're going, but when I unstick the hair from my face, I see two, three Dusty-strands stuck there too, blood-flecked.

"I'm not taking you to the nurse," she says. "If that's what you think."

"That's not what I think," I say.

And she finally stops when we reach the end of the west corridor, far from everything and everybody. She swivels the dial on her locker and yanks it open, tossing me a pack of gauze pads. That's when I see the red on her teeth and I remember that clacking sound, my elbow rearing up, punching her chin back.

I follow her into the girls' bathroom, watch as she spits the blood into the sink.

Looking in the mirror, I press the gauze pad against my eyebrow, looking at us both.

"I knew you had it in you," she says, her eyes flicking toward me, wiping her mouth with her hand. "You were always tougher than her."

I look at her, surprised.

Sitting on the bathroom floor, we're surveying our smashed bodies, their bloodied beauty.

I strip my kneesock down and let the air sting it, nettle-struck, the red streaks somehow thrilling.

"You lied," I say, because I feel like I can say anything now. "You and Evie didn't see Shaw out there together, did you? Why did you lie?"

"What's the difference?" She shrugs, barely interested. I'm

asking the wrong questions. This isn't the part where her heart is, her beating heart. "I wanted to make sure you believed me about her. I wanted you to know what she'd done."

I thrust the words from my mouth. What's stopping me now?

"Dusty, why do you think Evie got in the car with Mr. Shaw?"

She doesn't pause.

"Because she's disgusting. Because she's a disgusting little girl and she can't help herself."

I feel a flinch on me, fight it off.

"Were you there, Dusty?" I ask. It's my deepest guess. "Did you try to stop him? Or her?"

Dusty is still for a moment. She is so still, and I can hear the clack of the window blinds, the drilling moan of a distant lawn mower.

"Is that what Evie told you? That I tried to stop her?" she says, then shakes her head, adding, "She wouldn't tell you that."

"She didn't tell me anything," I say, my eyes on my knee, on the speckling red. "But you were there, weren't you? When Evie went with him?"

She pauses again, her head lowered slightly.

"I saw them," she says.

Then all the words come.

When she starts talking, it's like she's told the story a thousand times, practiced it, rehearsed it in her head. Not because it sounds fake, a pose, but because she's been trying, for months now, to put it right.

She talks, oh, she talks like Dusty never does, words falling helplessly, and I see it, right there. I see it like it's right before me:

Dusty had seen him in the yard, the swirl of smoke, the nighttime buzzing of katydids, the secret pocket at the center of the yard. From the back window, the half-moon in the upstairs hallway, she'd seen him.

She had to look for a long time before she recognized him. Is that Pete Shaw's dad? Mr. Shaw?

At first she thought it was for her. Why wouldn't she? Isn't that what boys did, watch her from afar and hope? Why not men? Didn't Dad always say she was too sophisticated for high school boys, that she was meant for men?

Then, one night, she saw him from her sister's window. She was showing Evie how to put the compression bandage on the right way, the bruised bone from their backyard practice, and the curtains were pulled wide.

It was even like she felt him first—how could you not? He radiated such awful heat, such a need, so raw, like a panting in your ear. Oh, it made her queasy and head-sick.

And then she saw it on Evie. Just a twitch, but she caught it. A quick twist of the head, Evie turning from the window and looking at Dusty to see if she saw him too. Or worse, saw her seeing him.

Dusty did catch it, those reflexes so fine. She saw and now she knew. Evie had seen him too, had seen him many times and didn't dare let Dusty know.

It sickened her, it did. Long nights in her bed, thinking of what it might mean, and why Evie wasn't disgusted, a man old enough to be her father. Why, instead of being disgusted, she seemed—

A man, a husband and a father, acting like some boy. Some mooning boy. She should be sickened.

But Evie wasn't sickened. Instead, it was like Evie wondered what it might be like, a grown man like that who wants only her. Maybe she convinced herself of all sorts of things, decided, like little girls do, that his love must be pure, and all he wanted was to gaze from afar, his heart in her little hands.

Of course, who knew what Evie thought, Evie who was always in the background, always interrupting, piping up, trying to be heard. Didn't she long to be the center? And now she was.

For him, she was.

Evie, she'd fallen for it.

Dusty wanted to tell her sister-things. Wanted to warn her that she didn't know what she was doing, that she was encouraging him and he was a dirty old man.

She wanted to stop her sister, but the words wouldn't come. Saying those words to Evie, *I know what you're doing, I know what you're feeling and it's wrong,* it'd make everything real, not some unformed muddle she could hide in her chest.

Because there was Dad to think about. There was Dad. And thinking of Dad, how she'd have to show him the sickness polluting his own house. His own daughter. The kind of girl who'd open her curtains, her blinds, everything that covers and protects her, for this man. This creeping monster.

And then it happened, just three days later.

Cutting across the long soccer field at the middle school, she saw Evie, perched on one of the flat-topped stone pedestals in front of the school, gazing out across the school lawn, swinging her hockey stick. Swinging her legs, one sock up and one down.

What's she doing? she wondered. Why isn't she home?

That's when she spotted the car parked across the street. A maroon Skylark.

Walking faster, nearly running, she knew who it was. Mr. Shaw, sitting there in his car, and Evie *knows,* she *knows* and she's giving him a show. Look at her there, giving him quite the show.

Look, look, look at me. A taunt, a tease, an invitation.

She couldn't bear watching it, her stomach turning.

She charged across the garden beds flanking the front steps, charged at her sister.

Spotting her, Evie nearly slipped from the high pedestal.

She grabbed Evie's leg, that little stick leg like you could break it, and she asked her what she thought she was doing. A man old enough to be her dad.

Turning fast, trying to pull away, Evie fell from the pedestal.

She took so long falling and Dusty did not try to stop her. She let her fall, the back of Evie's head snapping against the stone base, her face white and panicked.

It's sick, she shouted at Evie. It was the truth.

It's sick what you're doing, she said. *He's a pervert and now you're a pervert too.*

The look on Evie's face, it was like someone had taken a chisel to it. Like someone had split her in two.

The look, *It's like she's the innocent and I'm the one. I'm the pervert, ruining everything. How dare she?*

Evie scrambled to her feet, but not fast enough, and Dusty shoved her, heel of her hand on her shoulder hard, pressing Evie against the pedestal.

Oh, she pushed so hard, and Evie, helpless and wriggling, face reddening and trapped—why, she just started saying things.

Her voice gritted and quavering, Evie said everything, a bottled-tight lifetime of things, she couldn't stop.

It was like Evie'd spent her thirteen years waiting to tell her sister what she thought of her, what she thought of their happy home, which Evie said was like a prison. A prison. And what place was there for her, for Evie, there was only room enough for two. That Dusty made sure there was only room for two.

Dusty taking up all the space, all the air, and her need so great he—

Evie's voice hammering at her, *And you stand here blaming me, judging me, but look at you, Dusty, preening for him, twirling, dancing, the flirting and the winking and the curling up to him in our lawn chairs, I see how it is, Mom sees how it is. I know what you feel. You think you can hide it, but you can't. Who's the sick one, who is—*

She didn't even know how it happened. How it was that they were facing each other, and Evie saying those things, and then suddenly Evie's hand flew to her own mouth, like she couldn't believe what she had done. Like the words themselves burned her lips.

She remembers pushing Evie backward, the look on Evie's face, and the galloping in her own chest. She remembers Evie falling back, tripping over her field hockey stick, falling to the cement.

She doesn't know how she ended up on the ground too, knees digging into the grass, grinding into it, hands on Evie's legs, tight.

She doesn't know how it happened, but there was a surging in her chest, and her hands suddenly on that hockey stick, and that stick across Evie's throat, and Evie's eyes jumping, her head thrashing, and pressing harder to make it stop.

It was like a kids' fight, wasn't it? Over a nasty word on the playground. *Take it back! Take it back!* She would make Evie take it back.

Pressing so hard on the stick, pressing hard into the electrical tape circling it, her arms vibrating, her body vibrating, and Evie's face blooming a glorious red, and she knew suddenly that she could do anything.

All she could think was, *Look what I can do. I can push and push and push and those words will go back down her throat—my dad, my dad—and it'll be like she never said them at all.*

The color on Evie's face like no color she'd ever seen, and the feeling of the wood splintering under her thumbs.

I can do anything, I can do anything, and she didn't even feel Evie clawing at her arms, her chest. Long scratch marks that would last for days.

She didn't feel anything but the ending of things. She could seal up that moment, and it would be like it never happened at all, those words were never said. No one would ever know. She could end it all.

Then something shuddered into her, and she felt Evie inside her, felt her smallness and her weakness and the look in Evie's eyes like it was all over and there was nothing to stop it, the surrender there, and the handing over of everything.

She felt her hands let go, fling back, and she felt the horror in her, and that was when it happened.

The strong hands on her, the man's arms, grabbing her around the chest, grabbing her by the back of her neck like you lift a cat.

Lifting her off her sister, that face violet-shot.

That's how I see it. The way Dusty tells me.

Mr. Shaw's man's arms. I can feel them.

Listening to Dusty, it all shudders into place—Evie saying to me, *He saved me, so I gave him this thing.*

"He stopped you," I say, the recognition rustling against my neck. "Mr. Shaw."

"No, no, no. I'd already stopped," she says, the words breaking to shards. "I'd stopped."

"And then he took her away. Then he stole her away," I say, picturing Mr. Shaw hoisting Evie in his arms. A true rescue. At first, at the start.

Oh, Mr. Shaw, you might have been that knight if you had quit there. You might have been that knight, had you been able to stop your own sick heart from—

"No, no," Dusty says, her voice soft. "He pulled me away. She was on the ground and the sound, that...rattling sound from her throat, and I couldn't look. I couldn't look. We were both breathing so hard, but her breath, like when you put your ear on a seashell. Like your ear on a..."

"He took her," I say, pushing myself in.

"No," she says. And she tells me how it was. Evie shaking the breath back into herself, her face stunned, lost. The searing red on her neck.

How he'd started backing away again, like he didn't know what to do now. Like he was afraid to get near either of them. Someone could swoop in at any minute and point the finger at him.

Her face covered in her arms, Dusty hid herself in herself. She covered her face, and buried herself for...she didn't know how long. It felt like forever.

Hearing Evie stumbling to her feet, calling out to him, calling his name. Running to him, her breath that gruesome wheeze.

The car door slamming. The car kicking to life. The car driving away.

"You have to understand. The things she said," Dusty goes on, her voice splintering and going high. "They were so awful. Things no one should ever say about anyone."

Her thumb on the clotting blood on her knee, dancing there, touching the sealing blood.

"Lizzie, she said those things and it was like she...carved them into me. Because now I look at myself," she says, her hand lifting, nearly covering her mouth, "and all I see are those words."

"What words?" I ask, but somewhere in my head I know.

"I can't say them," she says, darting her eyes at me, her face breaking softly. "Do you think I can say them?"

"A-a-about you," I stutter. "About you?"

"She said, *How is it different from the two of you? From you and Dad.*
And I told her it was nothing like that, that I was nothing like her."

And Evie said to her, *No, you're right. You're nothing like me,
Dusty. It's not me you're like.*

*You're the one out there, just like Mr. Shaw. That's you under the
pear tree night after night, wanting things you can never have,* those last
words like a claw over Dusty's face.

Dusty, she'd said, almost a taunt, but a thousand times sadder,
you can want him your whole life and Dad's never going to give it to you.

I look at Dusty now and there's a howl in my head. I can't say
anything.

"She made it seem sick," Dusty says, her voice choking her.
"She made it seem like loving him was dirty. What could be dirty
about loving your father?"

"But why didn't she tell on you?" I say. "Why didn't she tell
what you'd..." My voice trails off.

"She'll never tell," Dusty says, her eyes lidding softly.

"She's protecting you," I say, but even as I say it, it doesn't
make sense. It doesn't make sense because they were never sisters
that way, were they? Only keening rivals, circling each other,
marking each other tightly.

A love was in it, I knew, but it was nettled and fearsome.

"It's not me," she says, shaking her head. "She's not protecting me."

I feel something stirring softly inside me. I think of Evie,
secrets held close to her chest, and I see it's not about hiding, it's
not about sealing herself up, sealing herself away from me.

She is raising the barricade so high, so he will never have to
know. He will never have to see what his daughter did to his
other daughter. What either of them has done. I think of Evie in
the car on the way back from the pool, *I'm sorry, Dad. I'm sorry.*

"I never told him about her either," Dusty says, as if reading my mind. "I pictured myself, so many times, going to him. Saying, Don't you see, it's all her fault. Everything's her fault. She ran to him. She ran away with him. Even if I had never...she was going to do it. Go with him. I know it.

"But I could never say it. I couldn't stand seeing the look on his face. I never want to see it."

She can break his heart, both sisters are saying, *but I won't.*

"I'll never tell either," I blurt. "I'll never tell." .

She looks at me, and it's such a tortured look, full of anger and despair and a flushy kind of warmth I've never seen on her before.

"It's like kids," Dusty says, and she's almost smiling. "It's like when we were kids. Blood sisters, right? Remember, in the back-yard, all three of us, thumbs to thumbs."

A memory hazes forth, Evie and me, maybe five or six, stretching our arms before golden Dusty, our thumbs jabbing, waiting for her silvery laceration.

"Blood sisters," I say.

She might even reach out to me, but she doesn't. She tilts her head, looking down at the tile, dragging her cleat against it.

"That day. The way I was. It wasn't me, you know?" she says, almost shaking her head in wonder.

I think of Dusty on the hockey field, ferocious and biblical, her stick slashing, saberlike.

"It's a thing to know about yourself," she says, quieter still.

She watches me.

"Yes," I say.

Then there's a ripple across her face, and she looks away.

"Lizzie," she says, a whisper. "I know how it's been. With you at our house. All that time with him. I know how it's been."

"Dusty, I..."

Her hands shaking in her lap, palms up.

"I know how it's been for you. With him. All those nights. I know."

"But I..."

"But that's over now," she says, her voice tiny, forlorn. "That's over. Do you understand?"

I don't say anything.

She turns and faces me, her hands lightly on my arm, light like Evie-light, but I feel a steel beneath them. I do.

"The way it is, for Dad and me," she says, "it'll never be like that for you and him. It goes so deep with us. You could never have that. You just couldn't."

I could not.

Who was I to imagine I could?

That's what I think, and then the thinking of it makes me feel sick. I feel sick.

"He always says to me," she says, smiling lightly, "'You're going to leave a string of broken hearts, Dusty. Remember I told you that. I saw it before anyone else. I was the first.'"

She smiles at me. "I have to be true to that, don't I?"

Then she puts her fingers to her lips, as if she just thought of something.

"But I never...he never...it's not like that," she says. "Like Evie said it was. That's just Evie's sickness. To see something so beautiful as dirty, as wrong. She can't help it, I guess. She's a sick girl.

"What Dad and I have, Lizzie," she says, fingertips resting on that lovely mouth of hers, "it's pure. It's pure and I never looked at it. It was just a feeling, always, my whole life."

Twenty-five

"I don't pretend to know the hearts of women." Mr. Verver said that once, long ago. He'd said it, laughing, he'd said it with a knowing slant of his head, and I remember Dusty, her face, the glow of it, because Dusty only ever glowed and gloried under his gaze. I think of Dusty and boys, those furtive thoughts of why she can never yield herself to them, doesn't even care to try. Mr. Verver, he gives her everything and asks nothing in return, except everything. Everything. There's nothing left for anyone else, she gives it all to him, his gaze rendering her beauty with such care. And then the struggle after Evie went away, and after she came back, oh, for Dusty not to have that gaze on her. Oh, any minute at all in her life, not to have that gaze on her...

It's nearly Labor Day. The sounds floating through the kitchen window, and it's like a thousand other nights, and Dusty's starry trill, Mr. Verver's throaty laugh, the swing of his voice, like his hand on your back, pushing you on the swing set, your feet in the air.

Everything is back. It's back. But it's all different and the laughs are different, aren't they? I nuzzle the screen door and look and see their tanned faces, their gleaming teeth and avid eyes, and the frenzy in the air seems a thing apart.

Everything looks different now, Evie once said. *But I don't think it's different. I just never saw it before.*

Dusty, the eagerness on her face, the grasping, the grappling. How hard she's trying, how hard he's trying too. It's desperate, but you believe in it:

We will make it so, we will make it as before, a fairy tale, handsome king and golden princess, surveying their kingdom from on high . . .

I think of Evie up in her room, and wonder if she's hearing them too and knowing she is.

If things had been different, Mr. Shaw may never have touched her. He may have gone his whole life never stepping from the shadows. Never going beyond a few shared words on the back lawn of the school. But then it happened, and she ran to him, and then he couldn't stop.

But I saved her, didn't I? Stringing clues together, tracing the breadcrumbs back. Dropping breadcrumbs myself. All to rescue her from him.

Rescued her, returned her, restored her . . . back to that house where now she lies, one thin, filmy wall from her attacker, from the girl who held herself against her neck, nearly pressing the life from her.

Would you let it all go on? Would you let both sisters hide their dark tales, their black-heart secrets? Or would you tell all, turn that enchanting, light-struck household inside out, lay open its mysteries?

Caught up in it all, in the slipstream of it, I've seen things. I've seen the massy heart of things.

They had made their choices, both sisters, hadn't they? Neither would tell what happened. Neither would ever tell.

They'd decided what mattered to them. And it was Mr.

Verver, it was him. The him of him, and the idea of him, and maybe they were the same.

And now they've drawn up the bridge, raised high the walls, and who was I to say? Who were the police, anyone, to say they knew better? That they could look at the gold-gleaming family before them and see its troubled center and say they knew better, could undream that beautiful dream?

These two girls, not princesses so much as palace guards, sacrificing all to keep their noble king safe. Up high in his tower. Golden-walled, immaculate.

I walk outside, onto the patio, and watch them. There he is, holding court, Dusty enthroned at his side, her legs curled tanly beneath her.

I watch for a long time before he sees me, but he does.

He rises so fast, my heart catches.

There's a warmth on his face that brings everything back.

I take a few steps toward him.

Calling my name, he flings his arm out to me, hand outstretched, his face open and ready, inviting me in.

She smiles too, the gracious victor to her former rival, and the two of them, their smiles are the same and so much radiates from them it takes my breath away.

He flings his arm wide.

Take it, he says, hand outstretched. *Oh, Lizzie, take it.*

It's Sunday morning and Dr. Aiken has left to get almond Danish and I creep into my mother's room and she lifts her arms above her head and says, Come lie with me, little girl, like she used to when I was very small and dainty.

We are tucked under the mauve bedspread with the satin border I rub between fingers and it soothes.

I could lie there forever.

"High school this week," she says, smiling at me.

"Yeah," I say. High school, the idea seems so small, after everything.

"I heard Mrs. Shaw and her son moved away," she says carefully. "All the way down by Point Cleary."

I feel a twitch at my temple, push my fingers to it.

"It's funny," she says, "because I was always grateful to him."

"Grateful?" I say. "To who?"

"Oh, I'm sure you don't remember. You were so little. It was at Green Hollow Lake. You and Evie, gosh, I can still see you in your matching suits. Evie had water wings, but your dad propped you up on your raft and you were having a fine time. Then that motorboat came by, and whoosh."

She sweeps her arm across the bedspread, making a shush.

"You fell and Harold Shaw was right there. He plucked you out and I still remember your little face, your eyes big as saucers. You were holding onto him so tight."

"That was Mr. Verver," I say, I nearly shout.

Mr. Verver scooped me up, shook me like a wet puppy, lifted me as if by my neck scruff, and saved me then and there.

She shakes her head and smiles.

"No," she says. "He was off taking Dusty on the Jet Ski. It was Harold Shaw. He had you, and you just did not want to let go. It was hard to unclaw you from him. And he seemed so touched by it."

She looks at me. "I always remember that."

I don't say anything.

"I guess it seems different now, after everything," she says. "The memory. It's not the same now."

"No," I say, but I'm not listening. She keeps talking, but I'm not listening. I am far away and can barely hear her.

Step-shuffle-back-step, step-shuffle-back-step.

Flashing before me, such visions: the photograph in the Shaw house, the one of Mr. Shaw and Pete at the lake, and me bobbing in the background, bobbing on my yellow raft. And Evie, and Evie, turning toward me on her sleeping bag, turning toward me and whispering, mouth to ear. *He saw me at the pool, doing dives. It reminded him of something that happened at the lake, a long time ago. How he'd seen me fall in the water. The most important moment of his life.*

He said watching me at the pool, it all came back. And he knew what it was to love. The most important moment of his life.

Both our memories self-spun, radiant fictions.

Me and my shadow.

Wanting something so badly, you make it so. He and I, we share that. It's a strange secret, sharing, and I'll never tell.

This I suddenly remember, from before everything:

Mr. Verver and Dusty sunning on lounge chairs in the backyard. Dusty, maybe fourteen, is wearing a polka-dot bikini and pink sunglasses, and Mr. Verver, he's wearing khaki shorts and sunglasses.

For a minute of course for a minute they look like brother and sister or something else that you know

And it's so hot and Evie and I are kicking the soccer ball around and Dusty is laughing at Mr. Verver, whose finger is running back and forth in midair, in the space above

Dusty's golden stomach, which he

never touches.

He's teasing her about the tiny gold down running in a narrow line down the center of her midriff, from the frilled bottom edges of her bikini top to the frilled top edges of her bikini bottom.

Evie and I pull up our T-shirts to see if we have the treasure trail

that's what Mr. Verver keeps calling it, treasure trail

see if we have the treasure trail too

Evie's is pale brown and mine's not really there at all

at least not so you could see

but if I run my hand along it I can feel something tickling under my fingers.

I can feel it just the same.

Acknowledgments

With deepest gratitude and greatest debt to Reagan Arthur, without whom. Special thanks also to Sam Humphreys at Picador UK, to Andrea Walker at Reagan Arthur Books for her keen insights and guidance, to Jayne Yaffe Kemp at Little, Brown for her inestimable assistance in the final stages, and to all the wonderful folks at Reagan Arthur Books and Hachette. And, at Writers House, to the invaluable Maja Nikolic, Angharad Kowal, Stephen Barr, and my agent, Dan Conaway, for everything.

Greatest thanks as always to my family: Phil and Patti Abbott, Josh, Julie & Kevin, Jeff, Ruth & Steve Nase, and Ralph Nase. And, as ever, to Josh, Alison, Darcy, and Kiki. And to Sara Gran, one of my earliest readers, favorite writers, and dearest friends.

About the Author

Megan Abbott is the Edgar Award–winning author of four crime novels. She has taught literature, writing, and film at New York University, the New School, and the State University of New York at Oswego. She received her PhD in English and American literature from New York University in 2000. She lives in New York City.